The Newcomer

Book One in the Sixpenny Bissett Series

Caroline Rebisz

No part of this book may be reproduced, scanned or distributed in any printed or electronic form without permission in writing from the author, except for the use of brief quotations in a book review. Please do not participate or encourage piracy of any copyrighted material in violation of the author's rights.

Any trademarks, service marks, or names featured are assumed to be the property of their respective owners and are only used for reference. There is no endorsement, implied or otherwise, if any terms are used.

The Newcomer is a work of fiction. Names, characters, businesses, places and incidents are either the product of the author's imagination or are used fictitiously. Any similarities to persons, living or dead, places or locations are purely coincidental.

The author holds all rights to this work.

DEDICATION

For Alan

.

CONTENTS

#

ACKNOWLEDGMENTS

Thank you to my family who support my writing journey. Alan, my husband, who puts up with my daily sales updates and accepts the hours I spend closeted with my writing. Danuta and Beth, my daughters, who read my books and give me valuable feedback. My Mum, Pam Evans, who encourages me when I have doubts.

Writing a book cannot be done alone. A big thank you to my Beta Reader, Beth Rebisz, who inspired a number of changes to the story. A special thank you to my friend Helen Mudge who proofreads my manuscripts. Her eye for detail and her insightful comments are invaluable.

CHAPTER ONE
ROSE COTTAGE

They had gone at last.

Jenni shut the door with a deep sigh, turning her back to rest it on the wooden frame and gradually sliding to the floor. She wrapped her arms around her knees as she rested her head upon them. Squeezing tightly, she gave herself a well-earnt hug. It had been a long, hard move, but at last she was in.

"What a day," she spoke out loud, realising how silent the house now seemed.

It was only an hour since she had arrived at Rose Cottage in Sixpenny Bissett to start her new life. The huge removal truck had been following her car as they had wound their way through some of the smallest lanes imaginable. How the truck had managed to get through without taking vast amounts of tree detritus with them was beyond her understanding. Jenni had pulled in the wing mirrors on her new BMW as a precaution. She had been so scared of hitting them against oncoming vehicles. The removal guys seemed so laid back as they swung the truck down the windy tracks. Let's face it, who is going to argue with a vehicle that size?

Sixpenny Bissett was deep in the Dorset countryside. Its main road was the only thoroughfare. Either side of the road were the most beautifully quaint houses with a mix of thatched and traditional slate roofs. No two houses looked the same, something which had attracted Jenni to the village.

The huge removal van was probably not the most welcome sight that afternoon. The road had been almost impassable as the four lads had heaved her furniture and boxes into the cottage. Jenni had kept a low profile, not wishing to face the possible annoyed looks of her new neighbours. She had camped out in the kitchen, unloading the kettle and cups, and making sure the team were refreshed after the long drive. Over the last few days, Jenni had seemed to spend all her time making copious cups of coffee or tea. She honestly couldn't believe a group of lads could drink so much and never seemed to need the loo. The benefits of being young and possessing a strong bladder.

Fortunately for Jenni, there had been no issues with the neighbours. Tuesday was a quiet day in Sixpenny Bissett. In fact, every day was a quiet day in Sixpenny Bissett. People didn't drive through the village to get anywhere in particular. It wasn't a main thoroughfare. The only cars usually out and about belonged to the residents and Tuesday was a day when nothing much happened.

The last hour had been frantic as Jenni organised Ryan and his team to place her furniture in all the right places. She was relieved that her early planning had made this exercise as pain free as it could be. It would prove to be a great decision when she came to face the unpacking alone. The last thing she wanted to do was move heavy items of furniture unnecessarily.

Ryan, the supervisor, and driver of the removal team had insisted on putting her beds together. He made a big deal of suggesting she might want a decent night's sleep after the drive. She caught him winking at one of his guys as he offered that. Irritatingly, he had spent most of the last few days flirting with her, instead of putting his back into it. He left all the hard work to his team.

Why do some blokes think single woman are simply gagging for their attention?

Creep!

Thankfully now all was silent.

Jenni gazed around the hallway with a huge smile on her face. This was her new home. The first home she had chosen alone. And she reckoned she had chosen well. The house enfolded her within its welcoming embrace. The hallway was certainly a feature of the house, with a curved wall which sloped away from the kitchen towards the dining room. Its quirkiness was one reason she had fallen in love with her new home, at first sight.

Suddenly she heard a faint cry from the kitchen. Pulling herself up, she opened the kitchen door to let Freddie out. He wandered across the hallway, sniffing the walls as he surveyed his new kingdom. He rubbed his cheeks against the doorway into the study, marking his scent as he claimed his new territory, before he noticed his mistress and wandered over for a head rub.

Freddie was a young black cat, only just over a year old. Jenni had taken him in as a kitten and had survived those training days with courage, as her arms were ripped to shreds with his play. Over the last year, he had learned to control his enthusiasm for her upholstery and her skin, confining his scratching to the huge cat tower. Freddie had kept Jenni sane over the last year. He was there at her side when everything got too much and could sense her need for a cuddle when grief got too much for her to bear.

"Come on then, Freddie. Let's find you some food, yeah?"

He was an intelligent cat. Freddie instinctively knew the word 'food' and was off back into the kitchen where he had spotted his bowls earlier. His plaintive wails told of his extreme hunger. Of course, he hadn't had anything since they left Birmingham in the early hours. There was no way Jenni was dealing with any messes in her new car. Freddie had slept most of the journey, courtesy of a sedative from her kindly vet. He had been shut in the kitchen as soon as they arrived at Rose Cottage and hadn't had a chance to explore just yet.

Dinner first.

Adventures second.

As Freddie snuffled his head into the food bowl, absorbing the food rather than eating it, he really was the messiest eater, Jenni opened a bottle of wine. She really was exhausted. Jenni had been up at 5am loading the last things into the car. She hadn't slept much last night. The blow-up bed didn't really help and Freddie, who was frustrated with being locked in, spent most of his time swiping her on the nose. The drive had taken hours, not helped by the level of concentration needed to ensure she didn't lose

3

the lorry behind her. All too often she forgot herself and steamed off, only remembering at the last minute, and was then reduced to crawling to allow them to catch up.

And now she was here.

There was no rush to unpack. It was just Jenni to worry about. Well, Freddie too, but he would shift for himself. She had a microwave meal, which she would pop in shortly, and then crash out on the sofa with a spot of TV. Ryan had also connected up her Sky box for her so she was good to go. Sometimes playing the impractical female card paid, even if it stuck in her throat to have to ask. Especially from Ryan. He had taken the role of gallant knight a bit too seriously. His suggestive comments had become tedious as they packed up her old home.

Needing help from others was a new challenge for Jenni. She had been so used to Reggie doing everything for her. Well that was behind her now. She would just have to learn some new skills, pretty quickly, if she was going to maintain her focus as an independent lady.

She sighed, turning her thoughts away from the painful past.

Jenni took a big glug of wine. As she savoured the wine's restorative qualities, the door knocker sounded. Quickly checking out her hair on her mobile phone camera, she applied a bit of lipstick. First impressions are so important. She had forgotten to lock the door. Shaking her head in frustration at her own forgetfulness, she pulled it open, letting the chilly breeze in. Living on her own meant that she needed to be a bit more thoughtful about her own security. Or perhaps she wouldn't need to worry so much out in the depths of the countryside.

Standing on the doorstep were a middle-aged couple proffering a bottle of red. "Hello, welcome to the village," said the chap. "My name is Jeremy. Jeremy Penrose and we are your new neighbours. The Rectory, next door."

"Kate," smiled his companion. "Welcome to Rose Cottage." Kate stuck her hand out towards Jenni, almost muscling her husband out of the way.

What struck Jenni initially was that Jeremy had the kindest smile. A brief glance also revealed his job. The dog collar gave it away. He must have been in his fifties, tall, slim with a fine head of wavy, brown hair. His outfit seemed to endorse the traditional country vicar look; brown corduroys with a knitted jumper. By contrast, Kate was very small and round. The role of a vicar's wife is often to play second fiddle as a supporter, but Jenni's first impressions were that this was a formidable lady who knew exactly what she wanted and how to get it. There was no sign of a wallflower here.

"Thank you so much," replied Jenni as she took the bottle. "Would you like to come in? Oh, by the way, my name is Jenni. Jenni Sullivan."

They all shook hands on the doorstep as Kate explained that the last thing they wanted to do was intrude on her first day. "We just wanted to pop round and say hello. And to let you know that if you need anything at all, then please don't hesitate."

"That is so kind of you. I think I am OK for now. I have a glass," laughed Jenni as she waved the bottle. "All the important things accounted for." Her attempt at humour was met with genuine smiles. A good start.

"Have you moved far?" asked Kate.

It was clear the conversation would continue on the doorstep, which suited Jenni. She was keen to get to know her new neighbours, as she may well need to call on their help in the days ahead. But on the other hand, she was dying to slip out of her tight jeans, pull on a set of joggers and collapse on the sofa.

Socialising was going to be a must in the weeks ahead, but she needed to be mentally ready for it. It was going to be hard putting herself out there as a single woman. Most of her neighbours were bound to be couples. Jenni had known this was a major downside of the choice she had made. Moving away from everyone she had known for years and years might be seen as a foolish decision, but Jenni knew it was the right thing for her.

"Quite far," replied Jenni. "Birmingham. It is quite a contrast, much quieter down here." Jenni smiled.

When she smiled her face lit up, changing her whole countenance. Kate gasped, realising what a naturally beautiful woman their new neighbour was. She will cause a stir, Kate thought. She will shine compared to the old fuddy-duddies who populate the village. This is going to be fun, Kate thought. She is going to attract attention and some of it may well not be welcomed.

"Wow, that is quite a change. Whatever made you move to Dorset?" asked Kate.

Jenni was not ready to go into detail just yet. There would be time enough to share her story once she had settled and got to know Kate a little better. She settled for a bland statement to cover any awkwardness.

"Just fancied escaping to the country. It felt like the right time."

Kate immediately picked up on the reluctance of their new neighbour to disclose the real reason just yet. There was no sign of a husband, but Kate had already noticed the huge diamond on her finger. Perhaps a boyfriend lived down nearer the coast and she was coming to join him? There was plenty of time to find out the gossip and, of course, the whole village would be vying to be the first to find out more about the beautiful woman who had joined their community.

"Look, we won't keep you any longer, Jenni. Why don't you pop round to us tomorrow for coffee? The Rectory, out of your drive and hang a left." Kate was gesticulating with her hands. "Get yourself settled tonight and then I can give you the lowdown on the village tomorrow. Give you all the goss," she grinned.

Kate was clearly used to getting her own way and confident that her invitation could not be refused. Jenni was secretly relieved. It would give her a chance to make a friend who could hopefully navigate her through the pitfalls of village life. Jenni and Reggie had lived in a busy suburb of Birmingham and her friendship group had been on hand all her married life, and especially during the school run days. The daunting task of making a whole new group of friends in Sixpenny Bissett was exciting and scary at the same time.

"That would be lovely, Kate. I look forward to it. See you in the morning then. About 11?"

"Perfect, see you then."

Kate and Jeremy were walking backwards as they waved goodbye. Jenni slowly closed the door as she saw them depart into the gloomy evening. Childishly, she twirled on the spot, enjoying the slippery feel of her socks on the wooden floor. Freddie came to join her, winding himself around her legs and declaring his love. Bending down, she picked him up into her arms, cradling him against her chest. The soppy cat gazed up at Jenni, enjoying the tickle he was getting behind his ears.

"This is home now, Freddie. We are going to be so incredibly happy here, my little friend." She kissed his furry head. "Anyway, let's explore before I eat."

Jenni cradled the cat as she walked through the additional rooms downstairs, noting all the features which had attracted her to Rose Cottage the minute she had walked through the door, all those months ago. A large, square living room was furthest from the kitchen, ideal for her big, cream sofas. The fireplace was made from cream stone, which, if she had designed it herself, would have been her perfect choice. An open fireplace held centre stage and Jenni almost longed for the cold of winter so she could cosy down with a log fire.

The dining room was big enough to cope with her large mahogany table, which only ever got used when entertaining, or when the boys were home. Next to the kitchen was a small study which Jenni would use when she finally got to grips with setting up the PC. The likelihood that its setup would wait until George next came to visit, niggled at the back of her mind. She was a dinosaur with IT unless it related to her mobile phone.

George was Jenni's eldest son. He was the spit of his father and, unfortunately, had too many of his father's characteristics too. He was a petrol head just like Reggie. He had grown up with cars. His dad had taught him to drive when he was thirteen, making circuits of an old airfield. Jenni's worries about the danger of starting so early didn't bear any consideration. Reggie and George were inseparable, both at work and play. George had turned down the chance of going to university so he could start working for his dad at the car showroom. His future had been determined from such an early age.

Fortunately, he was a natural salesman, just like his father. He could sell anything, ranging from a high-end Porsche to a battered old Ford Fiesta. Now at 26, he had found himself the perfect career and was earning enough to buy his own home. The one thing missing, in Jenni's opinion, was a girlfriend. George liked to play the field and always seemed to have a beautiful girl on his arm, but she never stayed around too long. George was far too independent for that.

Jenni sashayed her way up the curved staircase, another beautiful feature of the house. The balustrade was formed of ornate wooden columns and she could imagine the fun Freddie would have, swiping her as she travelled up and down stairs. He did love to ambush her when she least expected it. Meanwhile, Freddie had rolled over in her arms and was now adopting his default position, lying astride her arms with all four feet flopping. A picture of pure relaxation. He had obviously forgiven her for the hours spent in the travel box, thought Jenni.

The master bedroom was above the lounge and had a very serviceable ensuite. The corridor, running down the centre of the house, had three other bedrooms leading off from it, along with the main bathroom, which was located on the curve. There was plenty of room for guests. She was sure some of her mates would be knocking on her door next summer when they wanted to enjoy a break on the south coast, for free.

Jenni would set aside one of the rooms for Jimmy, her youngest. Jimmy technically still lived at home, when he was around. He had finished university that summer and had gone off travelling around the world. His last message had come from Chile, but unfortunately, he was never the best at keeping in touch.

Jimmy had been the most vocal about Jenni's move. He had even called his mother a stupid fool. However, his disgust at her leaving Birmingham was more to do with his desire to have cheap lodgings, rather than Jenni's personal needs. An example of his, all too often, spoilt nature. They had not done the best job of parenting Jimmy. The baby of the family had always seemed to have had his own way, too easily, and now simply expected everyone to bow to his desires.

They had had a blazing row over the move.

Jimmy had the cheek to say she was evicting him by moving because it would make it impossible for him to commute back to Birmingham. Commute to what? She had shrieked in frustration. The nearest Jimmy had got to working was a Saturday job at the local supermarket before university. His parents had funded him throughout his course and, unlike many of his contemporaries, he had had no need to work. He had plenty of spending money for drink.

That boy is spoilt, Jenni's mother was always quick to point out.

Perhaps she should be charging him rent for all his worldly goods, which she would be storing until he decided to hang up his travel boots and find himself a career. His degree had been in Maths and Jenni had no idea what her son would do with that. She really couldn't see him entering the car dealership. And whether he and George could work together was also debatable.

It was at times like this that Jenni wished she had a daughter. Her best friend, Elena, had two daughters who adored their mother and would do anything for her. Trust Jenni's luck to have two boys who either favoured their father or were so wrapped up in their own worlds to notice their old mum.

She could have done with a daughter over the last year.

Shrugging her shoulders, Jenni decided now was not the time to think about the past.

Today was all about new beginnings. A fresh start.

A chance for happiness again, after the trauma of the last few years.

"Come on, Freddiekins. Time for mummy's dinner."

CHAPTER TWO
ROSE COTTAGE

"Reggie, slow down darling," Jenni shouted over the roar of the engine.

The car held the corner with precision as Reggie changed down a gear. It should have been impossible to corner at 70mph, but his new car was high performance, that was for sure. Unfortunately, the weather was not playing ball; it was dreadful. The rain was making visibility difficult. It was also very late and a lack of streetlights made the lane gloomy in the extreme.

Reggie and Jenni had been into the centre of Birmingham to the theatre; Les Mis, which had always been Jenni's favourite musical. Reggie hadn't been keen but he was feeling in a good mood, so had humoured her. The good mood came about by him taking delivery of a new Honda S2000. He was keen to put it through its paces. Reggie always tried out the cars before he put them on the sales forecourt. He saw it as a perk of the job, even though, as the owner, he could do whatever he wanted anyway.

Les Mis had been as good as Jenni had imagined. The scenery, the costumes and, of course, the music had been amazing. As they drove home, she hummed along to 'At the End of the Day,' reliving the evening's entertainment. Humming was helping the anxiety she often felt when Reggie was putting a new car to the test, especially at speed. Jenni did not like it. Not one bit. But she would hold her tongue for now.

The car engine screamed as Reggie accelerated down the dark lane. They weren't far from home now, which was a blessing. Jenni hated fast cars. What is it about men who want to rev the bejesus out of an engine? The louder the noise, the better the car. Jenni just didn't get it. Which was surprising, seeing as she had been married to a car salesman for the last thirty years. You would have thought she would have learned to appreciate a slick body and the thrust of the drive by now. But no, Jenni was a philistine when it came to cars. They were a means for getting from A to B. That's all.

Reggie was passionate about his cars. That's why he had taken the risk, twenty-odd years ago, to set up his own business. They had piled all their savings into the venture, which had luckily paid off. Reggie had made his first million before he reached the age of forty. The car business had helped them build a lifestyle which had allowed Jenni to stay at home and look after the children. It had provided them with the means to travel the world, staying in the most wonderful hotels.

They were happy.

And, oh, so very lucky.

Jenni was in a world of her own as she thought about the theatre and the wonderful musical. She didn't see the deer as it strolled out in front of the car. The first she knew about it was hearing Reggie shout "Shit." He slammed on the brakes, but the road was too wet. The car wasn't stopping. The deer seemed to have frozen, in fear, right in front of their path. They were hurtling towards the animal at over 60mph. The tyres screamed as Reggie forced the brakes down with little hope of slowing in time.

It was at that moment that Reggie made a split second decision which was to prove fatal. He swerved to avoid the deer. The Honda veered off the road and hit a fallen tree, going airborne. For a few seconds there was silence, as the car flew through the night sky. Then the noise was overwhelming. The car landed on its roof and skidded towards a huge oak tree. The front of the car slammed into the tree at speed, folding the bonnet into the driver's side of the car.

Silence.

Darkness.

Jenni came to first.

She was confused, trying to work out where she was and what had happened. Her mind was in a whirl as she tried to figure out what hurt. She was hanging upside down in her seat, with the belt holding her from falling smack on her forehead. The pain in her head was pulsing. She realised she must had hit it against something hard. She could feel something dripping and a wetness stinging her eyes. Panicking, she decided it must be petrol. She reached up to wipe the liquid from her eyes. It was blood, thankfully. Calming down, now that the fear of the car exploding was retreating, she took stock of her injuries.

She couldn't feel her legs. But, now that she was becoming more alert, the pain started to kick in. Gradually she felt downwards, as far as she could reach with the limitations of the seatbelt. One leg was trapped under the crushed metal. That was where the extreme pain seemed to be coming from. She could sense the blood seeping out of numerous wounds. This is not good. I'm bleeding heavily, she realised.

She needed help, and fast.

Her mobile was in her pocket, which was fortunate. Trying not to drop it with her slippery fingers, she dialled 999. While she was waiting for the call to be answered, she tried to turn her head, looking for Reggie. She hadn't heard him moan or cry out since the crash. That was so unlike him. He should be cursing that damn deer which had destroyed his new car before he could get it out on the forecourt.

Her husband was lying across the steering wheel with his head at an unusual angle. His eyes were glassy. Blood had dried on his face. He wasn't moving. Her arms screaming with pain, she pushed herself across the gap towards her husband. She touched his arm, pushing him gently as she would do when he fell asleep in front of the TV, snoring his head off.

"Reggie, wake up," screamed Jenni. She reached out to shake him again. As she did his head flopped back showing the damage to his beautiful face. "Reggie," she cried.

"Hello, what service do you require?" the phone sprung into life.

Jenni reached for Reggie's hand. She held on fast as she explained to the operator where they were. "Please send help quickly. My Reggie doesn't look too good."

"We will be there as quick as we can, Jenni." The voice was reassuring. But Jenni was not reassured.

A cold feeling settled in her stomach as she looked at her husband. "I don't think he's breathing," she whispered.

Placing her palm over his mouth she desperately tried to feel for air being expelled. There was nothing. Remembering what she had seen on the trashy TV hospital dramas she loved, Jenni tried to find a pulse in his neck.

Nothing.

It was then that the screaming started.

Jenni woke up with a start, disorientated.

Where was she?

Scrambling around, she found the light switch and flooded the strange room with welcoming brightness. She was shaking. Dripping with sweat, the duvet was wound around her legs.

It was the same old nightmare.

That dreadful night. The night all her dreams came crashing around her. "Poor Reggie," she sobbed. The whole dreadful night was relived in her mind, with the clarity of reality. In the early days, she had taken sleeping tablets to try and forget, but the memories wouldn't leave her alone. They visited her far too often, denying her the chance to move on with her life. She really thought the move would have drawn a line under the horrible dreams.

Unfortunately not.

Freddie was awake and could sense the distress coming from his human friend. He did the only thing he could do, butt his head into her chest, looking for a comforting stroke. He purred loudly as if to break the silent tension. The act of stroking her cat would calm Jenni and allow the dark thoughts to recede.

Reggie had died instantly when the car hit the tree.

The doctors reassured Jenni and the boys that he wouldn't have suffered. The suffering was reserved for those left behind. Jenni had spent weeks in hospital with a fractured skull and three breaks to her right leg. Her life had never been in danger, but the pain, after the lengthy operation to fix her leg, had almost destroyed her. It would be followed by months of physio to support her to walk again, and the plastic surgery to hide the scars. If only there was a magic cure for the scars to her heart. That was the hardest pain to bear.

Sometimes she wished she had died with Reggie, rather than wake up every morning alone.

They had been inseparable throughout their marriage. He was her first love. She was a virgin when they got together and had never looked at another man since then. Oh yes, Reggie was a bit of a player. But it was all a front. Part of the salesman patter. He was devoted to her. He would never do anything to hurt her.

Except die.

Jenni missed him every day.

Her friends had told her it would get easier, but everything reminded her of Reggie. The pain did get easier to manage, but it never went away. It was the first thing that hit her every morning.

Moving house was part of the healing process. She could not continue to live in that old house. The one she and Reggie had made their home, had brought up the boys in, and had hoped to retire in together. She needed a fresh start if she was ever going to move on. She was only 50, so the thought of spending the rest of her life alone seemed crazy. But she couldn't make a fresh start with all their old friends watching on.

Or the boys.

George and Jimmy had found the death of their father incredibly hard to deal with. In the early months they clung to each other as Jenni was too sick to help them out. George had grown up rapidly. He had taken over the car dealership. Work had probably been the healer for him as it kept him busy. He was determined to keep the business strong as a testament to his father.

Jenni had signed over 50% of the shares in the company to George so that he had control over decision making. The remaining shares were split between her and Jimmy, maintaining the family involvement in the success of the business.

Jimmy dealt with his grief by running away. Just like Jenni. He escaped the sadness, which seemed to ooze from his mother, by heading off around the world. He had pitched his idea to Jenni as a learning experience before he had to settle down, but she knew that there was more to it than that. He was escaping the demons of that awful year after Reggie had died.

It was nearly two years now since Reggie had left her. The pain was controllable now but the memories were still sharp. She needed to live again and Rose Cottage was the fresh start she needed. The money from her investments, the money Reggie had squirrelled away over the years, and the sale of the family home, meant that Jenni would not need to work. She had the means to keep herself comfortably and then decide what she wanted out of the rest of her life.

She was determined to do something. She just wasn't sure what that was, yet. She was on a journey of discovery. A journey without Reggie by her side, but very much in her heart.

Lying back in the covers, she pulled Freddie in close and kissed his furry head. As she slowly stroked his head, she gradually slipped back to sleep.

CHAPTER THREE
THE RECTORY

Kate balanced the tray of biscuits, precariously, on one oven glove as she pushed the Aga door closed with her bum.

It was an act which required precision, battling with the heat from the oven blasting out, which made the door surrounds red hot. Kate had used an Aga for years but had still not perfected the most elegant way of opening and shutting the heavy, cast iron door without either slamming it or letting the dry heat seep across the kitchen. She could not do without her four oven cooker. It was her best friend. Kate loved it with a passion, probably not equal to her feelings for Jeremy, but it was a close run thing.

The ginger biscuits looked perfect and the smell was to die for. From experience, Kate knew they would be crispy on the outside and chewy within. She just hoped Jenni wasn't watching her figure, especially after all the effort Kate had made this morning. Not only had she been baking, but she had run the hoover round downstairs, another job which was well overdue. She was keen to make a good impression on her new neighbour.

Kate had taken the morning off, so that she could prepare for her visitor. As the owner of the village store, aptly named Kate's, she had the luxury of allowing herself leave without having to ask the boss. She had left the store in the capable hands of Claire, her assistant, who would no doubt manage without her just fine. Claire was very efficient and Kate secretly thought she loved it when the boss went out. Claire thrived on responsibility and took every opportunity thrown her way. She was keen to impress and prove her worth. She seemed determined to make her role indispensable to Kate.

The village store had a steady flow of business throughout the week. A range of customers frequented the place, from those more elderly clientele who purchased their daily provisions, to those who had run out of an essential and popped in for that. After paying for Claire's time, the store only just broke even. Kate wasn't in the business to make money. Thank goodness that wasn't her driving factor as she would have been pretty disappointed. Her determination was to ensure that the villagers had a vital resource open to them.

Five years ago, the previous owner had left the village under a bit of a cloud. He had been fiddling the books and the Post Office had investigated him for fraud. It was at that point that the Post Office element pulled out of the village and there was a real risk that the shop would become unviable. It was hard to make a profit out of just the grocery side of the shop. The village had been up in arms about losing their convenience store.

It was Jeremy who had suggested that they take on the shop. He felt it played an important role in the village. Despite his concern for his flock's needs, it was clear the vicar could not run the store. It really was outside his remit of leading the village's pastoral care. He did the next best thing and persuaded Kate to take it on. At first, she had been reluctant but, after he had thrown his weight into convincing her, she launched herself into the venture with her usual gusto.

She loved the daily conversations with her regulars. It was the perfect place to learn all the gossip. And Kate loved a good gossip.

On Mondays, she ran a knitting club in the shop, where her regulars could grab a cup of coffee and a slice of cake whilst clicking away at their needles. There was always a good attendance. Recently, Kate had been thinking about setting up a café to run alongside the shop. They had the room, as the old post office counter had been removed last year, allowing Kate to use that area for the knitting club. The only thing holding her back was time. And money. She couldn't contemplate putting more of their savings at risk to expand like that. The small amount of savings they had were allocated for the kids' university fees.

Kate placed the biscuits onto a serving plate as she made a swift check around the kitchen. Jack, the Jack Russell, was sat obediently in his bed. Why the hell had they decided on Jack as a name. So unoriginal. Jeremy was not overly inventive, a trait which could be tiresome, but Kate found so attractive. The cheeky dog could smell the biscuits and decided that if he sat quietly, perhaps one would come his way soon.

Unlikely at the moment.

His master, Jeremy, was out for the morning, visiting another local parish. Kate, ever the loving wife, would save him a biscuit for later. They were his favourites so it would be unfair not to. If there were any left over, then perhaps Jack would be lucky. He really shouldn't eat them, but Jack knew his master was a pushover to a sweet, doggy face. And he knew how to perfect the look, even raising one paw in supplication. Simply adorable and hugely successful in the biscuit stakes.

The doorbell rang, breaking into Kate's thoughts. Looking at her watch, she could see it was spot on 11am. Oh, I do like a person who is on time, thought Kate; I think we will get on just fine.

Greetings were exchanged at the door, before Jenni followed Kate into the kitchen. Kate proffered a seat at the vast, wooden table. It was the comfiest place in the house, enjoying the added warmth of the Aga. The two women engaged in small talk whilst Kate blustered around making coffee. While they chatted, Kate secretly observed the newest villager.

Jenni was very tall for a woman; she must have been over six feet. Her hair was immaculate, blond, straightened and cut with wispy bits at the side, which framed her face perfectly. Kate was struggling to determine her age. She had almost perfect skin, which was devoid of makeup. There are not many women who can carry that look off. And despite just moving house, her nails were elegantly painted, a dark blue colour. Kate's initial impression of Jenni last night was accurate. She really was the most beautiful woman.

Now let's see if her character matches her looks, she thought. I do hope so.

"How's the unpacking going, Jenni?" Kate wedged herself into the chair, sighing as she met resistance. These biscuits don't help, she thought. She really should cut down on the sweet stuff, but she found it so incredibly hard.

"Slowly," Jenni smiled. That beautiful smile again, which lit up her face. "I have started unpacking the kitchen, which is probably the biggest job. And the most needed, I guess. I cannot believe how much paper there is. The removal men packed up my crockery and there is virtually a rainforest of paper to get rid of."

"I can only imagine. If you need a hand getting rid of the paper, Jeremy normally makes a trip to the local tip with our garden waste most weeks, so I'm sure he would be happy to take it for recycling."

Jeremy was hugely accepting of his services being offered out. Kate was always doing that. He was far too kind for his own good sometimes. He would never turn down a request, especially if it had originated by an offer from his wife.

"That is so very kind, Kate. I may well take you up on that offer. Young Freddie, my puss, is finding it great fun playing with the paper. He loves the sound of it crunching under his feet, so just keeps jumping around the piles. I guess I must just accept I am going to be in a mess for a few weeks. It's so very hard on your own."

Kate watched as Jenni's eyes took on a sorrowful look. Her face settled on the look of a little girl lost, all of a sudden. Kate was intrigued about Jenni's situation. Was it too rude to ask? No. It was best to get it out into the open before the elephant in the room festered for weeks to come.

Kate went for it. "You don't have a partner then, Jenni. Any family?"

Jenni had deliberately dropped in the remark about being on her own because she secretly wanted to let Kate know about Reggie. The next few weeks were going to be difficult enough, meeting new friends and neighbours. From what she could tell, Kate, as the vicar's wife, could be a key influencer in the village, so would provide Jenni with a conduit to sharing her personal circumstances. Saves her talking about it anymore than she wanted to.

Jenni was learning to live without Reggie, but it was hard at times, especially when people asked the inevitable question.

"My husband died 18 months ago. Reggie. We had a dreadful car accident. I was lucky to come out alive, but poor Reggie died instantly." Jenni paused as she watched the emotions flit across Kate's face. It went from interest, to shock, and settled on sympathy.

"Oh, Jenni. That is dreadful. I am so sorry to hear that. It must have been a very difficult time. Do you have any children?"

"Two boys. George is 26 and James 22. Do you?"

"We have two as well. We were late starters. Tried for years and nothing happened then suddenly Joseph came along, followed by Mary." Kate could see the smile twitch at the corners of Jenni's mouth. "Don't laugh. Vicar with Joseph and Mary as kids' names." Kate couldn't help breaking out into laughter and even snorted as she enjoyed her own joke. "God knows why we did it. Seemed a good idea at the time. They get quite a ribbing about it at school. They are 15 and 13 so going through the dreadful teens stage. With yours being a bit older, I guess they were a big support after your husband died."

Kate was doing the mental maths. If George was 26 then perhaps Jenni was in her late 40s or early 50s. She certainly did look good for her age.

"I guess." Jenni wasn't very convincing. Her tone resonated with a hint of the loneliness she was feeling. "I was out of it for a few weeks, so the poor loves had to cope without me. Once I came out of hospital, Jimmy was designated as my carer, fetching and carrying until I could get around on my own. George took over running the business, which took the pressure off big time."

Jenni went on to explain about Reggie's car dealership. Kate was a good listener and let Jenni talk, making the odd gesture, a nod of the head to show she was paying attention. Jenni was finding it quite therapeutic to share her story with her new friend. And she felt Kate was going to be her friend. She had warmed to her already and felt very relaxed in her company. Once she had outlined her journey from married mother of two to widow, moving across the country for a fresh start, the conversation moved on to Sixpenny Bissett.

Kate was in her element talking about the village.

"You have picked a great place to live, Jenni. We are a small village, but a thriving community. I'm sure you will find most people are very welcoming to newbies. We haven't had anyone move here for a couple of years so you will be the focus of interest for a while. Sorry." Kate laughed.

She didn't say it, but she was sure that some of the men in the village would behave like bees around the honeypot. Overpowered by the beautiful new stranger. And waiting to see who would get stung first. Kate could put good money on which ones. The usual suspects.

"I am looking forward to meeting people." Jenni tried to sound more confident than she felt.

"Well, I have got the perfect first step for you. Ease you in gently. It's Harvest Festival this Sunday morning. It is a lovely service and most of the village will be there. We have coffee afterwards, so will be a chance to meet a few people in quite an informal gathering. Fancy that?"

"That would be lovely, thanks Kate." Jenni was not a churchgoer, or at least she hadn't been up to now. But this could be a safe way of dipping her toe into the social waters of Sixpenny Bissett.

"Well, I will come and knock for you if you fancy. Then we can sit together in church. Jeremy will be up front of course," Kate giggled.

"That is really kind of you. One of the things I have found so hard since Reggie died is going to things alone. I have always had a man at my side, so walking into a room alone is bloody difficult."

Kate had empathy for Jenni.

Her situation was similar, although under different circumstances. All too often she was parted from Jeremy in social engagements because of his job. Kate was incredibly confident, or so she looked to the casual observer. Sometimes she didn't feel it and the pressure of being the vicar's partner fell heavily on her shoulders. It was hard to have a bad day, especially when she didn't really want to be nice to people. The whole persona of cleric's wife was that of kindness and interest in others. Even when she felt the complete opposite.

With the weekend sorted, the two women chatted comfortably for the next hour. Jenni was reluctant to leave, but she was conscious of not overstaying her welcome. A pile of unpacking was beckoning her back to her new home. It felt the most natural thing of all for the two friends to embrace and exchange kisses as Jenni left.

Kate watched Jenni stroll down the path between the houses, smiling to herself. She really liked Jenni Sullivan and was looking forward to getting to know her better. It had been a while since Kate had felt so relaxed with another woman. She had loads of acquaintances, a perk of her husband's job, but few that she would regard as bosom buddies.

CHAPTER FOUR
ST PETER'S CHURCH

Sunday morning was going to be a warm one.

The late summer sun was pushing through the clouds, encouraging Jenni out into the garden. She had an hour spare before church so had made herself a jug of coffee. Old habits die hard, it appeared. Every Sunday morning, it had been a ritual for her and Reggie to spend time with the papers and consume copious amounts of caffeine. Settling for a magazine for a change, she let herself out onto the patio. Her sunglasses sat on top of her head as she poured a mug of strong Colombian coffee.

The garden of Rose Cottage was the perfect size for Jenni. A patio gave her ample room for summer entertainment. Surrounding the neatly maintained lawn were numerous border plants, most of which Jenni had no idea of their names. What she did recognise were the beautiful rose bushes planted around the walls of the cottage and scattered throughout the busy flower beds. She adored roses; another attraction for the house when she had first visited.

The last few days had been fruitful; she had made excellent progress.

Most of her boxes were unpacked and she was delighted that nothing had been damaged. Well, at least as far as she could tell. Her new house already felt like home. Of course, there would be work required to get it up to her normal, pristine standards. Jenni was determined to find a local handyman to help with decorating and the odd repairs which she had spotted already. Other than her bedroom and the lounge, she was lacking curtains and even some curtain poles. Sooner or later she would have to get that sorted, especially if she wanted to maintain her privacy. Jenni knew her own limitations and putting up curtain poles was certainly one of them. It would be the first job for her handyman. She needed to find someone reliable, preferably by word of mouth.

Last night she had a long conversation with George. He was, no doubt, checking up on his Mum, but it did make her feel better for talking with him.

He was full of news about the dealership and seemed jolly proud of himself. Jenni had absolute confidence in her elder son. He had been trained well by her Reggie. George said he missed her, but, deep down, she knew he was thriving without having to worry about his mum and how she was doing. Out of sight, out of mind. Jimmy had also emailed her overnight. He had made his way from Chile over to Argentina. He had managed to get himself some temporary work on a cattle ranch. Her baby, the cowboy!

It was good for her to know that her boys were coping without her. She carried the guilt that mothers always seem to be saddled with. Any of her choices had to be made with an eye to her offspring. How would they feel? Would they manage without her? This latest move had been one of the first decisions in her life where she had put herself first. But she still felt guilty about her selfishness. Crazy, isn't it? They are adults now and don't need their mum worrying over the impact her choices might have on them.

The coffee was delicious and mellow, providing the perfect recipe for a lazy Sunday morning. Jenni could not stay out in the sunshine for long. As much as she could quite happily do that, the question of meeting more of the village characters was uppermost in her mind. She could not turn down the chance to lean on Kate's support for that first meeting with some of the key members of the community.

The church service was due to start shortly, so a quick application of lipstick was required and then she would go and meet Kate. She chose a blush pink, something understated and more appropriate for church than her usual pillar-box red. She felt a bit nervous about today as she was sure that all eyes would be on her as the newcomer. With that in mind, she had dressed carefully for the occasion. Tailored, navy trousers with a lightweight jumper presented a fashionable image without being too showy. She had discarded about ten different outfits before she had settled on this one. For goodness' sake, it's only church, she had muttered to Freddie, who lay casually on the bed watching the parade of garments. He really was no help at all when it came to fashion choices.

Jenni's nervousness was held at bay as she and Kate walked into the church some minutes later. Having her new friend at her side was helping immensely. Entering via an impressive porch, they traversed the nave, looking for empty seats. Stone slabs, devoid of burial markers, led the way towards the chancel. The nave was busy with villagers greeting each other. Kate waved at a few people before leading Jenni to a seat near the middle of the building. There was method in her decision. Jenni could check out those neighbours sitting in front and, for those behind the two women, they could check out the newcomer. Everyone wins, decided Kate.

As Jenni took her seat, she managed a furtive glance around the congregation. Making eye contact with a number, she was met with smiles. Everyone seemed very pleasant. It was interesting to see a range of ages across the seated parishioners. Jenni had expected the church to be packed with oldies, but Kate had been right, most of the village had turned out for Harvest Festival.

Jenni was oblivious to the looks she was getting in return, especially from the menfolk. Some were gazing at her circumspectly, not letting their partners notice their interest. The newbie was definitely causing a stir. She may have thought her outfit had been chosen to blend in, but it did quite the opposite. Her tall stature and model-like figure was causing the blood to race in a few of the males.

Not the most appropriate activity, in church.

The service began. Jenni was listening intently to Jeremy as he conducted the proceedings in his jovial and kindly manner. It had been a long time since she had attended a service, other than Christmas festivities, and she enjoyed the format and the lack of stuffiness. She had been worried that the service would be very highbrow. Several children were involved in bringing farming produce to the altar in thanksgiving for a bountiful harvest.

The local farmer, Jenni didn't catch his name, gave a talk about the farming year. To be fair, Jenni was not paying attention at this point. She was fascinated with the copious amounts of nasal hair sprouting above his top lip. Unbelievable.

Beside her, Kate boomed out the hymns with gusto. Jenni could not help a small smile as she realised her new friend was totally off-key. Kate obviously did not have an ear for a tune but was not ashamed to perform at the top of her voice. Thankfully, the noise of the congregation singing completely drowned out Kate's caterwauling, except for those immediately beside her. Jenni caught the eye of a kindly neighbour who nodded and smirked at Kate's singing at the same time. She was obviously infamous for her performances.

Jenni's admiration for her new friend went up a couple of notches. She loved Kate's lack of conformity.

Once the service ended, a group of ladies shuffled quietly to the back of the nave, where a small kitchen area was set up. It was intriguing to see such a practical function in a traditional church building, but it worked, in Jenni's opinion. Over the noise of numerous conversations could be heard the chink of coffee cups and spoons. Jenni stood next to Kate, nerves starting to kick in. Now was the time to face her audience. No doubt she would be the centre of attention simply because of her newness.

As expected, it wasn't long before the two women were surrounded by villagers keen to learn all about the newcomer. The first person to introduce himself was a very elderly gentleman, who had appeared at Jenni's side within moments of the blessing. He was a portly chap, well-dressed in an immaculate suit. On his breast he sported a number of military medals, which glimmered in the sunlight bouncing through the stained glass.

He cleared his throat purposefully to attract Jenni's attention. "Good morning, young lady. Herbert. Herbert Smythe-Jones." The gentleman stuck his hand out as Jenni attempted to disguise the giggle which was fighting its way up her throat. "And you are?"

Well that was direct and to the point, Jenni thought. "Hello. My name is Jenni Sullivan. I have just moved into Rose Cottage. Lovely to meet you."

Jenni gave him one of her famous smiles and the poor man was lost. The blush started on his cheeks then moved down his neck until his whole face was a red beacon. His mouth opened and shut numerous times without him speaking. He just stared at the beauty in front of him.

Before Herbert could get his emotions under full control, a further parishioner wheeled his way into the small circle of people surrounding the newcomer. He was holding two delicate coffee cups, one of which he proffered towards Jenni.

"Hi there. You must be Jenni. Morning, General." He directed the last comment at Herbert. "Peter St John at your service."

Jenni nearly combusted as she tried to hold the giggles in. Did everyone in this village have a double-barrelled surname? Even the village was double-barrelled. She had expected the community to be a damn sight posher than Birmingham, but really!

"Hello, Peter. Lovely to meet you." That smile again, lighting up her face.

Her friendly grin was certainly having an unusual effect on her new audience. Peter saw it as a challenge he must accept. He knew with a certainty, which bordered on arrogance, that Ms. Sullivan would be his next conquest. He quickly looked around to see if his wife, Paula, was watching. Reassured that she was serving drinks at the opposite end of the church, he relaxed into a conversation with Jenni. Well, it wasn't really a conversation. Peter was blowing his own trumpet, espousing his talents as an architect. Jenni just listened and nodded in what she hoped were all the right places, whilst The General watched her.

Peter was a handsome chap but, unfortunately, he knew it. He stood beside Jenni, like a cockerel puffing up his chest, as he talked nonstop. He didn't seem to notice that Jenni's attention was wavering. She was looking around frantically for an escape route. She really wasn't listening to this dreadful man, who was in love with himself.

Meanwhile, Kate was enjoying the whole show.

She had expected that Jenni would turn a few heads, but to find these two men already performing like lapdogs was certainly humorous. She saw Jeremy approaching and decided it was a good opportunity to manoeuvre Jenni away from Peter. The last thing Jenni needed was that old lech sniffing around her so soon. Time enough for that once she felt more confident to deal with Peter's certain style of chat.

As Kate gathered Jenni under her wing and guided her towards the porch, Jenni caught the eyes of another man. His eyes turned away from her immediately, making Jenni gasp with surprise. She had recognised the look of sadness he wore. She understood that pain.

He was the most handsome man she had seen in years. As tall, or if not taller than her, he bore a passing resemblance to Richard Armitage. She smiled as she imagined she was in a scene from the Vicar of Dibley. She suddenly saw an image of Dawn French striding down the aisle, singing of her heartbreak.'

"Who's that?" she whispered in Kate's ear as she nodded in the chap's direction.

Kate followed her eyes and sighed. "That's Richard Samuels. He lives a couple of doors down from you on the other side. Juniper Cottage. Not that you will see him much. Spends most of his time down at his boatyard or out on his boat. Poor man."

Jenni was intrigued by Kate's words, but unfortunately another villager interrupted their conversation and they moved on. As they left the church, her eyes continued to follow Richard. I wonder why Kate said poor man, she thought? He really had the saddest expression, as if he had a world of troubles on his shoulders. He had tried his hardest to avoid eye contact, which was out of sync with the rest of the community. Everyone else was keen to attach themselves to her like a limpet, outdoing each other to spend some time with the new parishioner. By contrast, this gorgeous man acted as if he would do anything to avoid talking to her.

Well, finding out his backstory would have to wait for another day, thought Jenni. She was intrigued and determined to get to the bottom of the mystery gentleman. She was confused by her own feelings too. Since Reggie had died, she had not been interested in another man. She was far too young to give up on relationships, but the thought of another man in her life was just not on the agenda.

In spite of that Richard Samuels interested her.

Kate watched the emotions clearly written across her new friend's face. Oh dear, this will not end well, she thought to herself.

CHAPTER FIVE
LAUREL HOUSE

The cork slid effortlessly out of the bottle with a satisfying pop.

Peter carefully placed the bottle of Côtes du Rhône on the breakfast bar and picked up a Chardonnay. The work surface was almost obscured from view by delicious wines, ready for their guests. In truth, it was only a dinner party for eight, but Peter St John believed in showing off to his audience. There must be a bottle per person. Surely it wouldn't all get drunk, but never would it be said that the St Johns weren't generous with their hospitality.

After catching a glimpse of Jenni Sullivan at church, Peter had been on a mission. He was determined to engineer a further meeting. He was obsessed with Jenni already and he didn't even know her yet. Peter was a superficial guy. He was attracted to a woman by her looks not personality. Jenni was a beautiful woman so, in his book, fair game. The challenge of having her had obsessed him in recent days. It was like an itch he delighted in scratching. How to meet her without raising suspicion? The easiest way to do that was a dinner party, in his opinion. Then he could choose the competition for the lovely Jenni's attention. Or ensure there wasn't any competition, if he was sensible.

Paula had been happy with his plan for a dinner party. She loved to entertain and, unknown to her, played right into his scheming hands. She had been excited to meet the mysterious newcomer to the village. She decided she was about to get the greatest coup of the year, hosting the newbie first. Poor old Paula. She never saw what was coming until it was too late. Despite being married to Peter for over twenty years, she was still taken in by his scheming.

Peter St John was a player.

He had been all his life and was in no mood to change now. One woman was never enough for him. He had affairs on a regular basis. He really had no shame. Sometimes Paula suspected, but most times he got away without her knowing a thing. Those liaisons were the best, as he didn't have to face his wife's grumpy moods when she found out and railed against his promiscuity. It wasn't even the risk of getting caught that concerned Peter. The times Paula had found out, she had forgiven him far too easily. It was as if he was above criticism when it came to his sexual appetite.

Peter didn't understand women.

As much as he loved sleeping with them, he really didn't get how their minds worked. His wife, Paula, was a total mystery to him. She was an attractive enough woman, but with an exceptionally low libido. Sex was a chore to her, or at least that was how it seemed to her husband. Perhaps that was why she turned a blind eye to his liaisons. It wasn't that sex had disappeared from the St John household. When it happened it was very athletic, but it wasn't enough for Peter.

He was always after something more. Like a child, he wanted what he couldn't have. Not that he would chase for too long. If he had to put in too much effort, he would get bored and the attraction would wear off. Not that this happened often. He was rightly proud of his success rate. Peter always had the upper hand when it came to his mistresses.

He didn't do losing.

On the domestic front, life with Paula was good though. He would never dream of leaving her. They rubbed along just fine. They had never had children so their lives were centred around work and play. Paula ran her own upholstery business, which kept her occupied during the week, and at weekends, they played hard together. Golf was a shared passion and most Sundays were spent on the course. They loved to entertain, which was useful for both their businesses. Many clients of Peter's architect firm would be treated to the legendary entertainments at Laurel House.

Just at that moment Paula wafted into the room, her scent arriving before her. Wow, that's strong, thought Peter, as the heady perfume hit his nostrils. It wasn't unpleasant, but a bit much. Describes Paula perfectly, the man-bitch in him reflected. Paula was wearing a flowing kaftan dress, which wasn't the most flattering, and her arms were adorned with bangles. Paula was going through her bohemian phase. Hopefully, this phase wouldn't last too long as those bangles really jarred on his nerves.

"Darrrrling," Paula drawled in her attempt at a sexy voice. "Did you put the serving spoons on the table?"

Peter had been flat out for the last hour, whilst Paula beautified herself, and still he was getting criticised. For once he was keen to keep the peace and not get tonight off on the wrong footing. So he held back on the sarcasm.

"Yes, darling. Everything is ready and the starters are prepped to go in the oven as soon as everyone's here."

"Thank you, sweetie."

Paula made an obvious turn to look at the huge clock, which you could see from every point of the kitchen. The head turn was a clear message that their guests were now exactly one minute late. Paula was an absolute stickler for timekeeping.

As if on cue, the doorbell rang. First to arrive were Jeremy, Kate, and the lovely Jenni. Peter's mood perked up a few notches. She looked gorgeous in a slimline, navy dress and heels to die for. Her hair had been swept up into a chignon which showed off her shapely neck. Peter was desperately holding himself back. He would love to explore that slope between ear and shoulder with his lips.

Whoa, calm down mate, he thought. Don't give anything away to Paula. Not yet anyway. Wait until she has a few glasses inside her and she won't notice a bit of legendary St John flirting.

Woof, woof.

Resisting temptation, Peter threw himself into serving aperitifs. Whilst in mid jiggle of the cocktail shaker, Thomas and Winifred Hadley arrived.

Thomas owned Green Farm and was one of the most influential of Sixpenny Bissett's residents, and the owner of the amazing nasal hair. His family had owned the farm and land that surrounded the village for over a hundred years. He was in his early 60s but had no plans to retire anytime soon. His eldest son, Roger, worked with him on the farm, but didn't live in Sixpenny Bissett. Hadley tradition ensured that the farm moved down from father to son, but the farmhouse would not be handed down until Thomas officially retired. To Roger's frustration, that didn't look like happening any time soon. Until then, he would have to commute from his home some five miles away.

Their number was complete with the arrival of Alaistair Middleton. Alaistair or Al to his friends, was a builder and as he was introduced to Jenni, she took a mental note of that fact. A good person to know, especially as she had a raft of curtain poles which required fixing up.

The dining room table was a work of art, which Peter had spent hours over. Image was so incredibly important to the St Johns and nothing should be out of place or mismatched. His efforts were noticed by Jenni who made a suitable comment to Paula, assuming she was responsible. Peter was particularly pissed that his wife chose to take the praise without mentioning it was his hard work.

What a cow!

Although, all that effort to impress was not wasted as he had strategically placed Jenni on his right, with Al on her other side. Al had a reputation as a talker. Peter had decided that after fifteen minutes of Al wittering on about joists and brickwork, Jenni would be putty in Peter's hands. No pun intended. Thomas and Winifred were on either side of Paula at opposite ends of the table, with Jeremy and Kate on his left hand side. He had worked out the table plan purposefully, to keep his wife distracted whilst Peter did his thing.

True to form, Al started his usual diatribe about the perils of being a self-employed builder. Peter had known Al for years and they were the closest to best mates that Peter had ever warranted with another male. He was not a man's man per se. He was very much into women. Al was not just a talker, who could bore the pants of anyone, but he also wore the bitter scars of a recent divorce. His ex had left him two years ago, taking a substantial chunk of his company savings and their personal assets, but leaving him with the house. Al was the Hadley's neighbour, owning one of the old farm cottages. He also rented a barn from them which he used to run his business from.

Peter's ears pricked up as he heard Jenni's voice. He had been half listening to Al and Jenni's conversation whilst chatting with Jeremy. "Alaistair, could I ask for your help. If you have time, of course, as I appreciate how busy you are."

Peter could see Al's chest puff out as his mate took on the role of saviour to the damsel in need. "Well of course, Jenni. What can I do for you?"

Damn it, was there a hint of suggestion in the way Al uttered that last sentence? Peter would need to tell his mate to back off. He had seen her first so there was no way Al was getting first dibs. Oh yes, he may well be single, but Jenni Sullivan was far too classy for a hairy-arsed builder. Oh no, that would never do. She was white-collar potential and could not be seen slumming it with Alaistair Middleton.

Peter kept one ear on the conversation.

"I need a number of curtain rails put up. Probably not the sort of work you would do but perhaps you can recommend someone. The walls look a bit manky so need some filler at the same time, I think."

Alaistair would never entertain such a job, thought Peter somewhat relieved. He spent most of his time on renovations and extensions, where the big money was.

"Of course I can help you out with that, Jenni," smiled Alaistair. "I guess it's a bit of an urgent job if you haven't got your curtains up yet. How about if I pop round Monday morning?"

Seriously, where the hell did that come from? Al's eyes were fixed on Jenni's face and he had a sickly smile reaching from ear to ear.

"Thank you, Alaistair. I am so grateful to you. You are a lifesaver. Monday would be splendid."

34

This needs some serious intervention, thought Peter. He coughed loudly to break up the conversation and motioned to Paula to clear the plates and bring out the main course. The sheer arrogance of Peter's behaviour was not unnoticed by Jenni. Her Reggie would never have dared to humiliate her like that during a dinner party. They had been a well-oiled machine as they entertained. Jenni felt sorry for Paula. She hadn't come across as a doormat at first meeting, but at Peter's signal, had scurried off to the kitchen to do her husband's bidding.

While his wife was out of the room, Peter decided it was time to work his magic. "So, Jenni, how are you settling into Rose Cottage?"

Jenni flashed him that smile as she shifted her body position over to face Peter. "It is a lovely house, thank you. It already feels like home and it's only been a couple of weeks."

"Couple of weeks, already? Wow, how time flies," laughed Peter. "Probably has got some work to do internally to modernise things. Old Joe, whom you bought it from, had let the house go a bit. If you need an architect to plan the house of your dreams, then I will give you mates' rates." Peter winked as he tried to seal the deal.

Jenni winced at this smarmy man. She seriously hoped her face didn't betray her thoughts. Jenni was not accustomed to being rude in company. It didn't pay to ostracise anyone in the village when she was such a newbie, but this man was really insufferable. She attempted to smile sweetly, whilst cursing him inside.

"I love the old-fashioned nature of the cottage." Jenni was determined not to let Peter bloody St John anywhere near her plans for the cottage. "It's got some really quirky features, especially the curved walls, which I love. To be totally honest, most of the work required is superficial. Decorating and changing some of the colour schemes, which are a bit dated."

"Well, if you change your mind, I would be happy to show you some of my designs. I have a great reputation around here for stylish and modernised homes captured inside the shell of an old cottage. It really is a sight to behold."

Jenni smiled again as she thought, "what a tosser!"

Peter was encouraged by the smile and launched into a long, one-sided conversation extolling his skills. He was on a roll and clearly did not see the boredom written all over his intended conquest's face. When it came to talking about himself, Peter held a gold medal. How he managed to obtain the contracts he did, was difficult to understand. Perhaps half of his work came about because the client could not take any more of his bull so just signed up to shut him up.

The evening progressed satisfactorily.

Copious amounts of wine were drunk. The volume of conversation got louder and, at times, a bit risqué. Kate was the worst once she'd a few glasses of wine, and she had one of those laughs which was so infectious that everyone was in tears when she got going. By the time the brandy was being passed around, Peter was pretty pissed. He was conscious enough of his inebriated state that he knew he would pay for it tomorrow. Perhaps he would pass on golf in the morning and stay in bed, nursing a hangover and dreaming of the delightful Jenni.

Jenni was tiddly but keeping it under control. She had employed her usual tactic of drinking copious quantities of water in between sips of wine. There was no way she would disgrace herself tonight. However, she was enjoying watching the others getting drunker and drunker. Alaistair, next to her, was almost slumped in his chair, holding his head up with arched arms on the table. On her other side, Peter continued to waffle on. He really was a dreadful bore and so full of himself.

Suddenly, Jenni felt a leg touch hers under the table. Thinking it was just a mistake, she didn't move her leg as she was keen not to make a fuss. But then the leg started to move. It stroked up the inside of her calf in a slow, but deliberate fashion. Once it reached her skirt, it made its way back down in a very deliberate way. She was stunned at the blatant violation of her body, not something you would expect at a neighbourly dinner party.

Jenni was flabbergasted. Who would do such a thing?

Looking around the table, it was clear that there could only be two suspects. Peter or Jeremy. Jeremy was deep in conversation with Kate and was facing his wife so, unless he had the longest and most dexterous legs ever, then it could not be him. As she looked at Peter, he grinned and then winked.

The cheek of that bloody man, she thought. What the hell does he think he's doing? And so blatantly. And then even winking at her. What the hell!

The evening was over as far as she was concerned. She needed to extract herself from a difficult and awkward situation without embarrassing her hosts. Not that she had any regard for Peter, but his poor wife, she did not deserve the humiliation.

"Paula, Peter," she interjected the various conversations. "Thank you so much for your hospitality this evening. The food has been wonderful, Paula. But I really must call it a night."

Jenni started to push her chair back, confirming her intention to leave. Peter was devastated. He had hoped to continue his little game of footsie. Perhaps she was embarrassed and didn't want to give in to his charms too quickly.

Ah, she's going to play hard to get. What a tease! If she wants to play games then that will make the whole thing much more exciting. He was turned on big time now. And up for the challenge of Jenni Sullivan.

Let the conquest commence.

Challenge accepted!

Jeremy got to his feet, prompted by his neighbour's call to action. He was still sober as Sunday was his workday. He would need a clear head in the morning. Nobody liked to take communion from a vicar who stank of stale wine breath.

"Yes, come on Kate." He took the back of his wife's chair as if to encourage her upright. "The evening is late. We must get to bed. Jenni, we will walk you home."

The St Johns only lived the other side of the church from Jenni, so it was not much of a walk, but she was grateful for the company. One of the first things she had noticed since moving to the village was a total absence of streetlights. The village was pitch dark at night and she would need to remember to carry a torch whenever she ventured out after dark in the future.

As their guests departed, Peter sunk onto the sofa with another large brandy in his hands. The night had been a resounding success. He had spent hours working on Jenni Sullivan. It was only a matter of time now before she succumbed to his charms. Rolling the brandy around the glass, he imagined the gorgeous woman lying beneath him as he banged her good and proper. Wow, that would be amazing.

He was so excited that he decided Paula would have to do tonight. Paula was slumped on the sofa opposite him, sipping on her brandy. She looked pretty far gone, so he was confident of a blow job tonight. Once she'd a few, Paula lost all her inhibitions and could be pretty damned wild.

Just the thought of that made up for the disappointment that it was Paula rather than Jenni he was taking to bed. Oh well, if he had any problems maintaining his passion tonight, he could imagine the beautiful neighbour as he screwed his wife.

"Come on, woman," Peter sighed, trying to sound sexy. The use of the term woman would normally have Paula incensed, but tonight she really hadn't got the energy to argue. "Up those stairs now and let's celebrate a successful evening with some hot sex."

Paula secretly loved it when Peter went all caveman.

She smiled sexily at him as she levered herself out of the sofa and followed him up to bed. Tonight she was in the mood for sex too and, unfortunately, Peter was the only man available. He would do for now.

But he was no longer the man of her dreams.

Paula had a secret fantasy. She couldn't believe it, but she actually had a bit of a crush on Alaistair. The feelings had crept up on her over recent weeks. Every time she was in his company, she got all unnecessary. Not that she would ever be unfaithful to Peter.

But it wasn't wrong if she imagined it was Al rather than Peter in bed with her. Was it?

Despite Peter's obvious shortcomings, he was her husband and she was a stickler for loyalty.

Unfortunately, her husband didn't live by the same standards.

CHAPTER SIX
ROSE COTTAGE

Jenni sighed as she lay back into the soft folds of her bed.

She was surrounded by fluffy pillows, which lovingly embraced her in their luxury. A cup of coffee was steaming beside the bed and her book had been discarded whilst she pandered to Freddie's needs. The young cat was keen to get out of the house and explore the gardens. He couldn't understand why he was shut in the house and he was making his complaints known to his lord and master, or should that be mistress. He was very disgruntled to have to use the litter tray and had left a present downstairs for Jenni. Most of the litter was strewn across the utility room floor. Knowing that soon Jenni would notice the mess and get angry with him, Freddie was taking advantage of the situation and settling in for a good belly rub.

As she stroked the cat, Jenni reflected on the previous evening. She had really enjoyed the company. Well, most of it. Paula seemed a lovely lady, poor woman. She must have the patience of a saint to put up with that prat of a husband. Paula had laid on a wonderful meal and had been the perfect hostess.

What little time she had spent chatting with the farmer and his wife had been very pleasant. They seemed to know everyone important in the village, and the idea of buying fresh food from the farm shop appealed to Jenni. She also had a great result in organising a visit from Alaistair to sort out her curtain poles. Another good contact made, which hopefully would be useful in the days ahead as she got the house improvements planned out. And of course, Jeremy and Kate had been wonderful. She genuinely believed she had found a firm friend in Kate.

The only fly in the ointment was Peter St John.

What an absolute creep. He had been so full of himself and flirted outrageously with her. Right in front of his wife! How disrespectful. The final straw had been the seductive rubbing up of her leg. She honestly could not believe the cheek of the man. She had given him no reason to suggest his attention would be welcomed. Surely men didn't do such things in polite society. Even when drunk.

Jenni really disliked men like Peter St John.

They had such an inflated opinion of themselves and believed that everyone else saw them as they liked to see themselves. There is something quite sad in not knowing what an idiot you are. Even if he were single, Peter was not her type at all. He was arrogant and bombastic. She liked her men with a damn sight more humility. Not that Jenni was even looking for another man just yet.

She had moved to Dorset to start a fresh life. Not to find a man. She needed to escape the constant reminders of Reggie. All their friends carried shared memories of Jenni and Reggie as a couple. It had tormented her whenever she had met up with their longest-known friends as there was an uncomfortable level of awkwardness, especially when no-one seemed to know what to say or do.

Moving away gave her a fresh start with strangers who didn't know Reggie. She didn't have to explain about Reggie's untimely death. And now that Kate was fully armed with her backstory, she was certain the community of Sixpenny Bissett would soon be aware and, hopefully, be polite enough not to ask too many questions of the newcomer.

Jenni was keen to make new friends. Just friends. It may be nearly eighteen months since Reggie died, but she was not ready to replace him in her heart. And certainly not with a married man who made her skin crawl.

Her thoughts were interrupted by the ring tone of her phone. Looking at the screen, Jenni saw an internet call coming from Jimmy.

"Jimmy, darling. How lovely to hear from you."

"Howdy Mum," laughed Jimmy with a nod to his current job as a cattle herder. Jenni smiled as she imagined him slapping his chaps as he jumped from his horse.

The line was surprisingly clear, considering her younger son was backpacking in Argentina. He tried to ring her every Sunday. Firstly, to update her on his exploits and secondly, and most importantly, to reassure Jenni that he was still alive. Jimmy was the closest to his mum and he understood that she worried constantly about him. She had always been a bit of a worry mummy, checking in on him when he went to university as if he could not manage without his mother's ministrations. Her need for reassurance that he was safe and well had increased, understandably, after his father's death.

Despite all that, Jimmy loved his weekly chats with Jenni.

She was an excellent audience as she just sat quietly whilst he rambled for ages. She didn't interrupt but let him run his course. Jenni lay back against her pillows as she listened to Jimmy excitedly recount all the adventures from the past week.

The only one not happy with this familiar conversation was poor Freddie.

He was hoping for some breakfast and would have to wait.

CHAPTER SEVEN
LAUREL HOUSE

Peter slammed the front door a little too loudly, his usual method of announcing his return to the matrimonial home. He did not see Paula wince at the sound. He was totally oblivious to the annoyance it caused her. He did it every day without fail. It was one of the numerous things which got on his wife's nerves. That list of things seemed to be growing rapidly recently.

Peter was exhausted.

He had been on the road all day, visiting clients. His meetings had been hugely valuable, but he could feel the impact on his body from being sat in the car most of the day. His back ached and he could feel a tension headache forming at the base of his skull.

Paula was in the kitchen, preparing dinner.

The News was playing in the background as she stirred a sauce on the hob. Creatures of habit, they exchanged a kiss on the cheek as Peter helped himself to a large whiskey. It didn't even occur to him to offer one to his wife. It never did.

"How was your day, darling?" Paula placed the spatula back on a spoon holder as she decided to give her husband her complete attention.

Peter groaned.

Unusually, he didn't want to elaborate on his successes. Usually, he was only too willing to blow his own trumpet, but tonight he just felt washed out. He settled for the briefest summary of his excellence.

"Good thanks. I nailed down three new contracts which will keep me busy for the next few months. A further 50k coming our way in the new year."

"Wow, excellent news, darling. Happy Christmas to us then." Paula picked up her wine and chinked her glass against Peter's. She never doubted her husband's ability to bring in quality work. He had the 'gift of the gab' when it came to persuading wealthy clients to part with their cash. "Thinking of Christmas, your Mum rang."

Peter groaned again.

"Oh God, what did the Wicked Witch of the West want?"

"She's invited us for Christmas." Paula's voice faltered slightly, anticipating the response.

"She can fuck right off. I hope you told her that."

Peter refilled his whiskey glass. His mother was always a sore point for Peter. He hated her with a passion. And it didn't help one bit that Paula seemed to enjoy her mother-in-law's company. He was convinced Paula did that out of spite.

"Oh come on, Peter. When are you going to drop this stupid feud with your mother? I said yes, by the way. It will be nice to have someone else do the catering for a change." Paula returned to stirring the sauce and didn't see the look of horror on her husband's face.

"Bloody wonderful. Thanks for spoiling my Christmas, Paula."

Peter flounced out of the kitchen before he said anything more. His history with Julie St John, his beloved mother, was something he had never shared with anyone. Even his wife. Some things should be buried deeply, never to see the light of day, and never discussed. It never occurred to Peter that he might find some sort of closure if he had shared his deepest anxieties with his wife.

That would make him vulnerable and Peter didn't do vulnerable.

Julie St John was a nasty woman. She had been widowed young when Peter was only five. Peter didn't really remember his father. All he could recollect, from that time, were the noisy arguments between them. And the violence. His mother took a regular beating from his father. One of his earliest memories was of him sitting at the top of the stairs listening to screaming voices and then the slap of his father's fists and his mother hitting the wall.

How his father died was a mystery and one his mother would no doubt take to the grave.

Once free of her abusive husband, you would imagine that Julie might have cherished her only son, providing him with the stability missing from his childhood. But no. Unfortunately, Peter then became the target of her anger. Julie always had a different guy hanging around. Peter got used to listening to the disturbing sounds of his mother and the latest boyfriend going at it all night long. It was made very clear to Peter that he must never leave his room at night. He was left to lie in bed, listening to the groans of the rickety old bed and his mother's cries of passion.

Peter could do nothing right as far as his mother was concerned.

She was quick with her fists if he spoke out of turn, was late home from school, or was caught out of bed during the night. School became his sanctuary. He was safe there. In fact, his mother was reported to social services a number of times, but no-one came to save the poor child from the trauma of his childhood.

Once he was old enough to leave home, Peter ran as fast as he could towards his future. He enjoyed university as it suited his studious nature and allowed him freedom from the bitch of a parent. He never went back home, finding things to do during the holidays. Julie didn't miss her son and never asked where he was outside of term time. In fact, she forgot he even existed until Paula came along.

Peter hated his mother.

Peter loved his mother too but would never tell her that. He rarely even told Paula he loved her. That would make him vulnerable and Peter didn't do vulnerable.

The damage Julie had done to him as a child festered over the years. It was always there in the background and never spoken about. Strangely, Paula and Julie had bonded on first meeting. As Peter could not share the trauma of his childhood with his wife, Paula could never understand how deep his hatred for Julie St John festered in his heart.

Oh well, he would have to stomach a couple of days of festive cheer with the bitch and the latest boyfriend. God knows what his name was. Peter could never keep up with his mother's latest conquests. He would keep his head down and probably get pissed for the whole visit.

Why the hell did Paula have to say yes?

CHAPTER EIGHT
ROSE COTTAGE

Alaistair decided on his small truck for the trip round to Jenni's. It fitted nicely on the narrow street, tucked up next to the drive of Rose Cottage.

Putting up curtain poles was not the sort of job Alaistair would normally entertain. He wouldn't get out of bed for the money he was likely to earn for this morning's job. But money wasn't Alaistair's motivation today. Oh no, money did not come into it today.

He was purely motivated by the lovely Jenni Sullivan, his damsel in distress.

Alaistair had been living in a woman-free zone since his ex had left. Ruby had screwed him over good and proper. She had been the one to leave him, but she still managed to fleece him of a good chunk of his capital. The whole split scenario had made him especially bitter. How was it fair that he had to pay out a large amount of his hard-earned assets because that bitch, Ruby, had decided the grass may be a bit green over the other side of the valley?

Ruby had moved in with Teresa, a rather butch bodybuilder.

Blimey, Alaistair had not seen that one coming. He had never imagined his wife was into women. Not only had he had to face the gossips when Ruby left, but when the village tattlers had realised she had decided to bat for the other side, his embarrassment was complete. For months, any conversation would stop when he walked into the local shop. It was obvious that he and Ruby were the main topic of conversation. It certainly took some time for that to quieten down. Thank goodness he never had children. He could not imagine the impact it would have had on small ones. Neither he nor Ruby had been interested in babies or continuing the Middleton line. The dog had been disturbed enough when its 'mummy' had left. She had wanted to take the dog, but there was no way that bitch was taking his puppy. That was a definite no-no.

Meeting Jenni on Saturday night had piqued his interest.

She was a stunning looking woman with the most beautiful smile. A cracking figure and a seemingly nice personality to go with the looks. And she was alone. And by the sounds of things, totally unable to do anything practical for herself. She needed Alaistair. He liked a woman who was dependent on him. Ruby lost all her fascination when she branched out on her own. Alaistair was not one of those men who could just wander over to a girl in the pub and chat her up. His confidence had taken a huge knock when Ruby hit him with that bombshell. Having a damsel in distress, asking for his help, was nectar to him. It gave him a real buzz.

He hadn't been out with another woman since Ruby. Over two years on his own. The talent in Sixpenny Bissett had been non-existent up until now, and having a new, beautiful woman in the village was going to attract interest from all the single guys. Not that there were many in the village. At last count it was just Alaistair and Richard Samuels. Well you couldn't include those old fogies who were sitting in God's waiting room. He was talking about red-blooded males with an active pulse.

Alaistair was also very conscious of Peter St John, his best mate. Peter was the total opposite of Al. He was confident, far too confident for his own good. All too often he had used Al as his wingman whilst he was preying on female talent. Al had thought he might pick up some of Peter's cast-offs, but he wasn't even very good at that. Hopefully Jenni Sullivan had a bit more sense about her. She would not fall for Peter's charms. Surely.

Jenni answered the door sporting a tight fitting pair of jeans and yellow fleece. She personified a ray of sunshine on a dull Monday morning. His spirits lifted a notch further as he gazed on her loveliness. What a catch she would be if he could win her over. The whole male population would be jealous of him. It was a long time since he had felt so excited about a prospect.

"Good morning, Alaistair. I am so happy you could fit me in today. You are an absolute lifesaver."

Jenni chatted on as she showed Al around the house, indicating the various poles and locations. It was an exceedingly small job, in Al's opinion, but he was sure he could string it out for most of the day. Mondays were usually his admin days when he would do his books or cost up new jobs. He was making a special exception for the lovely Jenni. Wouldn't it be the most rewarding way of playing truant from the business, spending time with the beautiful newcomer?

"Let me put the kettle on while you get set up," said Jenni. "Tea or coffee?"

"Coffee would be lovely, thanks. Black no sugar."

Al set about checking his tools and drawing up the locations he would need to drill. No point in rushing the job, he thought. Need to pace himself to make sure it lasted the day. He wouldn't take the mickey in terms of billing Jenni. Today was about personal satisfaction, not about making a quick buck.

Before long, Jenni was back with a steaming cup of coffee. She had made one for herself too which looked promising. Perhaps she would join him while he worked. Al was always much more confident with women when he was in his customary setting with drill or screwdriver in hand. He could chat in a more relaxed manner when he had the comfort of a power tool in his mitts.

"Oh, hello little one." Al might be a dog owner but he had a secret admiration for cats. "What's your name little man?"

Freddie, as usual, was loving the attention. He curled himself around the stranger's legs, purring loudly. He rubbed his cheek against Alaistair's trouser leg, leaving a nice trail of dribble behind.

"This is Freddie," responded Jenni as she picked up the ball of fur. "He loves the attention, little tart. Oh gosh, I'm sorry. He has made a mess of your trousers."

"Honestly, don't worry. Just old work clothes. My little puppy makes a much worse mess." Alaistair perched on the edge of a chair as he supped his hot coffee, blowing on the surface to cool it down. He was terrible when rushing to gulp down a short of caffeine, often burning his mouth.

Jenni smiled as she placed Freddie on her lap. Instinctively, she stroked his head as she watched Alaistair appreciating the fragrant coffee. She had never seen anyone able to drink a boiling mug of any type of liquid so fast. Before she knew it, he was back to work, empty cup handed over.

Jenni was intrigued to understand whether Alaistair had noticed the behaviour of his friend at the weekend, so moved the conversation onto that. "It was a lovely dinner party on Saturday. Did you enjoy it?"

"Yeah, it was good," grunted Al, who had a couple of screws in his mouth, as he fixed one half of the pole in place. "Drank too much. Felt like shit all day Sunday. I never learn. Did you have fun?"

"It was good fun. Lovely to meet a few more neighbours. Paula seemed really nice. She is such a good cook. Loved the food. Not so sure about Peter though." Jenni felt she was being a bit daring bringing up her opinion of her host. It was clear that Alaistair was good friends with Peter, but it was a risk she felt was worth taking.

"What Pervy Pete?" laughed Al.

"Pervy Pete?" Jenni decided the name suited him well.

"Well, I know he's my friend, but he is a bit of a ladies' man. Poor old Paula puts up with him and she doesn't know the half of it. He likes to play the field and, unfortunately, leaves a trail of devastated hearts behind him. Word of advice Jenni, steer well clear."

Jenni was not surprised. Her first impressions obviously were spot on. "I have a confession to make," she giggled, still thinking of the name Pervy Pete. Classic.

"Confess away." Al was groaning internally. Please God she is not interested in Peter. He really couldn't bear that.

"Pervy Pete lived up to his name Saturday night. He had the cheek to rub

50

his leg up and down mine." Jenni saw the look of shock on Alaistair's face. "At first, I thought it was Jeremy, but can you imagine the vicar touching up a woman under the table?"

Al broke into a loud guffaw as he tried to imagine Jeremy Penrose doing anything sexual. He must have, once or twice, as he had two kids, but he was so strait-laced it was untrue. "What the hell did you do? Stamp on his toes?"

"I wish. I was so shocked I didn't know what to do. Unbelievable. You just don't expect something like that, especially with his wife in the room."

"Well, like I said, he is a player. He really doesn't care what anyone thinks, especially poor Paula."

Al was secretly happy. Pervy Pete had shot himself in the foot, quite literally. Jenni was a classy dame and there was no way she would fall for such crass behaviour. His old mate had done him a favour and smoothed his path, that's for sure.

The conversation flowed as Alaistair continued his work. Jenni relaxed in his company and started to prepare her curtains as he finished each pole. The heavy fabrics were heaved into position, with Alaistair quick to help her put them up. His small stepladder was a godsend. Like a good boy scout, he was always prepared, especially when there was a single, attractive woman to impress. Oh, he had thought of everything to show his worth to the lady.

As lunchtime approached, the job was almost finished. Alaistair could not string it out any longer without making it obvious. He had put up five curtain poles in about three hours, which surely had to be the slowest on record. Thankfully, Jenni hadn't seemed to mind and had appeared to enjoy his company.

Now was the time to go in for the kill, figuratively speaking. "Do you fancy joining me for dinner one night this week? We could pop to the King's Head. They do an excellent supper."

Jenni was a little taken aback. But dinner would be nice. Alaistair seemed good company and with both of them being single, where was the harm?

Just as friends, of course.

"Thank you, Alaistair. That would be lovely. My treat though, as a thank you for dropping everything to help me today." Jenni smiled warmly.

Alaistair's excitement was slightly tainted as he wondered whether Jenni thought he was doing the job for nothing. He may be interested in getting to know the lovely Jenni a bit more, but he certainly wasn't a charity.

Luckily, Jenni noticed the pause and realised what she had said. "Obviously, I am paying you the going rate for your work today, Alaistair. Dinner is a thank you for dropping everything to help me at such short notice." She gave him that beaming smile again and he was lost.

Alaistair was flummoxed as he stuttered his words. "Perfect. How about Thursday evening?"

Jenni had a clear social diary and knew she wouldn't need to check for a clash. "Lovely. Shall we say 7pm? Do we need to book?"

"Leave it with me, Jenni. I will book something in. Geoff, the landlord, is a mate so he will squeeze us in even if it's busy. That's a date then."

Oh no, I really hope Jenni didn't take that literally, thought Al, as he saw the look on her face. He really didn't want to scare her off. He laughed, making a big joke of things as he started to pack up. It had been one of the best days ever and he was already excited at the thought of dinner together.

So far it had all been incredibly easy. He was rusty at this game, but Jenni seemed to have fallen for his charms.

How wrong could he be?

CHAPTER NINE
ROSE COTTAGE GARDEN

The noise of a lawnmower powering up confused Jenni.

Surely that's in my garden, she thought, striding through to the kitchen. She was frustrated that the back door keys weren't to hand, reminding herself, yet again, to buy a rack for the keys. She could never seem to find them when she needed them. Especially in a hurry.

As she stepped out into the back garden, she was greeted by a vision. A young man was pushing a lawnmower across her lawn. He was dark and mysterious, with olive skin and wavy, brown hair which curled at the front in a kiss curl. His face was framed with a stubbly beard and moustache; a look which appeared to be casual, although he probably shaved it into that design, achieving the rugged look. He was wearing tight jean shorts with a black t-shirt. From what she could see, his physic was as chiselled as his face.

He was gorgeous.

But what the hell was he doing in her garden?

After she had taken her fill of gazing, it seemed appropriate to wave him down and question his antics. Jenni made a quick check in the mirror. It always paid to be looking your absolute best when faced with such an Adonis. Waving her arms around, she finally got his attention. The lawnmower spluttered to rest. He strolled over towards Jenni, with the sexiest walk ever. Blimey, he really was sex on legs.

"Hello," Jenni started. "Not being rude, but what are you doing?" Jenni waved her arms towards the mower as if to emphasise the meaning to her question.

"Hola, Señorita. My name is Henrique. I am your gardener."

The accent was even more sexy. His voice was soft and tuneful, as only the Spanish can deliver. An English accent really doesn't have that mournful, lustful tone. Calm down woman, Jenni thought. Why was she getting all discombobulated by a good-looking chap?

"I'm sorry but I didn't know I had a gardener."

Jenni found herself speaking extra slowly and enunciating every word. Why do we do that when faced with someone foreign? It's so British. And so rude.

"I work for Joe. He pay me each month." Henrique obviously was not aware that the house had changed hands. "I been back to España for last month. Where is Joe?"

"Ahh, that explains it. I bought the house from Joe some weeks ago. Hi, I'm Jenni. I live here now."

Jenni reached out her hand to shake his. With Mediterranean flare, the young man took her hand and pressed his lips to it. The gesture was powerfully sexy. Jenni could feel a warm tingle travel up her arm and into her core. Wow, his lips felt warm and soft on her skin.

Her mind jumped fifteen steps ahead and imagined those lips caressing her body. She quivered with excitement.

Stop.

Henrique coughed as if to rouse her from her fantasies. "You want me to work for you now?"

The tone was almost pleading. Jenni was a soft touch. She probably didn't need a gardener, but one as beautiful as this would not be a hardship. She had been excited at the thought of tinkering in her beautiful garden, but it would seem rude to do Henrique out of a job. Perhaps he was a treat to herself?

"How much do you charge, Henrique, and what did you do for Joe?"

"I cut grass and trim your bush for you." Jenni spluttered, trying to contain her laughter. She signalled to him to continue as she hid her face behind her hand. Desperately trying not to cry with laughter, she could feel her sides about to split. "Joe had me every week. Twenty of your English Pounds is my money for an hour of my time."

Jenni continued to smile at his disjointed English. Of course she could not have managed to hold a conversation in Spanish, so she really shouldn't laugh at him. It was so endearing though. Well, twenty quid was not too bad. A cheap price to pay for the pleasure of watching his model-like body prance across her garden.

For goodness' sake, she thought. He doesn't look much older than George. What the hell has happened to me? Lusting over a lad, young enough to be my son. I think I need a cold shower to calm down.

"OK, Henrique. You have the job then." Jenni smiled at him. As he returned the smile, another spark fizzed in her belly. His smile was amazing, revealing the whitest teeth she had ever seen. "I was just about to put the kettle on. Do you fancy a cup of tea?"

"Tea, black no milk please, Señorita." He literally bowed to her as he wandered back to the lawnmower and picked up where he had left off.

Jenni took her time with the tea while she cooled down. She was a menopausal woman, fantasising over a young stud who probably wouldn't look twice at her. How sad! Despite that, she couldn't help but watch his movements as he walked up and down the lawn. "I think I am going to enjoy having a gardener," she whispered to Freddie, who had come to see what all the fuss was about.

Henrique, meanwhile, was thinking about the lovely lady as he pushed his clunky mower in front of him. She was a much more interesting customer than Old Joe, who moaned all the time. This could be fun. She was an extremely attractive lady for an older woman. Henrique liked the older ladies. They were always more grateful. Henrique was not averse to some extra duties, if the clientele appealed to him. Jenni was certainly his type. He could come to enjoy this job, much more than working for Joe.

Very interesting.

Jenni set out the tea on the garden table. She had baked some scones that morning so had positioned a couple on a plate as an offering to the Spanish god. Henrique wiped his hands down his shorts as he took the seat proffered opposite Jenni. The sunglasses, which had been propped upon his mop of dark hair, dropped onto his nose as he stretched his long limbs out in front of him, enjoying the autumnal sunshine.

"Where do you live Henrique? Are you local?" It was only polite to get to know him. Wasn't it?

Henrique smiled as he took a sip of tea, nodding at the taste. "Caravan over in the woods." He gestured in the direction towards the other side of the village shop. Jenni hadn't ventured over to the woods yet, but understood it was a popular dog-walking area. "Farmer, he rent it to me. Houses round here too expensive for a gardener."

Jenni listened intently as Henrique explained that he had moved to Dorset from Barcelona after university. He had studied in Bournemouth as part of his degree course so was familiar with the area. He wanted to learn English, while continuing his love of all things horticultural. Jobs in Barcelona were in short supply, especially since the crash of 2008, so many young Spaniards resorted to moving abroad to get a leg up the career ladder.

He had found his way to the Dorset countryside when a friend had told him he could charge more for his services to the rich people. Honesty always being the best policy, he delivered that part of the conversation with a cheeky grin. Farmer Thomas had agreed to rent out a small caravan on his land, which was basic, but sufficient for this young man. It meant that he could save his wages for the future.

The whole conversation was pieced together by Jenni as she picked out the pertinent points from his pidgin English. Henrique stuffed his face with the scones, hoovering up three in quick succession. What with his unique accent and a mouthful of scone, it was challenging to get the gist of his story. Jenni managed though. Perhaps the years of listening to teenage boys mumbling had set her in good stead.

"The cake is good, Señorita." That grin was so endearing. He must break all the girls' heart's, decided Jenni.

"I'm glad you like them, Henrique. Why don't I put a few in a bag so you can take them home with you? Have them for tea tonight." Her motherly instincts told her that the young man probably didn't have a very balanced diet. The way he had devoured the scones told her he hadn't had any breakfast yet.

Little did she know that Henrique was an excellent chef. He had a part-time job at the pub, a few nights a week working for Geoff and Jacky Smith. His Thursday night tapas nights were very popular.

"Thank you, Señorita. Must get back to work now." Henrique stood up, towering over Jenni. His smile lit up his face as he took her hand again, kissing her palm gently. "Lovely to meet you, Jenni. I like to work for you."

Wow, thought Jenni. I am going to love you working for me. Jenni sat for a few moments watching the man toil. She blushed as he bent over, showing her the top of his Calvin Klein briefs. He definitely did that on purpose. This was a young man who knew he was beautiful and certainly knew how to work it. He had a captive audience and was prepared to flaunt his wares.

Gathering up the tea things, Jenni departed to the kitchen. Nice as it was, she couldn't waste the morning watching Henrique work. He would think her some sort of pervert.

She wouldn't want to get a reputation like Peter St John, she sighed.

CHAPTER TEN
KATE'S GENERAL STORE

Herbert eased his leg over the saddle, gently placing his decrepit old bicycle against the shop wall.

For a seventy year old, Herbert Smythe-Jones was still very active. He would normally bike to the village store each day from his home, Manor House, located at the other end of the village. If the weather was particularly bad, he might use his old Jag, but he was reluctant to get the vehicle out of the garage, unless he really had to. It had to be severe weather for that to happen.

Herbert was no longer keen on driving and his eyesight was not the best anyway these days. No doubt if he visited an optician any time soon, he would probably get banned from using the car. He hadn't made that sensible visit yet, because keeping his license and the car was vital. Not the most responsible choice, but living out in the countryside without a car was impossible, in his opinion.

The General was thus named as he had spent his whole career in the Army, eventually earning those four stars. Herbert had travelled the world with his career, seeing active service in a range of conflicts, from the Falklands to Iraq. The Middle East had been the straw which had literally broken the camel's back. The horrors of war in the modern age were so vastly different to the world Herbert had fought for, in the early years of his career. He had decided it was time to rest his bones and settle back home in the UK.

His wife, Bridget, was fully supportive of his decision to retire. She had travelled the world with Herbert, bringing up their children pretty much on her own. She had to keep the continuity for the children, despite them having to adjust to different schools, and even languages, during their formative years. The idea of settling in the Dorset countryside was like nectar to the bee for Bridget. She grabbed the chance and delighted in making a home for the family in the ancient Manor House. It would be a home full of love and happiness, where their grown-up children and growing number of grandchildren could come and stay.

Their happy retirement was short lived.

Bridget got sick suddenly and was diagnosed with pancreatic cancer. She was dead before they had the chance to understand what was happening. And Herbert was left alone in that big old house. That was ten years ago. But it still felt like only yesterday for The General. He couldn't face leaving the huge Manor House and moving into something more suitable for a widower. Even if that was the most practical thing for him to do. His home held all his memories of Bridget. Every room resonated with her touch. He hadn't changed a thing since she left and would still wander from room to room touching her things. It kept her close, in his thoughts and everyday actions.

He often caught himself having a conversation with Bridget. Mad as a Hatter, he would mutter, if he found himself doing that.

The bell over the door tinkled as he eased it open. The village shop was quiet this morning with only Kate behind the counter, who was chatting happily with the newcomer, Jenni. The General waved at Kate as he picked up a basket and started to work his way around the store. Herbert didn't do a big weekly shop, preferring the joy of purchasing all his needs from Kate and her team. It was probably more expensive, but money didn't really come into it for The General. He couldn't plan ahead in terms of meals. He was the spontaneous type, so the ability to shop locally was vital for him. How he would have coped if Kate and Jeremy hadn't saved the shop, he didn't dare think about.

In the cold cabinet, The General picked up some beef sausages, thinking they would go nicely with some mash potato and onion gravy. Having selected some tins, including a rice pudding for tonight, he made his way to the counter. Kate was still chatting with the newcomer, so he hung around not wanting to interrupt.

He took a few moments to observe the new villager. She was an extremely attractive woman. So stylish, her clothes just seemed made for her, in fit and style. Not that Herbert was a clothes expert, but his Bridget had carried that same sort of natural style. She could wear almost anything and look good. Jenni Sullivan certainly did remind him of his wife. They were similar in looks. It was quite uncanny.

"Morning General." Kate interrupted his musings. "You met Jenni at church, didn't you? I don't need to make formal introductions, do I?"

Herbert placed his basket down on the counter so that he could take Jenni's proffered hand. She exhibited elegantly painted nails in a ruby red colour which showed off her expensive-looking rings. He noticed the huge diamond on her ring finger. Intriguing. He was certain he had heard she was on her own. Not the sort of question you could ask at first meeting. It would have to wait. Or he could ask Kate, he thought.

"Enchanté, Madame," Herbert shook her hand as he looked directly into her eyes. Oh, the resemblance to his Bridget, at that age, was striking. A shiver passed down his spine as he recognised, in Jenni, a kindred spirit. Her eyes spoke of loss. A loss which had changed her forever. He would have to find out what had caused the pain in her beautiful eyes. "Delighted to meet you again. How are you settling in?"

"Very well thank you. Umm." Jenni looked a bit confused as to how to address the old gentleman. Could she really call him The General? Sounded a bit cheeky. Kate was quick to jump to her new friend's assistance.

"Let me clarify. The General is really called Herbert. That's his actual name. But everyone calls him The General," laughed Kate. "You don't mind that do you, Herbert?"

"Not at all," replied Herbert or The General. "Says what it does on the tin." He laughed as he could see Jenni relax. "You must come round for coffee some time, my dear. I do like to grill all the newcomers to the village. Make sure they know what's what."

Kate interrupted again. "The General is chairman of the Parish Council. He will have you volunteering for all and sundry before you know where you are."

Jenni gave Herbert her legendary beaming smile. The General blushed a deep, rosy red colour as he fell under her spell.

"I would love to get involved in the village," she said. "It is a wonderful way of getting to know people and will help me settle in quicker."

"Super. Well why don't you pop over for a cup of coffee or tea next week and I can tell you all you need to know?"

Kate laughed as she nudged Jenni. "Careful what you agree to, Jenni. The General is very persuasive."

Herbert grinned. He was already excited about the thought of getting to know this lovely young lady. Perhaps he could get her involved with the council. God knows it could do with some fresh blood, and a woman's mind would be ideal.

Jenni and The General made arrangements while Kate scanned his basket of goods. She placed them into a wicker basket which The General always carried with him. It fitted easily on the back of his bike, leaving him hands-free to steer the ancient wheels. He really should invest in a more up-to-date model, but, as with most things, Herbert found it so hard to let an old, faithful companion go.

"I will leave you two ladies to it then." The General heaved the basket onto his good arm. His left arm had taken shrapnel some years back and wasn't so strong. "See you next Tuesday then, Jenni."

"Lovely you to meet you, General." Jenni smiled. "Look forward to coffee next week. I'll bake something to bring."

Herbert made his way outside, smiling to himself. It will be wonderful to get to know the lovely Jenni Sullivan he decided. I bet no-one else in the village has managed to get time alone with Jenni yet, he thought.

That would be a coup he could boast about down the pub later.

He may well be in his seventies, but perhaps there was life in the old dog yet.

CHAPTER ELEVEN
THE KING'S HEAD PUB

The King's Head was a thatch, the predominant roof style in Sixpenny Bissett.

It was a long, white, brick building, which was set back off the main road, with a generous car park at the side. The thatch was incredibly thick and appeared to slope down over the first floor of the pub. It was the most quintessentially British looking hostelry Jenni had ever seen. Today was her first visit and she was excited to learn more about its history.

Alaistair had called for her just before 7pm and they had walked back down the hill to the pub. Despite her efforts to convince Alaistair that she could meet him there, especially as his home was the opposite side of the pub from hers, he had refused. Ever the gentleman, Alaistair had insisted. He was out to impress. And it worked.

Jenni was touched by his efforts. It was quite refreshing. Jenni did miss the gallant attention of a man. Reggie had been the perfect gentleman without making it feel creepy and overpowering. She missed having a man to lean on. Despite feeling really proud of her achievements since she had moved house, it was pleasant to let a chap take charge for the evening.

Jenni had dressed carefully for the occasion. Without knowing how posh the pub might be, she had settled for a pair of black jeans with a soft, pink, wool jumper. Black, heeled boots and a leather jacket completed her look. It obviously received her companion's approval as she noticed the appreciative nod of his head as she had closed her front door and walked towards him down the path.

As they entered the pub, Jenni noticed everyone turn to look at them. Heads swivelled around in the most obvious way, like a celebrity had just walked in. It would have been amusing if it wasn't so obvious that she was the centre of attention. Jenni would have felt quite intimidated if she were alone. The pub was busy, with nearly every table taken by couples, and a fair number of guys sitting at the bar. There was a moment of agonising silence as the couple were watched. Then, like a light switching on, normal service resumed. An outbreak of noise, which crackled with numerous conversations, quickly resumed after everyone had taken their fill of the new arrivals.

Alaistair made his way across the lounge bar with Jenni following. He seemed to know instinctively where their table was. Impressive, she thought. Jenni had not seen the unspoken signal between Alaistair and the barman, who had wafted his arm towards a table at the back of the bar. It was secluded, just as Al had asked for.

He had anticipated that his arrival, with Jenni, would have stirred up a good deal of speculation. Secretly, he was bursting with pride at the glances coming his way. That will show them, he decided. However, Al was keen to have as much privacy as possible, as he tried to woo the lovely Jenni. And the pessimist inside him knew that if it ended with humiliation, then at least it wouldn't be played out to all and sundry to be dissected at their leisure.

Alaistair rushed to help her with her jacket and hung it carefully across the back of her seat, even pulling the chair out for her to sit down. It had been some time since Jenni had been treated with such care and attention. Again, it was refreshing and really quite lovely.

"What would you like to drink, Jenni?" asked Alaistair.

"I would love a glass of Rioja please. That would be lovely."

"Sorted. I'll grab a couple of menus too while I'm at it. Hope you are hungry. It's tapas night tonight. The dishes are usually delicious."

Alaistair made his way to the bar, leaving Jenni to look at her surroundings.

The walls of the pub were panelled in a dark wood which should have made the place look dark and oppressive. Excellent lighting had been used to add warmth to the atmosphere and each of the pictures, hanging at regular intervals, had individual uplighters. Towards the side of the bar area was the most enormous fireplace with an open fire raging. Horse brasses surrounded the hearth, adding to the quintessential country pub look. The area in front of the fire was the only part of the pub which was devoid of tables. The heat from the flames being the obvious reason.

Jenni recognised a few customers as she gazed around. Some familiar faces she had seen at church or when taking a walk around the village. She honestly couldn't remember many of the names which corresponded with the faces. That's one of the big problems with being the newbie. Everyone else only has to remember one name, whereas she faced the challenge of getting to know the whole village. It will come in time, I guess.

A few people smiled back at her as she scanned the room.

What she didn't notice was the furtive looks from several villagers. They were intrigued to see Jenni out with Alaistair Middleton. The man who could 'Bore for Britain' when he got chatting. A few smirks were shared as a number of diners imagined the night ahead for Jenni. Those smirks came from the poor unfortunates who had been caught by Al in the past and had had to listen to him drone on about Ruby Middleton.

Alaistair was not immune to the stares. It certainly didn't faze him. If anything he was chuffed to be seen out with Jenni. The gossips can put that in their pipe and smoke it, he thought. 'He who dares, Rodney,' in the famous words of David Jason. Balancing both drinks and a couple of menus, Alaistair made it back to the table with no spillages.

"Here we go," he said, placing a large Rioja in front of Jenni.

She took a long sip, savouring the wine. It was a good one.

Full bodied and rich.

The wine that is, not Alaistair! She smirked, hiding her look behind the menu.

Jenni scrutinised the choices. As Alaistair had mentioned, the food was totally Spanish-focused this evening. The selection of tapas dishes was extensive and, for those unfamiliar, an explanation of each dish was included. The broken English wording reminded Jenni of someone. Her lusty gardener would be proud of the descriptions, so familiar to his disjointed grammar.

Between them Alaistair and Jenni agreed on five dishes to share. It wasn't clear whether they mutually agreed or whether Alaistair just agreed with Jenni's suggestions. Fried calamari, chorizo in a red wine sauce, spinach, and sweet potato tortilla, patatas bravas and a seafood paella would give them variety of both taste and texture.

Alaistair let Jenni make the order. She was insistent, especially as she had promised to pay for the evening. He liked her, but that didn't mean he wanted to get stuck with the bill.

As she waited at the bar to be served, a couple of locals exchanged greetings with her. Going up to the bar was something she had got used to in the years since Reggie died. He had always insisted on doing that job. Reggie was a traditionalist and would never countenance his lady going to the bar. Paying for the food would have been crass in the extreme, in his view. Times had changed and there was no way that Jenni could be waited on anymore. She had had to learn new ways since becoming a widow and one of those had been independence. Some women craved it, especially if in a coercive relationship, but for Jenni it was an unnecessary consequence of the death of her husband.

A reminder of all she had lost.

It didn't take long for the food to arrive, all served in small, terracotta, pottery bowls. The dishes were beautifully laid out, artistic in design. Florence, the landlord's daughter, took her time arranging each dish to show it off to its best. Conversation stopped as the couple helped themselves to generous servings of each dish. The taste was out of this world, bringing the warmth and excitement of Spain to this corner of Dorset.

Once the initial rush to fulfil the needs of their appetites was met, Alaistair decide it was time to get to know Jenni a bit more.

"Jenni, I hope you don't mind me asking, you look like you have a ring on your finger but you've clearly moved here on your own? What's the story?"

A bit forward.

Jenni knew that this was always going to be the first question most people asked. Surprisingly, she hadn't needed to discuss her circumstances at the dinner party the other night. In fact she didn't have to talk much that night at all, as she was listening to Pervy Pete preach.

"My husband died 18 months ago." She paused as she watched the emotions change on Alaistair's face. He settled on an expression of sympathy. "Car accident."

"Oh, Jenni. I am so sorry to hear that. How dreadful. I think I can understand why you would move. Escape the memories."

Jenni was quite touched by his remark. Many of her closest friends had struggled to understand why she would want to escape familiarity, whereas this stranger understood her rationale.

"You are so right. It was the main reason for moving away. It was hard to leave my husband's business and our family home, but I think the kids understood. I have two grown up sons, George and James."

Al was imagining how the friends of her sons must have lusted after a MILF like Jenni. Not the most appropriate thought. He quickly dismissed it from his brain, just in case his mouth kicked in inappropriately. Sometimes words slipped from him without the appropriate filter being applied. So tonight he was being extra cautious.

"What line of business was your husband in?"

"Car dealership. Reggie bought and sold second-hand cars. My son, George, is running the business now. Reggie was a typical petrolhead, I'm afraid. It was his undoing." Jenni tried hard not to think about the scene of their accident. Just talking about it brought memories flooding back. "What about you Alaistair? Married?"

Jenni knew the answer to this one as Kate had mentioned Ruby before the dinner party. But it was good deflection tactics.

"Don't get me started!" Alaistair groaned. "Divorced. My wife ran off with another woman, would you believe it?"

"Oh dear. I bet that was hard," said Jenni. "Are you still on good terms?"

Alaistair reflected on that question before he put his mouth into gear. He hated Ruby with a passion, especially after what she had done to him. Not that he had still been in love with her when she had told him she was off. It was the humiliation of her running off with a woman. His male pride was severely tested. That hurt more than her leaving. It was the thought that every red-blooded male in the county was laughing at him behind his back.

Bastards.

"Not really," he shrugged. "Think I'm well shot of her. She fleeced me for as much as she could before going. What a bitch. Anyway, don't get me started on her or that cow, Teresa. Her lover. She looks like a bloody rugby player. Most red-bloodied men imagine lesbians as beautiful blonds with huge tits, not a butch rugby player."

Jenni was shocked by the vehemence of his words. Kate had mentioned he was bitter, but the venom which had just spouted out of his mouth was quite surprising. It was a bit of a conversation stopper. Unfortunately, it was too early in the evening for her to escape gracefully, without causing offence. Jenni was not the sort of person who felt comfortable showing her true feelings, especially when they were negative. She would have to smile sweetly and get through the rest of the evening. Perhaps a change of conversation would help.

"Anyway, how is your business going, Alaistair? You made such a beautiful job of my curtain rails so I'm sure you must be very busy with work." Trying a bit of flattery may swerve the conversation away from his ex-wife.

Now Alaistair was in full swing. For the next hour, Jenni didn't have to say a word. Alaistair launched into a long explanation of the ins and outs of his work. He went into the minutest detail of every job he had completed in the last six months. The level of detail went over Jenni's head and she tuned him out, smiling and nodding at various intervals.

Jenni was experiencing first-hand Alaistair's reputation. His 'Bore for

Britain' nickname was on full display. Jenni treated herself to a second glass of wine, along with a Guinness for Alaistair, without him stopping for breath.

Oh goodness, I cannot wait for this evening to end, thought Jenni.

As she sat there, gritting her teeth, she was not aware of another pair of eyes on her.

Henrique had popped into the bar to grab his nightly pint. Service was over and he was as dry as the Sahara Desert. As he sipped on his drink, he spotted Jenni with that builder chappie. He grinned as he watched her face. She was bored rigid. And trying incredibly hard not to show it. What a lady! Polite in the face of extreme boredom.

She really needs a red-blooded Spanish male to excite her, Henrique reflected. Perhaps he should go across and help her out? No, let Alaistair destroy his chances, once and for all, and then Henrique could swoop in and save the day.

Poor Jenni.

All these men wanting her.

And those desperate men not at all aware that she didn't want them. These English men are useless, decided Henrique.

CHAPTER TWELVE
ROSE COTTAGE

A log fire was burning merrily, creating twinkling patterns across the lounge carpet.

Kate eased back on the sofa, sipping the chilled Chardonnay which Jenni had just served. The two friends were enjoying a Friday night in together. Jenni couldn't face the pub two nights in a row and had asked Kate to join her for supper. She had, of course, invited Jeremy too, but he had cried off. Jeremy had seen the look in his wife's eye which told him, in no uncertain terms, not to even think about accepting the invite. It was clear that Kate wanted to catch up on the gossip, without her vicar husband alongside behaving like some sort of tittle-tattle gooseberry.

"So tell me. What happened?" Kate shuffled towards the edge of her seat as she fixed her gaze on her new friend. "Spill the beans."

"Oh, Kate. It was a nightmare." Jenni was still getting over the events of last night. "The meal was lovely and if it hadn't been for that, and a delicious wine, I would have got up and gone. Seeing what happened later, I wish I had."

"Now I am intrigued. Come on, dish the dirt." Kate took a deep glug of wine, excited to hear what happened.

"Well, the evening was long and hard. First, he ranted about his wife and her affair with another woman. Then he bored me senseless about his job. The only saving grace of the whole night was the food. It was delicious."

"It was tapas night, wasn't it?"

"Is that a regular thing on Thursdays then?" asked Jenni, easily distracted from the original question. If it was the case, she was keen to go again, but perhaps with different company.

"Every Thursday. It's young Henrique, your gardener. He's chef on a Thursday. It's something Jacky put in place a few months back and it's been a roaring success." Jacky and Geoff ran The King's Head with the help of their daughter, Florence.

Jenni was certainly intrigued. That Adonis, with his lawnmower, was an expert chef too. Now that was good to know. How come some people have it all? Looks and talent. It really isn't fair.

"Good to know. Anyway, after putting up with Alaistair chuntering on for hours, he insisted on walking me back home. I honestly didn't expect him to. I even came prepared with my torch, the latest vital accessory for my handbag." Jenni grinned, thinking how her life had changed in so many small ways since the move. "Well, we got to my door and, you are never going to believe it, but he only tried to kiss me."

"Bloody hell. Seriously?" Kate's mouth dropped open in shock. She hadn't seen that one coming.

"Seriously. It was like being attacked by an octopus. Arms like tentacles grabbing me and a big sucker squelching my lips. Disgusting, and he tasted of beer which didn't help either. Oh, it was horrible."

Kate burst into raucous laughter, visualising Al as some mystical sea creature, all legs. "My God, how did you react? Did you give him a slap? I would have done."

Jenni wished she had. She had tried to stay calm under his unnecessary attention, and with a struggle, she had managed to extradite herself from his tentacles.

"I think I made it pretty clear that I am not after that. I tried to let him down gently, especially after everything he had said about his wife. I was super conscious that he is quite damaged after all that, but that doesn't mean I'm prepared to put up with that sort of behaviour. I mean, I never gave him any indication that our meal was anything more than a thank you.

All in all, it was a dreadful end to a boring evening."

"Damn, Jenni. I never would have thought Al had the balls to try something like that. What an idiot. I don't remember the last time I saw Al with a lady friend. But going in for a kiss like that. I can't believe it." Kate started to giggle. "Sorry. I know I shouldn't. But Al trying to snog you. Unbelievable!"

"It was like kissing a sink plunger. I thought he was going to suck me dry. It was all dribble and drool. God, I think Freddie would be a better kisser."

Jenni was laughing too now. Their giggles only served to increase the humour and before they knew it, they were in tears. Kate ended up with hiccups. Which then made them laugh even more.

"Shit, I need a wee," cried Kate. "My bladder cannot cope with this."

Kate shot through to the downstairs loo before she could disgrace herself. As she sat with her knickers round her ankles, she thought about what Jenni had told her. Well, well, well. Al Middleton. Who would have thought it? He was definitely punching above his weight. But good on Jenni, standing up for herself.

I wonder how Al is feeling after another humiliation, thought Kate. He must be so out of practice if he thought a meal and a couple of glasses could win over Jenni. I'm not sure I will be able to look him in the eye when he next pops into the shop, she reflected.

Al the octopus!

Kate stifled another giggle.

Such fun.

She had guessed that Jenni would attract a fair amount of attention, with her stunning looks and friendly personality. In her wildest dreams, Kate had never anticipated that Al might have been the first to try it on. The likelihood of that happening was definitely not on her radar. Unfortunately, rejection would probably set Al back years. He had lacked confidence even before the debacle of last night. This would make things ten times worse.

Perhaps she ought to pick up with him and see if he was okay. Just in her pastoral capacity, of course. As a friend. As the wife of the vicar.

Not because she wanted to find out more.

Not because she wanted to get all the gossip. That really wasn't her style.

Seriously.

Kate could convince herself, but even her saintly husband, who saw the best in everyone, could see the truth. Kate loved being at the centre of everything which went on in the village. She just couldn't help it.

CHAPTER THIRTEEN
THE MANOR HOUSE

The front door knocker was as impressive as the house itself.

Jenni had been overwhelmed as she walked up the long drive, taking in the wonderful view. The General's mansion was set back from the main road and not visible until you made your way up the winding drive. As she had turned the last bend, the sight was something to behold.

The Manor House was a beautiful Georgian property, symmetrical in design. Red brick with four huge windows on each of the main two floors, facing the drive. A circular window graced the third floor which, in the past, would probably have been the servants' quarters. The front door was approached up an impressive staircase bordered with ceramic plant pots, teaming with autumnal flowers.

Roses grew up the face of the house and had been trained around each window, in an intricate design. Late summer colours of pink and yellow roses set off the Manor House wonderfully. Sculptured trees surrounded the property. Jenni wondered if Henrique had the job of maintaining this garden. If he did, it would be one hell of a challenge compared to her modest needs.

To the right side of the main building was a vast barn, which remarkably was thatched. Who thatches a barn, thought Jenni? It looked beautiful but seemed a bit excessive for storing your gardening equipment. Unknown to Jenni, the barn was an extension to the living accommodation. Herbert and Bridget had originally planned to use it as a granny flat for Herbert's aged mother. Unfortunately, she had died soon after they moved to Sixpenny Bissett and the annex had never been used for its original purpose. The

General's children loved to stay in it when they came to visit. It gave them the chance to stay independently, somewhat like a holiday cottage, and spare Herbert the disturbance of his noisy grandchildren.

Back to the door knocker.

It was huge, made of brass and extremely weighty. As Jenni dropped the clanger down, the booming sound it made broke the peaceful silence. The noise reverberated across the hallway within. It seemed like ages before Jenni heard movement. Firstly a shuffling noise, then the grating of locks being turned and, finally, the groan as the huge door eased open.

"Jenni, my dear. You found me okay?"

The General opened his body up, in a welcoming motion, directing her into the vast hallway. The floor was tiled with a light grey marble slabs and, set off further, with dark grey marble columns, dotted at regular intervals. There was even a vast fireplace at one end of the hall, before the staircase. A circular table held pride of place in the centre of the room, with a huge display of blue-leafed flowers adding a statement. It was a hall to be proud of.

Jenni reflected that most of her downstairs living accommodation could probably fit in this hallway. She gazed around her as she took in the opulence.

"What a beautiful home you have, Herbert. It truly is magnificent."

As she spoke, Jenni handed over a cake tin. Inside was a coffee and walnut cake she had pulled together that morning.

"Thank you, my dear." Herbert smiled, clearly happy that she was impressed with her surroundings. He loved his home, another reason why he couldn't contemplate downsizing. "And thank you for the offering. You will be impressed but I did some baking myself. I'm afraid you are the guinea pig," he chuckled.

The General led the way into the lounge. This room faced the rear of the property. Four huge sofas dominated the area, giving the room a cluttered feel. It was vastly different from the magnificent hall. The General obviously used this room for living, whereas the entrance hall was for show. A red, patterned rug covered the remaining floor space. A square coffee table sat in the centre of the room, in front of the brick fireplace. Dotted around the walls were various family photos, adding to the homely ambiance.

"You will excuse me, my dear. I will just go and fetch the coffee. Make yourself at home," said Herbert, as he left her to her own devices.

Jenni couldn't resist checking out the photos. She did love to be nosy, especially as it would help to build a picture of this friendly gentleman, who had obviously taken a bit of a shine to her. Learning a bit about his history would help her to get to know the person better.

An array of pictures, she assumed were Herbert's children, populated the cream-painted walls. It was clear that Herbert had several grandchildren too. Once she had checked out the photos, Jenni wandered over to the patio doors which opened out into the garden. A terrace was dominated by a large garden table and chairs, which looked out over a vast lawn. Everything was manicured beautifully. It was clear that The General was passionate about his garden. Towards the far end of the lawn, Jenni could make out a small lake, with reeds growing tall from its waters.

The door opened. Herbert returned, carrying a huge tray loaded with cups, coffee pot and what looked like scones. Setting the goodies up on the coffee table, Jenni watched as Herbert 'played mother.'

"Milk? Sugar?" Herbert passed Jenni the milk jug so she could serve herself. "I made some fruit scones this morning. Please try one. If you don't mind, I will save your lovely cake for my supper."

"Of course I don't mind, Herbert." Although, Jenni was suddenly wondering how much cake one could eat for supper, when one lived alone.

Turning her attention back to Herbert's offering, Jenni looked longingly at the warm scones covered with jam and cream. She knew she really shouldn't. A minute on the lips and all that. But it would have been terribly rude to decline. Trying to pick the smallest one, she took a bite.

"Oh, Herbert. These are delicious." Jenni licked her lips as the cream squelched. "Do you bake often?"

The General had learnt many new tricks when his wife had died. They had had a traditional marriage, with Herbert as the main breadwinner. Bridget had brought up the children, kept the house and cooked. Once she had died, The General had to find a way of supporting himself. He had briefly considered a housekeeper. He was lucky to have had a hefty pension pay out, which would keep him comfortably for the rest of his life, even in this huge house. Whilst he had employed a cleaner who kept the home tidy for him, he had baulked at someone taking over Bridget's passion, the kitchen.

Cooking was a new skill for Herbert and one that he really enjoyed. Initially he had had a few disasters, but he was only inflicting those failures on his own belly. It took some time before he was willing to share his attempts with friends, who were suitably impressed with his flair for flavour. In life, Herbert usually made a success of everything he turned his hand to. He relished being the best he could at any task. But not in an annoying way; it was an endearing characteristic which Bridget had loved in him.

Herbert and Jenni sat in companionable silence as they enjoyed the scones and sipped the coffee. Jenni sensed that Herbert was watching her intently, not in an uncomfortable way, but as if he were sizing her up. When the conversation started, Herbert did briefly ask her about her personal circumstances, but didn't push for detail. That was a comfort to Jenni. She had politely asked about Herbert's wife, but neither of them seemed keen to open up the wounds to further examination.

They both tiptoed around their grief and all too soon they were on more neutral ground.

"Well, Jenni, when you move into a village like Sixpenny Bissett it is common practice that you get about a year before you are roped in."

"Roped in?" The expression on Jenni's face clearly showed that she had no idea what The General meant.

"Volunteering for all and sundry, my dear. It has been some time since we had fresh blood in the village, so you will be in demand. I wanted to get to you first." The General grinned, including the slightest wink. It was a kindly wink, nothing creepy. Herbert was no 'Pervy Pete,' that was abundantly obvious.

Jenni felt flustered. She had time on her hands for sure, but did she really want to throw herself in to the community so soon? Of course, it would be a great way to get to know others, but her natural shyness burst to the fore, warning her not to push herself forward, just yet.

The General noticed the indecision on Jenni's face before he had even revealed his ask. May as well push on and put it out there. "Don't be worried, Jenni. I'm not going to push you into anything you wouldn't want. I'm just thinking you would be an asset to the Parish Council."

Now that was not what Jenni had anticipated. She had no idea how local government worked. "Really? What did you have in mind?" she quizzed him.

The General was chuffed that her first response was not a straight 'no.' "The Parish Council needs a woman's touch. We are a group of four men who are all a bit stuck in our ways. The meetings are getting terribly similar and stale. We need a fresh viewpoint." Herbert paused to allow Jenni to absorb his opening gambit. "I have been thinking for a while now that we need a bit more diversity on the council. I think you could be a real asset. And coming from a bigger city, you could challenge our thinking away from small village syndrome."

The General felt pretty proud of that last statement. It had only occurred to him in mid dialogue. As he had pondered on the benefits of adding a female touch to the council, he could also see the merits of a city mindset, where people might be less engaged with their local politicians. One of the many challenges The General found with the Parish Council was how decisions can become very personal in such a small community.

Jenni didn't dismiss the ask immediately. "Well what does it entail, Herbert? I really have no idea what a Parish Council does at all. Not something I have ever been exposed to before. Reggie was the man for politics in our house. It never really interested me, but I guess local stuff is different."

The General nodded slowly. "Very different, my dear. Our meetings range from dog poo bins to planning decisions. There are some serious topics we need to work through, including setting the precept for the year, that's the

Parish Council element of your council tax. But we can also get tied up in issues affecting the village. Obviously, we try our hardest to keep out of neighbourly disputes. Not that we get many of those."

Jenni could sense the enthusiasm for his role as Chair. "Sounds interesting, Herbert. What sort of commitment are we talking about?"

"We meet once every two months on a Wednesday evening. So not too much of a commitment. Outside of the meeting there are some actions, but most are dealt with by our clerk. Occasionally we have a few ad hoc meetings, if there is an issue to follow up, but it honestly wouldn't take much of your time."

"Ummm," Jenni wasn't dismissing things out of hand.

"Tell you what. Why don't you come along to the next meeting and see what you think? We have a vacancy so, if you find you are interested, it will be easy for me to sort out getting you on board. What do you say?"

Just going along and trying it out wasn't a sign of commitment, thought Jenni. It might be good to get involved in something new and meet more of the villagers at the same time. Perhaps she would have a chat with Kate too. See what she thinks.

"Ok, I'm not promising anything, Herbert, but I will come along and see what I think. When is the next one?" Jenni felt proud of her spontaneous decision.

"In a couple of weeks' time. I will email you the details if that's useful. I don't think you will be disappointed, my dear, and we definitely won't be. I can see that you would be a real asset to this community."

CHAPTER FOURTEEN
THE MANOR HOUSE

The General always had his evening meal at 6pm sharp.

The regimented structure within the Forces, over his many years, was a hard habit to shift. Routine had been his comfort during the dark days, when he struggled after the dreadful loss of poor Bridget. Knowing what he needed to do, and at what time, helped him put one foot in front of the other. Gradually that routine pulled him through his grief and out the other side.

Tonight, dinner was liver and bacon served with creamy mash potatoes. The General sat at the head of the kitchen table with his napkin tucked neatly into his shirt collar. Knife and fork rested neatly on his plate as he chewed each piece twenty times. He had read somewhere that this was a good ploy to ensure one didn't over-eat. Another habit he had perfected over the years. This one was a habit Bridget had hated. She loved to eat her food steaming hot and really couldn't understand Herbert's propensity to chew slowly. As he neared the end of the dish, any remaining food was almost always cold.

As he ate, Herbert was thinking about Jenni.

She really was the nicest person he had met in many a year. When Bridget had died, he had made a vow to himself that he would never love again. Bridget was the other part of his soul. A part which would remain missing for ever.

So why was his mind obsessed with Jenni?

She reminded him so much of his late wife. The way she walked and carried herself was as if he was watching Bridget come back from the grave. Jenni spoke with the same kindly and soft-textured voice. She was a classy woman, incredibly sexy and beautiful. Yes, she was probably twenty years younger than him, but what is age? Just a number. Herbert knew that he was virile and strong, despite his advanced years. He could provide financially for Jenni, without impacting on his beloved offspring's inheritance.

What would Fraser and Eleanor think of Jenni? He was sure his two children would grow to love her too. Herbert had been alone for so many years. Surely his son and daughter would want to see him happy again.

Picking up his wine glass, he took a sip of a very adequate Beaujolais. He swilled the liquid around the glass as his mind pondered his current predicament.

Jenni may not feel the same way as he did. She may want a younger man. But from what he had heard from Kate, she had been devastated by the loss of her husband, Reggie. Perhaps she would like a bit of companionship, rather than a lusty young stud who would be after her body rather than her mind.

He believed they were kindred spirits.

She had lost her childhood sweetheart who had been with her all her adult life. Her grief was fresher than his, but they both mourned their loved ones. Joining forces in a marriage of mutual respect and appreciation would be a formidable match.

Herbert might be naive when it came to the whims of women, but he really wasn't thinking about what Jenni might want right now. He had a goal in mind and was determined to work towards that.

He planned out this possible relationship as he would a military operation. Identify the target. Determine what weapons he had in his armoury to establish a superior position. Agree his strategy and then approach the target.

His main strategy would be friendship. He would cultivate his friendship with Jenni so that she could see for herself the benefits of their alliance. Hopefully, that would ensure that she could see the advantage in their union and an early treaty could be agreed between them.

All he had to do now was to convince Jenni of her destiny.

CHAPTER FIFTEEN
THE KING'S HEAD PUB

The two women chose a couple of comfy chairs by the log fire.

The pub was quiet for a change, which would give them a chance to chat without being disturbed. Relaxing back in their seats, Kate and Jenni raised a virtual toast to each other. A chilled wine cooler sat on the table between them, holding the remainder of the bottle of Chardonnay.

It had been Kate's idea to come for a drink at The King's Head and Jenni had jumped at the invitation. Their friendship may have been in its infancy, but they shared so many characteristics which seemed to draw them to each other. Jenni had numerous friends in Birmingham, but what she had lacked in her life was a best friend, a confidant with whom she could share thoughts and feelings. Reggie had previously fulfilled that role. After his death, Jenni had found it hard to talk to any of her mates about the depth of her loss. Having only known Kate for a few weeks, she knew they shared a bond where secrets could be nurtured.

Kate took a large sip of wine as she stretched her feet out in front of her, her toes enjoying the heat from the burning flames. "Now, Jenni, tell me, how are you settling in then?"

Jenni mirrored Kate as she stretched her toes towards the grate. "Surprisingly well." She smiled, taking a sip of the refreshing wine. "I honestly cannot believe how quickly the house feels like home. It has such a lovely feel to it. Do you know what I mean?"

"Of course. Home is such a special place. It's more than just bricks and mortar." She smiled. "I am so glad you love your new house. It must have been such a big step to move so far away from Birmingham. No regrets then?"

Jenni contemplated her answer before she continued. "It is strange but moving wasn't as hard as people think. I think many of my girlfriends said I was running away from everything I held dear. I wasn't. I just didn't think I could move on when everywhere I went reminded me of Reggie."

"I get that. You are so very brave though. I cannot imagine how much courage it takes to reinvent your life in another part of the country."

Kate had been thinking about Jenni's situation recently and had even talked to Jeremy about it. His role in the church often led to grief and loss being part of the day job. He had a very stoic view of death, which was grounded in his beliefs. Kate, on the other hand, needed to have her family and friends around her, supporting the major decisions in life. She was full of admiration for Jenni's courage to leave her support network behind and step out into the world alone.

"Bless you, you are too kind," grinned Jenni. "I don't feel very brave. I'm not sure how much I am enjoying being the centre of attention since I moved in. I guess I thought I could just hide in my new cottage undetected."

Kate guffawed at that remark. "No chance, lovely. The men in this village have not had someone as beautiful to gaze at for years. They are behaving like bees around the honeypot, wanting to taste your nectar."

Jenni coughed as she swallowed down her surprise. Kate certainly hadn't been that risqué before. But Jenni liked it. She loved that her new friend had a sense of humour and wasn't afraid to use it. Kate was no typical vicar's wife. And she was definitely not PC. She spoke without any kind of filter; words just came out of her mouth, as she thought them. Refreshing for Jenni. Most of their friends in Birmingham had been far too careful in sharing any controversial views. They very rarely shared an opinion unless it was about fashion or cosmetics.

"I honestly cannot see what all the fuss is about. I'm just an old, worn-out widow," laughed Jenni.

She knew she had kept herself trim over the years, but her face and body knew the passing of time, which wasn't always kind. Take her slap off and her face bore the wrinkles of age, despite the expensive creams she used to conceal the ravages of time. The body can be disguised with clothing, but when she struggled out of bed in the morning, her whole being reminded her of advancing time.

Kate saw something different.

Jenni had a natural beauty. Her long, blond hair was cut professionally and was layered around her cheek bones, complementing her oval-shaped face. Her skin had the look of someone much younger. She had obviously looked after it over the years. Kate would kill for Jenni's body shape. She had never been that shape, even before the kids. Despite carrying too much weight, Kate was quite happy with her own look. And she could appreciate the look of a more beautiful woman without a trace of jealousy.

"Old and worn out?" Kate scoffed. "Let me tell you, the men around here have been sent into a turmoil with your arrival. They are not used to elegant, city types. The nearest they get to glamour with their womenfolk is a clean pair of wellies. I've been watching them and you have got most of them all unnecessary."

Jenni giggled.

"Now, I know you have had the misfortune of meeting Peter St John. He's the village lech. He thinks with his knob and it's been twitching like mad ever since he met you. He's easily handled though. He really hasn't got the balls to stand up to Paula so you are safe there."

"Oh, no thanks," laughed Jenni. "He defo gives me the creeps. I really hate men who think they are amazing. Don't they ever look in the mirror and realise they are not all that. Such arrogance."

"Peter fancies himself, that's for sure. Trouble is, too many women have fallen at his feet so he believes his own propaganda." Kate filled their glasses up. The wine was starting to have an effect as they both relaxed. "Then there's Al, who fancies the pants off you, but will not repeat the mistake he made of kissing you. He lacks so much confidence that one rejection will see him off."

"It's a shame about Alaistair." Jenni jumped in. "He is a lovely man, despite being a motor-mouth. But anyone that kisses with that much moisture really stands no chance with me. And he's not my type. Do you know, I would have put him and Paula together rather than Paula and Peter. They seem well suited."

Kate nodded. "Interestingly, the three of them and Al's ex-wife, Ruby, used to hang around together before they paired off. Think they may have buggered up the pairings." She laughed at her own observation. "OK, so then we have The General. He just wants to protect you and care for you. He has been on his own too long to see you as some sort of sex object. He would rather take you to bed with a warm cup of cocoa."

"Herbert is a real gent. I like him but not like that. And I don't like cocoa." Jenni laughed. "But seriously, Herbert reminds me so much of my late father. He is adorable. I could really see me leaning on him emotionally, which worries me a bit. I miss my dad so much and it wouldn't be fair on Herbert if I took advantage of his better nature as my mental crutch."

Kate nodded, understanding the dilemma. The conversation had turned a bit too serious for her liking so she was quick to move it on.

"That leaves Jeremy and you can keep your hands off him. He's spoken for." Kate winked. She would never suspect her husband of straying. He was her soul mate.

"You have forgotten the best-looking man in the village, haven't you? Apart from your Jeremy, of course. Richard, the guy who lives a couple of doors down from me. Now he is gorgeous. I could break all types of resolutions for him."

Jenni took a big sip of wine. She was trying to keep it light and humorous. Richard Samuels intrigued her. He was very handsome and definitely her type. He just didn't know it yet.

"Forget it. Honestly, babe. He is damaged goods. Not for you."

It wasn't the first time Jenni had been told that, so she brushed over it quickly. Lifting the bottle from the cooler, she jiggled it in front of Kate. "Fancy another?"

"Oh God, we shouldn't. Not on a school night." Not that Kate had to worry about the school run. The kids were perfectly able to get themselves up for school in the morning. "Oh, go on then."

The night was young and the wine was flowing. The perfect recipe to get to know each other and gossip about the village. Jenni was really enjoying herself tonight and honestly didn't want the evening to end too early. Her friendship with Kate was something she already valued highly. Kate was such a laugh, which cheered Jenni no end.

Life in Sixpenny Bissett was going to be fun, especially with Kate at her side. Not for the first time, Jenni reflected on what a good move she had made.

CHAPTER SIXTEEN
THE VILLAGE HALL

The General tapped his pen on the side of his water glass, bringing the meeting to order.

There was a good turn out tonight. The four councillors included Thomas Hadley, the local farmer, who was deputy to The General. Between them, they managed the village with razor-sharp precision. Both gentlemen displayed a keen grasp of local politics and an absolute passion for the village. The other two councillors were Peter St John, who just wanted to influence matters, rather than any desire to support the community, and, finally, Richard Samuels.

Richard had joined the Parish Council some five years ago. As a prominent businessman, he added a huge amount of value to the team, including his knowledge of procedure and risk. Since the loss of his wife, Richard's performance had been patchy to say the least. His head wasn't really in the game. It was one of the reasons that The General was keen to get Jenni on board. To bring some life back into what was a rather stale committee.

"Good evening, ladies and gentlemen," Herbert started.

There were at least twenty villagers in attendance. Jenni was sat right at the front, notebook in hand and a look of total concentration on her face. Kate and Jeremy sat beside her. Jeremy usually attended such meetings in his capacity as 'esteemed clergyman' of the community. He also had a reasonable grasp of any upcoming problems and would normally tip the wink to Thomas or Herbert in advance.

Forewarned is forearmed, the soldier in Herbert reflected.

"Welcome to the meeting tonight everyone. For those of you who have not attended before, the first part of our session is open to the public to raise any issues and concerns."

The General paused and allowed a charged silence to reign. Usually silence forced someone to talk and tonight the audience didn't really need any stoking. First to raise her hand was Anna Fletcher.

"Yes, Mr Chair. I have an issue which I would like the Parish Council to take forward."

Herbert inwardly groaned, hoping that the noise hadn't escaped his mouth. Anna Fletcher was the village busybody. A retired school mistress, Anna had time on her hands and used that time to wind others up. If she wasn't spreading gossip, she was moaning. If Anna walked towards you down the high street, most people would cross the road rather than get caught in her tirade of moans and groans. Sixpenny Bissett was a lovely place to life. It would be an even lovelier place if Anna Fletcher would move on.

"The bushes outside Green Farm Cottages are severely overgrown. It is making it almost impossible to walk past on the pavement. It is a serious death-trap and needs cutting back."

The General looked across the room, judging the atmosphere of the community before he responded. All he could see were smirks and grins as regulars sympathised with Herbert. That woman was unbelievable, thought Herbert, especially as he was trying his best to impress Jenni. If she thought the council only dealt with petty matters like unruly bushes, then what chance would he have for winning her support. He would have to handle this one carefully. In normal circumstances, he would dismiss Anna's moaning with a few mealy words to pacify her. But tonight he was just not in the mood.

"Anna, thank you for raising the matter, but as you well know, neighbourly disputes should not be raised at the Parish Council. Can I suggest that you speak to Mr Middleton and ask him to trim his bush?"

Jenni spluttered as she tried her hardest not to belly laugh. She glanced across at Kate, who had her hand over her mouth, stifling her giggles.

What is it with the community of Sixpenny Bissett and double entendre when discussing their foliage? They were not alone in their mirth. The General had gone a puce colour. He had just realised his faux pas and was pleased to see Jenni enjoying it. He even risked a cheeky wink her way, which resulted in her bursting out into laughter. Quickly Jenni converted the laugh into a cough, disguising it well.

Anna Fletcher was not taking rejection well. Her voice took on a very 'schoolmarm' sound as she enunciated each word, slowly and condescendingly. "Thank you, Mr Chair. But I must disagree. One of your councillors is the owner of the neighbouring property in question, so I do think this matter should be addressed here and now."

Thomas cleared his throat loudly. "Mr Chair, may I address the room." Having received a nod from The General, he continued. "Ms Fletcher. As Mr Middleton is my neighbour and tenant of my barn, I will talk to him as both a friend and a landlord. As Mr Smythe-Jones has quite rightly explained, this is not council business and will be dealt with outside of council governance. Madame Clerk, please minute to that effect."

There was a collective sigh as the matter was closed down expertly. Anna Fletcher had been put back firmly in her box and the meeting could continue.

As Herbert conducted the business of the day, he continued to focus his attention on Jenni. He was keen to see her reaction to the proceedings. He tried not to make it too obvious although, unknown to him, Kate was watching The General and taking it all in.

She sighed as she realised he was far too keen on her friend. That will not end well, she thought. His suit would be rebuffed, but hopefully Herbert might realise the futility of his plan before he got hurt. Kate loved Herbert. He was such a decent guy, but not what Jenni needed. She needed him as a father figure and certainly not as a love interest.

Jenni was not ready for her pipe and slippers, just yet.

Meanwhile, as The General watched Jenni, her eyes were focused on Richard Samuels. He seemed to be in a world of his own for most of the meeting and had no idea that the possible newest addition to the Parish

Council was having her decision to join swayed by the mysterious man. Jenni didn't take her eyes off him. Unfortunately, Herbert was sat next to Richard and took her stares as directed at him.

What a pickle of emotions.

Jenni, the newcomer, who attracted interested when it wasn't necessarily wanted. She had done nothing to attract the stares. She was an innocent in this game of desire. The fools were falling at her feet and she couldn't even see it.

But the object of her interest had not even noticed her. The one person in the village who could ruffle her feathers, was the one man who was unobtainable.

CHAPTER SEVENTEEN
KATE'S GENERAL STORE

The shop was empty.

Jenni was relieved. She wanted a gossip with Kate, without an audience. She secretly couldn't wait to meet up with her for a chat, so was engineering another opportunity in 'Kate's' the village store. She made a pretence of picking a few bits off the shelves as she waited for her friend to finish a call. It sounded like she was speaking to her wholesaler. Wouldn't be the right time to interject.

Kate replaced the phone into its holder as she spotted Jenni lingering around the pasta. "Hello there, Jenni dearest. Recovered from last night?"

The Parish Council had been an eye-opener in more ways than one.

Jenni had lain awake for hours last night, mulling things over. She had decided to join the council and not just for altruistic reasons. True, she felt she could add some value, especially as the team was far too male, except for the clerk who didn't contribute to the discussion and took minutes. Jenni could come across, to people who didn't know her, as quiet and unassuming but, when she felt passionate about something, she was not afraid to push herself forward.

Jenni had decided she was far too young to step into the background of life. To shuffle off into celibacy and early retirement was no longer her life plan. There was life in this old widow yet. She was sure Reggie would have wanted her to live again, even if his sons may want her to disappear into widowhood quietly. Reggie may not have supported her need to spread her wings far from the previous role of the household matriarch, but he wouldn't have wanted her to hibernate completely.

She had been a wife and mother for the whole of her married life and, whilst she loved being those two identities, she felt like she was missing something. Whenever she had expressed those views to Reggie, he had just suggested another holiday or shopping trip. He really didn't get it. He was very much the alpha male, who believed in the woman being the support structure to his successful businessman life. She had loved Reggie with every bone in her body, but she also loved him enough to know his shortcomings. One of her main challenges had been trying to change Reggie's thinking.

All too often she gave up and didn't push the issue. She had missed out through her own lack of drive. Jenni was determined not to let that happen again. It was time for a change.

Going back to her decision about getting involved in local politics, Jenni had another motive on her mind. She had seen Richard Samuels a couple of times walking around the village and, more recently, at church. He seemed the most elusive guy she had ever known. His head went down when he walked past her and he avoided eye contact like a practised art form. She was determined to get to know Richard and, if the Parish Council should be the vehicle to drive forward that plan, then she would kill two birds with one stone, as the expression goes.

Realising she hadn't answered Kate yet, she directed her attention back towards her friend. "Interesting. Very interesting. Was it a typical meeting?"

"If your question is, does Anna Fletcher always have something to say and some challenge to raise? Then the answer is yes," laughed Kate. "But seriously, the format is fairly standard each meeting. But what they are missing is a woman-specific viewpoint. If I wasn't married to the vicar, I would have considered it myself. Put a bullet up their arses."

Jenni loved it when Kate got right down to earth with her expressions. The words simply fell out of her mouth and she very rarely sugar-coated her views.

"I agree that it needs something to spice things up a bit." Jenni nodded, as her mind stacked up the pros and cons into piles. The pros pile did seem to be more top heavy. "The lack of a woman's thinking was just far too obvious. Why has no one else put themselves forward?"

Jenni understood why Kate might be put off. Her best friend certainly had her hands full with teenage children and a business to run, alongside the role of vicar's wife, which must bring its own challenges. But there were plenty of other women in the village who could get more involved.

"I think they have all run scared, if I can be totally frank with you," sighed Kate. "It needs a woman with balls to take on the old fuddy-duddies of Sixpenny Bissett. Years of men running the show, especially men with a military background, or those local landowners, leads to a certain culture. I mean, I love The General to death. He is a sweetie, but he's a certain type. Add him and Thomas Hadley together and you have a village set in its ways."

"A woman with balls? I'm not sure I could live up to that, Kate. What experience have I got that trumps all the other women in this community that won't try?"

"You, Jenni Sullivan, underestimate yourself." Kate came around the counter and put her arm across Jenni's shoulder. She gave her a squeeze of encouragement. "You have balls. Never doubt your strength, sweetheart. To have survived what you have and then move halfway across the country to start again, shows me that you are just so very much stronger than you think you are."

Jenni pulled Kate in for a hug. She had only known this woman a matter of weeks and already she was a friend for life. Kate got her. Really understood her. It had taken 50 years of life to find a friend that truthfully knew her. Jenni's biggest problem was self-belief. Kate provided that in spades. Kate had more confidence in Jenni than she had in herself and would be behind her all the way.

"Thank you, Kate. I needed that."

"Cup of tea? I think it's time for a quick break, so let me put the kettle on and we can chew the cud to our hearts' content."

The shop was especially quiet this morning, and the friends were able to make tea and pull up a couple of chairs in the back room with a clear sight of the shop floor. If anyone came in, the bell would give them warning.

"Kate, I wanted to ask you about Richard Samuels."

Kate sighed as she looked at her friend. The smile on Jenni's face revealed a gamut of emotions. All of them extremely dangerous. If the eyes held the window to a person's soul, Jenni's spoke of desire. A desire which would no doubt be rejected. How should Kate handle this one? Her friendship with Jenni was at the forefront of her mind. A true friend would not stoke Jenni's desire, but did she really want to be the person to burst Jenni's bubble?

"Umm, Richard. Now there is a troubled man."

"Why so?"

Jenni was even more intrigued now. He was clearly a man with history. But what was that history? A dark secret, by the look on Kate's face.

"He lost his wife, Nicola, to brain cancer two years ago. He is a broken man if you ask me. Never recovered from the loss."

"Oh how incredibly sad. Was she very old?"

"Nicola was 48 when she died. It was so sad. And quick. At Christmas time she started having problems holding onto things. Was constantly dropping stuff and then the headaches started. By the time she saw a doctor, the cancer was fairly advanced and untreatable."

"That is no age at all. Younger than me." Jenni's eyes filled with tears for a woman she never knew.

"There was nothing they could do for her. The cancer was going to kill her. This horrible disease has a way of twisting the knife on your suffering. The poor woman lost her mind quickly. She didn't know who Richard was in the weeks leading up to her death."

Jenni understood the pain on that man's face now. It must be dreadful watching someone you love slowly drift away. When Reggie passed, she was in so much pain herself she didn't witness the moment he left her. The pain of loss ripped her apart, and the only blessing was that she didn't have to watch him die.

"Richard was alone with her when she died. Jeremy arrived soon after, but she had gone. To add to his pain, the authorities insisted on a post-mortem and inquest, just in case he had helped her pass. Can you imagine?"

Kate had brushed over the events of that awful day, holding back much of the detail.

To be suspected of killing your wife, when she was terminally ill, was the final straw for Richard. He had gone into a dark place for months afterwards. Jeremy had tried so awfully hard to offer comfort, but Richard had been angry with the world. He had railed against any comfort. Jeremy had been concerned enough for his parishioner's safety that he had spoken to the doctor's surgery.

After a number of visits from the doctor, Richard was encouraged to spend some time in a mental health hospital. Encouraged was perhaps the wrong word. He was committed against his will. A fact that hung like the 'Sword of Damocles' over Jeremy's head. Jeremy struggled to forgive himself for his part in Richard's breakdown, even though, on reflection it was the gift of life he provided. Without that support, Richard could have done himself harm. His life had depended on someone caring enough to risk his anger and do the right thing.

"That is so sad, Kate. He must have been devastated. I can only imagine the pain. I sort of understand why he is a bit standoffish now."

Jenni had that look on her face. A look that spoke of kindness and care for others. Unfortunately, to Kate, it also spoke of a deeper desire for the man, who now she knew was damaged and needed looking after. There lies danger, Kate thought. Richard was not the man for Jenni. She was certain of that.

"Jeremy and Richard are good friends."

Kate was keen to tackle this issue carefully. Sure, Jenni hadn't made out that she was interested in Richard as a love match, but the look on her face was enough. Kate cared so much for Jenni and was concerned that her new

95

friend would be hurt by this emotionally-destroyed man.

She continued. "Jeremy has tried to help Richard find his way back to peace. It's not an easy path. I honestly don't think that Richard will ever find happiness, even if the right woman came along. He is just too damaged."

If Kate thought that she had done enough to discourage Jenni, she was sorely mistaken. Unfortunately, Jenni was now even more intrigued about the man and determined to be the one to mend his broken heart. She figured it would take some time and effort, but Richard Samuels looked worth spending time on.

Reggie was the love of her life, but 50 was no age. She was far too young to shrivel up and die because her love was dead. Jenni had always been a passionate woman and adored the company of a man. Loneliness was not a comfort to her. She just could not imagine her living her life alone for ever more.

Perhaps it was too soon for either her or Richard to fall in love again.

But they could be friends.

And wait and see where that friendship would lead.

CHAPTER EIGHTEEN
THE KING'S HEAD PUB

The King's Head was busy with the usual after-work group.

Peter was sat on a bar stool facing Alaistair. The pair of them were regulars on a Wednesday evening. Wednesday was not an evening for romantic dinner dates and didn't have the hubbub of a weekend. It had become Peter and Al's night. Their tradition reached back many years. The two friends would grab a pint and chew over the latest news and gossip.

Being men, they rarely talked about relationships. Well, especially not about their wives. Occasionally, Peter would share the gory details of his latest exploit. His intention was never to seek advice from his oldest mate. No. It was mainly just to boast. Alaistair Middleton was a loser when it came to relationships and Peter would not be a true friend if he didn't rub his nose in the fact every now and then.

Peter wasn't really listening to his 'so-called' mate right now. Al was droning on about the footie. He had been down to Bournemouth at the weekend and was ranting about the price of the ticket and the cost of his half-time burger. If he had been listening more intently, he may have caught the score of the game and the highlights, but Peter really wasn't paying attention. Anyway, he was a Liverpool supporter and had no time for those chaps who supported a local team. They just exhibited their lack of ambition for life in general. If you wanted to be a success, then choose a team who thought likewise.

Peter was thinking about Jenni Sullivan.

Since the dinner party, he seriously could not get her out of his mind.

She was a classy bird and ripe for the plucking. At night he lay awake, into the early hours, thinking of all the delicious things he would do to her. He would get so horny that he often resorted to giving Paula a good seeing to. You couldn't call it making love. There was no emotion in the process for Peter. Not that Paula was complaining. In fact, their sex life had been full on of late. Paula had never had it so good, he decided. The fact that it wasn't a desire for his wife which was the driver of his passion was irrelevant. It was because of Jenni Sullivan, who was occupying his thoughts and desires.

Last week she had come to the Parish Council.

Man did she look tasty! Sitting there all prim and proper with her notepad in hand, sucking on her pen, all suggestive. He had to hold down his passion, as the image of her doing likewise to his cock had shifted his concentration away from the meeting and onto her lips. It was enough to drive a man wild. If he didn't get into her knickers soon, he would go crazy.

On a couple of occasions, he had caught her eye. She had held his gaze with a confidence which said she was ready for him. Was she thinking of him in the same way as his thoughts were fixated on her? It was only a matter of time. It had to happen. And soon, or he would probably burst.

He would need to engineer a way of making his move without raising suspicion with Paula.

God, Peter enjoyed the chase.

Normally, he was not a man to risk his secure homelife for a bit of skirt. Peter loved the chase of a new encounter. The excitement of cornering his prey and having them panting for him, turned him on. Once he had slept with his new quarry a few times, his boredom threshold soon kicked in. He definitely moved on if the latest object of his interest started to get clingy. He had a clear rule set when it came to extra marital attachments. Peter liked sex. He didn't want a relationship. He had a perfectly good one with Paula. He was certainly not risking his life with Paula to jump into another attachment. So 'love them and leave them' was his methodology.

And it had worked pretty well up until now.

Unfortunately for her, Jenni would just be the next notch on his bedpost. He would enjoy enticing her in. He was intrigued to know how good she would be in bed. Once he had had his fill, then they would end it all very amicably.

The sheer arrogance of the man; he did not consider that Jenni might have a say in the matter. No, the affair would be brief and all about his own self-appreciation. Once his goal had been achieved, it would be done. It would not do to have any emotional stress too close to home.

The last thing he wanted was for Paula to find out.

It wasn't that he didn't want to hurt Paula. Peter was not that kind of man. He didn't care about Paula's feelings, in the same way as he didn't think she cared about his welfare. It was just a damn sight easier to keep the peace. And of course, there were financial considerations. Poor old Al had taken one hell of a hit when that bitch Teresa had sneaked off to her lesbian love nest.

There was no way Peter wanted to give half of everything he had to Paula.

No way.

Suddenly, Peter realised he was being asked a question.

"Another pint mate?" Alaistair wafted his empty glass, breaking Peter out of his lustful thoughts.

"Cheers, mate."

CHAPTER NINTEEN
THE KING'S HEAD PUB

"Another pint mate?"

Al realised Peter wasn't listening. Sometimes he wondered why he went drinking with Peter St John every week. They might be friends, but Peter was not the most attentive of listeners. Tonight he was even worse. Al had been enthusiastically regaling him with a story about the Bournemouth v Arsenal game last weekend, and Peter was noticeable by his mental absence from the conversation.

Their relationship was all too often one-sided.

Al would listen, attentively, whilst Peter boasted about his latest affair. The man was a beast when it came to women. He could not keep it in his trousers. Why the hell did women fall for his smarmy charms? Al could not understand what they saw in Peter St John. OK, he was a decent-looking chap, but he was nothing special. He had the gift of the gab which some girls may fall for, but he was not boyfriend material. He just wanted sex.

Alaistair had spent far too many evenings as his wingman.

When Peter needed an alibi, it was always his old mate, Al, who stepped up and gave him a cover story. All too often, Al wondered why he was loyal to Peter. He had enough dirt on him to hang him out for all to see his true character. But Alaistair was too nice. He defended his friend, even when he was disgusted with his behaviour.

Alaistair really didn't understand why Peter could put his marriage at such risk.

Paula was the perfect wife and really didn't deserve to be treated the way she was. Al had always had a bit of a thing for Paula. She was his type. A real-woman's figure, with amazing boobs which seemed to defy gravity. It wasn't just her body which Al appreciated. He cautioned himself, secretly, about following Peter's sexist attitude. He was not like that. Paula was a successful businesswoman who wasn't afraid of hard work. She was a feisty character, which was probably a key requirement for living with Peter St John.

Many a night he had imagined Paula and himself together.

He dreamt of running away from Sixpenny Bissett and all the unhappy memories. Running off into the sunset to set up their new home-making business. He would do the building and structural work and Paula would design the fixtures and fittings. They would make a formidable team together.

Well, in his dreams they would.

But Paula St John could not see further than her bastard of a husband. Her biggest shortcoming to becoming Al's perfect woman, was her gullibility. How could she not see what a rat she was married to? If she could have seen through Pervy Pete, Al was certain that she would leave her husband. She just needed to see through him. But how? The woman had blinkers when it came to her husband.

Once Peter finally realised a second pint was on offer, the two friends settled down to appreciate the amber nectar. Al gave up on the conversation about the match, sensing Peter's disinterest. It was very unusual for Alaistair to be silent on their nights out, and that unusual behaviour had led Peter to take up the narrative. Initially, Al wasn't really paying attention, as he expected the usual drivel about some bird Peter had plans on shagging.

But suddenly his interest was piqued.

"That Jenni Sullivan is one tasty bird, don't you think Al?" Peter was almost salivating with lust. It was embarrassing.

Al was shocked to hear Jenni described as a bird. She was the least likely person to be described thus. "She seems a very lovely lady," he jumped to her defence. "We had a lovely meal together the other week."

"Of course, I forgot about that." Peter lent forward on his stool as he whispered. "Did you?"

"What do you mean, did I?"

"Shag her."

"Bloody hell, Pete. Of course I didn't." Alaistair was genuinely disgusted in the crass way Peter spoke about women. If it wasn't for the fact that he lacked male friends, he would probably ditch Peter completely. "We had a lovely meal together and I walked her home. That's all."

There was no way Al was going to let on that he had gone in for a kiss. He was deeply ashamed of that. He would never normally try something that forward on a first date. It was probably the drink which had given him a bit too much Dutch courage. Of course, Jenni had been so sweet about it. But it had probably put back his chances of a second date by some weeks.

"Oh, that's good news. Wouldn't want to step on your toes, mate."

"Don't know what you're talking about, Pete. What's up?"

"I'm going to have a try at the lovely Jenni."

The grin on Peter's face literally went from ear to ear. He looked chuffed with himself. Al felt sick. What had Jenni Sullivan done to deserve the attractions of Peter St John? Poor woman. Although he reckoned she could probably handle herself.

"I'm not sure she's your type, mate."

That was the understatement of the year.

"Not sure I have a type, mate." Peter laughed. "She's one sexy lady. That's reason enough to give it a go. I'm sure she will be all over me once I lay on the St John charm. Don't you think?"

Al groaned as he realised his friend actually believed his own bullshit.

"Good luck with that, mate. Isn't it a bit dangerous, you know? Shitting on your own doorstep?"

Peter laughed even louder, causing a few fellow drinkers to glance over to see what was occurring.

"I will be the epitome of discretion. No need for Mrs St John to find out anything. I'm thinking the Christmas party may be a good opportunity to work my magic."

The Sixpenny Bissett Christmas party took place in the village hall and was notorious for being a boozy affair. A sore head was the main takeaway from the evening. It was a night everyone attended, hence the use of the vast village hall. Geoff and Jacky from The King's Head supplied the booze and every family was encouraged to bring food, which led to a huge variety of tasty morsels.

Alaistair could not believe Peter would seriously consider making a move on Jenni at such a high-profile event for the village. At least, being prewarned he could do his best to protect Jenni from his friend's drunken desires.

And poor Paula. He could not imagine how she would feel seeing her husband flirting with the new neighbour in front of all her friends.

What a tool!

Not for the first time that evening, Alaistair wondered why he bothered with Peter St John. He really didn't like the guy. Just someone to drink with. That's all.

"Another beer?" asked Peter.

"Go on then," replied Al.

CHAPTER TWENTY
ROSE COTTAGE GARDEN

It was one of those days when Henrique hated living in England. When he wished he was working the sunny gardens of Northern Spain.

The rain was falling steadily now. His hair was soaked and stuck to his face in clumps. Despite his waterproofs, he could feel the damp seeping through to his clothes. Any other day and he would have rolled over in bed and stayed there. Snug and warm in his caravan rather than working in this dreadful weather.

But today was his day at Jenni Sullivan's.

He loved working here. Not only because Jenni always provided a steaming cup of tea and some form of cake accompaniment. He had other reasons. He had a bit of a crush on the lovely Jenni. She really was a MILF. That was the expression he had gleaned from one of his many university mates. Every day he worked for Jenni was a bonus. Luckily, she never noticed him watching her surreptitiously.

Not in a creepy way of course. She was like a fine piece of art. To be admired from a distance, to appreciate her qualities and commit them to his memory.

He had engineered positions around the garden which gave him a decent view into the house. He observed Jenni tidying the house, doing her ironing, and even working away on her computer. He loved being able to watch her going about her daily business, totally oblivious to his gaze. Henrique could then imagine himself strolling in on her and enveloping her into his arms. She would fall into him and give herself completely.

It was all very strange. This crush of his.

Henrique could have his pick of the girls. His track record at university was one to be proud of. The girls loved his Hispanic good looks and the accent was guaranteed to get them into bed. Things were somewhat slower in pace when he moved to Sixpenny Bissett. Other than Florence in the pub, who was definitely off limits, there was a shortage of women of his age group. Regular trips back to Barcelona gave him some respite from his celibate state. He had a regular girlfriend back home, who waited patiently for his return. Or at least that was what she told him.

Since meeting Jenni, he had become obsessed with her. Older women held an attraction for him and Jenni was an older woman who oozed allure. He just couldn't get her out of his head. At night, he lay alone in his caravan imagining he was inside Rose Cottage. He imagined Jenni naked in his arms as he showed her what a Spaniard could offer.

Henrique thought English men were useless when it came to lovemaking. They did not know how to woo a woman. A woman was like a precious stone, to be handled with care, cherished, and stroked in all the right places. Henrique was a master in the art of lovemaking. He was good with his hands. Not only did he possess green fingers, but also very dextrous ones.

The rain started to drip down the back of his neck, sending a shiver down his spine. Looking towards the house, he realised Jenni wasn't in the kitchen. Normally she would have a cup of tea ready for him by now. Perhaps she didn't expect him to be working on such a dreadful day.

He saw a light was on in the bedroom, a bright glow in the gloomy morning. The curtains were open, giving him a clear view into the room. Suddenly a shape moved across the room towards the window.

Realising that he didn't want to be caught as a voyeur, Henrique moved behind a large, twisted hazel bush, which provided him with sufficient cover. If Jenni spotted him, he could pretend that he had intended to trim it today.

Jenni moved to stand in the middle of the window, looking out over the garden. She was partially dressed, only wearing a lacy bra on her top half. It was a vision. Black lace cupped her breasts, pushing them up into a cleavage. Henrique sighed as he took in his fill.

"Oh my, what a woman" he whispered to the hazel.

He could feel the passion rising as he imagined removing that lacy bra and delving into her magnificent chest. He was transfixed on her as his breathing got faster, sweat forming on his brow. His foolish crush was getting worse by the minute. All too soon, she turned away from the window, picking up a jumper and pulling it over her torso.

The show was over.

Henrique groaned with disappointment. He struggled out from behind the hazel and attempted to make himself busy. Turning his face into the rain, he cooled his ardour with its chilly drizzle. Henrique realised Jenni would be at the back door before too long, and the last thing he wanted was for her to find him lingering in the bushes. His mind continued to fantasise as he carried on with his jobs.

Luckily for him, Jenni was completely unaware of his infatuation.

She regarded him as a young boy, albeit a beautiful young boy, who could do magic with her garden. His reward today was a large slice of homemade chocolate cake. Little did she know that he wanted oh so much more than that.

But that would have to live on in his dirty thoughts. He could never have told this classy woman what he would love to do to her. It just wouldn't do. She would probably sack him if he did. At least, admiring her from a distance gave him something to cling on to.

His real reward from this wet afternoon would not be the delicious chocolate cake, which was amazing. It would be the sight of Jenni and that lacy, black bra. Once he was back in his caravan later, he would unpack that image and play it over in his mind. He wouldn't need a porn magazine tonight to keep him company in the cold, lonely night, just the image of Jenni Sullivan.

CHAPTER TWENTY-ONE
THE VILLAGE HALL

The night of the village Christmas party had arrived.

Jenni was finishing the last touches to her make-up, conscious that Kate and Jeremy were due to call for her in half an hour. She had thought long and hard over her choice of outfit for the evening. Not too dressy had been Kate's advice, but one never knew what to expect at such a do. Jenni was keen to make a good impression. It wasn't vanity. Purely a need to fit in with her new community.

One of Jenni's weaknesses was an overriding need to be liked. She lacked confidence at times. The need to be one of the crowd and accepted by others was important to her. She never sought confrontation and, all too often, she found herself being taken advantage of, purely because of her need to be nice to others. Jenni would much rather be taken for granted than be disliked.

Back to her wardrobe choices.

Jenni had chosen a safe option, a little black dress with a sweetheart neckline and plunging open back, which had required some strategic brassiere choices to avoid unnecessary straps. Black hold-up stockings were a must, to avoid any visible lines beneath the dress. Jenni had looked out her old Christian Louboutin heels. Reggie had spent a small fortune on them some years ago when they were going to a trade event. He had wanted to show off the success of his business by the status of his wife's expensive shoes.

And it had worked.

As she applied her eyeshadow, Jenni thought about her conversation with George earlier. Her elder son had been full of gusto as he shared news of the pre-Christmas sales turnover. He had had a whopping month and had suggested the shareholders take an extra dividend, to share out some of the profit. Jenni was expecting a nice bonus just before the holiday season, which was lovely to know. It would also mean that Jimmy would be able to draw down some extra funds to keep his travels moving along. He had talked about working his way into North America next and then Australia, which would be more expensive and would require a bigger budget.

George had agreed to come to hers for Christmas.

Jenni was excited to show off her new life to her elder son. He hadn't seen the house yet and she was hopeful he would approve of her choice. It would just be the two of them together for the festive period, which would be a change from the big family do's of before. Reggie loved to entertain. The house was always full of friends and relations, drawn by the wonderful food and copious amounts of alcohol. Jenni had accepted the noise and chaos because Reggie was in his element but, if truth be told, she preferred it when it was just the four of them.

Half hour later, Jenni, Kate and Jeremy made their entrance into the village hall. The venue was perfect for a party. A high, vaulted ceiling provided great acoustics and the huge timber frames were festooned with Christmas decorations. The bar area was packed with villagers queuing for drinks. At one end of the hall, a DJ was pumping out tunes from his position on a raised platform. Luckily, the sound balance was just about right. The music was loud enough for dancing, but not too loud to prevent conversations. There was a fair smattering of people on the dance floor already, which was good news as it was so early on in proceedings. Jenni was sure that the floor would be heaving once the drink began to take control.

Jeremy returned from the bar with wines for the ladies and a beer for himself. Kate was already wiggling her hips to the tunes. It was infectious. Jenni could feel her toes starting to tap along to the 80s music. An excellent choice of playlist, especially as the majority of those at the party were of a similar age to Jenni.

Before long, Peter and Paula St John joined them. Peter was clearly the worst for wear already. Poor Paula had a look of resigned acceptance on her face, knowing a long night was ahead. Peter slurred his words as he tried to hold down a conversation with Jenni and Kate. Honestly, Jenni found she only got every other word. Not much of a conversation. It was quite embarrassing.

What a mess he was.

Noting the situation, Jeremy became the kindly knight to the rescue. He cleverly orchestrated a move to peel Peter away from the ladies and over to a group of men, hanging around the bar area. Jenni spotted Alaistair amongst them as he waved across at her. She gave him a beaming smile in return, grateful that he would have to entertain the drunken Peter.

A narrow escape.

Once Peter was out of the way, Paula came into her own. She was animated as she discussed her upholstery business, offering Jenni advice and guidance. Rose Cottage had the basics finished off, but Jenni needed more curtains and cushions. For the next half-hour, the two women were deep in conversation, discussing the pros and cons of curtains versus roller blinds.

Jenni really liked Paula. She seemed an interesting woman who had a real passion for her work. The only fly in the ointment was her husband. Well, she couldn't be blamed for him, other than perhaps poor judgment in her choice of spouse. Jenni couldn't understand why someone as sensible as Paula could be married to such an idiot.

"Come on girls," shouted Kate over the opening bars of Wham's Club Tropicana. "Let's dance."

The three ladies shimmied their way into the centre of the dance floor. Kate was not the sort of person to dance on the periphery. She was a centre-of-the-dance floor kind of person. Jenni would never have chosen to push herself into the centre of things, but with Kate at her side, she acted as if all her inhibitions had disintegrated in the mist of the dry ice swirling around the crowd of revellers.

Jenni sang the opening bars to the song at the top of her voice.

Smiling across at Paula and Kate, she moved her body in time to the music. Joy was plastered across her face as she danced, sang, and sipped her drink. She really couldn't remember the last time she had felt so free and uninhibited. She was totally absorbed with the music and a love of life. It had been a hard road she had travelled so far without Reggie, but, like a chrysalis bursting open, she could feel herself unfurling into a beautiful butterfly.

Kate nearly burst with excitement when the iconic Human League track kicked in. She beckoned at Jeremy suggestively as she screamed out the words of the song. Her husband followed her lead on to the dance floor.

Kate's husband was a typical dad dancer; slightly awkward, but throwing himself in to it with an enthusiasm for his art. All personas of respectability were discarded as the middle-aged folk of Sixpenny Bissett partied to their hearts' content. Faces smiled at each other. Voices belted out the words to each song.

Drinks were spilt on the floor, adding to the challenge of staying upright, especially for those who had been drinking solidly for the last few hours. Jenni didn't dare think about the state of her Christian Louboutin's. She could feel the soles sticking to the wooden floor. Her beautiful shoes. Her heart would break tomorrow when she saw the state of them, but, right now, she was in the moment and loving it.

The DJ suddenly pulled out the heavyweights as Nirvana's Teen Spirit pumped out of the speakers. It was one of those renowned songs where no-one really knows the words, but one was compelled to belt out a load of garbage with confidence and gusto. Jenni was not alone in screaming out the words of the iconic song whilst pogo dancing up and down on the spot. Kate was by her side. Jenni was stunned to see her friend so animated. How she didn't end up with two black eyes from her bouncing boobs was impossible to tell. Kate grabbed hold of Jenni's hand as they bounced together, screaming at the top of their voices.

"Whoo-hoo" shouted Peter St John, as he sauntered into the group of friends on the dance floor.

Peter was no Kurt Cobain.

He swirled around with his arms outstretched, nearly taking out Jeremy. He positioned himself in the middle of the group, the centre of attention, just where he loved to be. His fellow dancers grimaced, but Peter didn't seem to care. He was in a world of his own.

As if the DJ recognised an idiot when he saw one, he moved from Nirvana to Madness and Baggy Trousers. Peter was inspired. Or should that be obsessed. With hands in his trousers, he perfected an imitation Cossack routine. How he didn't end up flat on his back was anyone's guess. He threw himself into his dance with an enthusiasm which did not equate to any form of skill for movement.

He may be a prat, thought Jenni, but he is a fun prat.

CHAPTER TWENTY-TWO
THE VILLAGE HALL

Al was watching Peter make a complete tit of himself.

He was out there on the dance floor, behaving like a teenager. A middle-aged man with a beer belly who suddenly thinks he can move to the beat. Peter just had to be in the centre of everything, even if he was looking like a total prat. Gyrating his body against Paula in an obviously suggestive way, as she looked decidedly uncomfortable. Then twirling around in circles with that stupid grin on his face.

It would only be a matter of time before he turned his attention to Jenni.

Earlier, Al and Peter had propped up the bar, sharing a drink together. Peter was drinking heavily this evening. Well, he was a fast drinker normally, but tonight he was excelling himself. He had downed two pints in the first half hour, followed by whiskey chasers. Peter was infamous for his love of drink, but tonight he seemed like a man possessed. Al didn't even attempt to keep up. He wanted to enjoy the evening and, more importantly, remember it.

As they sipped their beers, Peter was full of himself, yet again. "Tonight is the night, big boy." He punched Al on the arm, not with force but in a chummy manner.

"Oh yeah?"

"Tonight I'm making a move on Jenni. Watch and learn, mate. Watch and learn." Peter grinned. A creepy, beer-soaked grin.

"Don't be an arse, mate," groaned Al. "Paula is here. What the hell? Have you got some sort of death wish?"

"I will be the soul of discretion," slurred Peter. "This place is packed. She won't suspect a thing. Watch and learn."

Much as he disliked Peter when he was like this, Al did want to protect his friend from total humiliation. "Do us a favour, mate. Just have a few drinks and a laugh and leave it at that. I don't think Jenni is your type, Pete. She's not interested."

Al was more than confident in his words. Jenni was far too classy to fall for Pervy Pete's banter. She had even told Al what her first impressions of Peter were, when they had met for dinner. And they were not good first impressions. Pervy Pete was not on Jenni's shortlist of possible partners. Not by a long chalk.

Unfortunately, Peter couldn't imagine any woman not wanting him.

"She is gagging for it, Al. Take my word for it. She puts on a front, you know. But I can see underneath the smokescreen. She wants me, mate. Big time."

Al shrugged his shoulders in an admission of defeat. The man believed his own bull. Desperate.

Back in the present, Al watched Peter dance around Jenni.

He beckoned her towards him, in a suggestive way. Fortunately, Paula was looking the other way and Jenni just laughed. Probably thinking he was a right idiot, thought Al. He really was making a fool of himself. His dancing was so exaggerated, flinging arms and legs around like some form of St Vitus' Dance. Other dancers were watching him now, trying to avoid the swinging arms.

Gradually Kate and Jenni moved away from his gyrating hips, taking Paula with them. They were soon at the side of the dance floor. The three of them danced their way towards the bar, leaving Peter nonplussed in the centre of the crowd of revellers.

Like a guppy fish, his face displayed his shock at being abandoned.

Al couldn't help laughing as he watched his friend left alone and stranded. His dance moves slowed; his arms hung, dejected, at his sides. His audience had left him. But even now that he had been so obviously rejected, he was still watching Jenni intently. He didn't care that people saw him gawping at the object of his obsession. He was too far gone.

His eyes followed her. Creepy eyes watching her every move.

Al noticed that Jenni was making her way towards the back corridor, the location of the ladies' loos. Peter was watching her go. In one swift movement, he left the dance floor and made for the nearest entrance to the corridor.

There was no way Al was going to leave Jenni alone to have to deal with Pervy Pete. Not wanting to be the one to break things up, he found Paula at the bar and whispered in her ear.

"Paula, love, I think you should go and find Peter. He was heading for the loos. Not sure he is very well. And he was heading to the ladies'." He shrugged his shoulders. "We don't want him to get caught in the wrong bog, do we?"

Devious, of course, but he couldn't exactly say, I think your old man is on the prowl and his prey is on her way to the bathroom.

Paula shrugged and shouted back in Al's ear. "Serves him right. The amount of booze he has put away tonight." She shook her head in disgust. "Okay. I'll go and find him. Maybe take him back home before he disgraces himself."

Al sighed as he watched Paula make her way in search of her degenerate husband. Poor Paula. She doesn't deserve a fool like Peter St John.

CHAPTER TWENTY-THREE
THE VILLAGE HALL

Jenni was looking hot with a capital H tonight, thought Peter.

He had watched her surreptitiously as she walked into the hall. That dress was stunning and really showed off her curves. And the back, with a vast expanse of skin exposed. He wanted to touch her, run his fingers down the back opening, feeling down her spine. She was one sexy woman and tonight he was on a mission to show her a good time.

Tonight would be her lucky night.

With a few beers inside him, he hit the dance floor. He would show these young'uns how they did it in the 80s. His drink-fuelled confidence drove him to places, or should that be, to moves he would never contemplate when sober. The ladies were loving him gyrating. They were all over him. In his head!

He had an audience and Peter loved an audience.

While he was twirling around and perfecting the moonwalk, his best Michael Jackson impression, he suddenly realised Jenni had retreated to the bar. Without breaking stride, he danced around to face the bar so that he could watch her movements. She was with Paula and Kate and it looked like they were getting another round in. It would be far too obvious if he followed them over there, so he continued to dance and watch. With laser precision, he locked Jenni in as his target.

She could not escape him. Not tonight.

He watched Jenni put her drink down and wander over towards the loos. The corridor, leading to the ladies,' was dimly lit and ran alongside the main hall. There were two entrances. One by the bar, which Jenni was heading towards; the other was by the stage area, just to the left of the DJ. Peter danced his way over towards the DJ. If anyone was watching him, they would think he was lining up a request. At the last moment, he peeled off and into the corridor.

A master of deception. Or so he thought.

Sadly, he was wrong.

Another set of eyes watched him.

His wife.

Once he had managed to sneak his way into the corridor, he hung around in the gloom, waiting for Jenni to finish her business. It's never a good idea to get between a middle-aged woman and the need to pee. Well, that's what Paula always said. Not that he really saw Jenni as middle-aged but perhaps her bladder was, even if the rest of her looked as buff as a teenager. The workings of the female body were a mystery to him. It was on a need to know basis only.

The corridor was quiet, which was fortunate.

It's never a good look being caught hanging around the ladies' toilets. He found a doorway inset into the wall, which provided him with cover and a vantage point to watch the ladies' toilet door. Leaning against the wall was a support, especially as he was swaying from the copious amount of alcohol, which was now starting to take effect. He would not let the booze bring him down. Not when he was so close to the prize.

Peter sensed her before he saw her.

A waft of expensive perfume filled the gloom and the click of heels struck the tiled floor. Peter was hiding outside some sort of maintenance cupboard, by the sound of it. He could hear the whirring of a machine through the door. His senses were heightened as he listened to her approach.

He timed his move to perfection.

In one swift movement, he swung out into the corridor, capturing Jenni in his arms, and pushing her gently back into the hidden doorway. Jenni gasped. He could feel her trembling within his arms. She was obviously excited, turned on by his spontaneity. His arms explored up and down her torso, taking in her curves. Her trembling continued.

"Peter," she gasped again.

Oh God, she is desperate for it, he thought.

Not letting her speak anymore, he bent his head slowly, his lips touched hers. The taste of her lip-gloss hit his senses with a strawberry burst. He pushed against her lips, forcing them open with his tongue. She resisted for a moment, but he knew she wanted him. His tongue invaded her mouth, filling the space as he explored her taste. His right hand found her breast. He squeezed, feeling the softness of her flesh against his fingers.

They were magnificent breasts.

He didn't notice Jenni squirming beneath his embrace. Well, he noticed, but in his twisted mind, she was writhing with ecstasy. Peter had no idea that the kiss wasn't welcomed. Much less the juvenile fumbling of her breast. He had convinced himself she was panting with desire for him.

More importantly, he didn't notice they were no longer alone.

Whack.

What the hell?

A second blow hit the side of his head. Letting go of Jenni, he turned to face his assailant.

"Bloody hell, Paula. What the hell?"

Paula stood before him looking like a maniac. She was seething, with fists clenched, ready to belt him again. "You bastard." She screamed at him as she slapped him around the face again. "Can you not keep it in your pants, just this once?"

Peter shrivelled in front of the demon who had taken over his wife. He had never seen her so angry. This needed careful handling and quick. His face was sore and still stinging from the last couple of blows. He didn't think he could take another one and retain any form of dignity.

"It was her," he cried, pointing his finger at Jenni.

It was the most idiotic thing he could have said, but he was desperate. Laying the blame on the woman, surely Paula would understand how hard it is to resist when a beautiful woman throws herself at you. Even the most faithful husband would be challenged by that.

What an idiot!

Jenni shook her head as she turned towards Paula. Tears had started to well at the corner of her eyes as she wiped her hand across her mouth, trying to rid his saliva from her face.

"Paula, you must believe me. He grabbed me when I came out of the loo and tried to kiss me." She turned on Peter then. "You horrible man. First you try touching me up under the dinner table and now this. You are a sad, sad man. I could have you done for assault."

Those last words hit Peter hard, even harder than the blows he had just taken from his wife.

How could she even imagine he had assaulted her? It was just a bloody kiss. He slumped further down the wall coming to rest on his heels. His head was spinning, both from the drink, and the slaps he had taken from Paula. Suddenly his stomach decided to add to his disgrace. Bringing up its contents, he sprayed vomit across the floor, hitting the precious Christian Louboutin's.

For Jenni that was the final straw. Groping and uninvited kissing was one thing, but ruining her favourite shoes was a whole new ballgame.

"You bastard," shouted Jenni.

She spotted a few villagers had joined them in the corridor, attracted by the noise. Great, even more humiliation. Grabbing her clutch bag, which had fallen onto the floor in her struggle, she slotted it under her arm and flounced down the corridor.

"Jenni," cried Peter. "Don't leave me with her."

If he could see the watching faces, Peter would have an idea of the forthcoming scandal which would run riot across the village. Known drunk who has a reputation for womanising, found in flagrante with beautiful new resident. Wronged wife walks in on them. And then it all kicks off.

Of course the gossips wouldn't necessarily seek out the truth. They had seen it with their own eyes. Peter and Jenni caught in the act. Paula betrayed.

The innocent party would be Paula, the wronged wife. Everyone knew about Peter's reputation as a cheater. Paula had been far too accommodating to her husband's faults, but surely even she didn't deserve this humiliation.

Jenni, as the newbie, would be portrayed as the wicked woman enticing poor Peter, who everyone knew, could not help himself. She had wafted into the village with her good looks and money, turning things on their head.

Pinching someone else's husband was just not the 'done' thing in Sixpenny Bissett.

Not the 'done' thing at all.

CHAPTER TWENTY-FOUR
ROSE COTTAGE

Jenni fled from the village hall as fast as her heels would carry her.

In her haste, she didn't stop for her jacket. It didn't take long for her to realise that was a big mistake. Rain was driving horizontally down the road, hitting her face with its icy blast. Within seconds, her dress was sopping wet. Her arms and legs drenched with rain, as her feet slipped within her shoes. Her running motion became gangly and disjointed. Forgetting any sense of propriety, she kicked off her heels and ran barefoot.

She shivered as the pent up sobs erupted. Jenni hadn't cried like this since Reggie's funeral. The sobs came from deep in her body, from deep within her core. Her body was racked with pain as she ran home. Her feet stung with numerous small cuts from the pavement. But that pain was nothing compared to the sense of betrayal and humiliation.

Jenni had regarded the move to Sixpenny Bissett as a fresh start. A chance for her to move on from being Reggie's widow. A chance to integrate into a new community which didn't know her past, who would like her for being Jenni, not Reggie's poor wife. She had settled in so well to the village and had started to make some really good friends.

And now that was all destroyed.

By that stupid bastard who couldn't take no for an answer.

And how dare he try and make out that she was the instigator.

Her front door was thankfully in sight. Jenni gathered every last essence of strength to charge down her garden path as she fumbled for her keys. She dropped them onto the flagstones and frantically felt around in the dark for them. She had just grabbed hold of the key ring when she heard footsteps behind her. Within seconds, she felt herself being pulled into the ample chest of her friend, Kate.

"Come on, sweetheart. Let's get you in the dry."

Kate took the keys and fiddled with the lock. The two women practically fell through the front door. The warmth of the house was a welcoming hug to Jenni. She was so cold that her whole body was shaking. It wasn't just the cold, but a huge dose of anger filled her with rage. Jenni stood in the hall, dripping, seemingly unable to move.

Kate took control.

She could see her friend was struggling with the events of tonight, so Kate ran up the stairs, grabbing a big, fluffy towel along with Jenni's PJs. Jenni had remained standing in the exact same position, now crying quietly. Within moments, Kate stripped Jenni from her little black dress and began buffeting her body with warming towel caresses. Once satisfied she was dry, Kate pulled Jenni's PJ top over her head and helped her into her bottoms. Jenni was acting like a child, fully dependent on someone to help her, whilst she wallowed in sadness from what had just happened to her. In contrast, Kate embraced her natural motherly demeanour. Her buxom figure was also the best thing ever to cling to, when in pain.

Before long, Jenni felt the warmth creep back into her body, tingling as her body temperature rose slowly. She collapsed into her favourite chair, which seemed to hug her whole body as it supported every emotional ache. She had bought this chair soon after Reggie had died. It was described as an adult bean bag, even though it had the appearance of an armchair. Its polystyrene filling moulded to your shape as you relaxed into its depths. This chair became her go to place when she needed a virtual hug.

Kate poured both of them a generous slug of brandy and took the armchair next to Jenni.

"What the hell happened, Jenni love? I saw you run out like you were being chased by the devil. I had to come and check on you. I was worried." Kate rubbed her hand up and down Jenni's arm, reassuringly.

Jenni was still heaving with sobs, gasping as she tried to calm herself down. "That bastard Peter St John." Jenni looked directly into Kate's face. "I didn't do anything."

"Sorry, love, I don't understand." Kate's face had a look of confusion as she tried to piece together the events of the evening. "What did he do?"

"He grabbed me when I came out of the toilets. He bloody kissed me. I never asked him to, you must believe me."

The penny dropped. Kate had seen Paula disappear after Jenni. Things were starting to become clearer. "Oh sweetheart. Tell me."

Jenni took a deep breath. "He grabbed me and stuck his tongue down my throat. It was disgusting. I was just so shocked. I had no idea he was waiting there in the dark. Scared the shit out of me." Jenni shivered as the memories came flooding back. "The bastard even grabbed my boob. What the hell?"

Kate hadn't seen that one coming. Peter St John had a reputation, of course. But on his own doorstep? What sort of idiot tries that? "And I guess Paula caught him in the act?"

"Yep, she whacked him round the head. Serves him right. But then the weasel tried to make out it was me grabbing him! Can you believe it?"

Kate laughed at the sheer ridiculousness of Peter's defence. Paula would never be stupid enough to fall for that one. Surely?

"What a stupid man. I am so sorry this has happened to you, Jenni. Please, you must believe me, this is not normal behaviour in Sixpenny Bissett. We are usually a very welcoming community. Not one which gropes you on a night out."

Jenni tried a smile. It came out more like a hiccup. "I do hope Paula believes me. I really like her and she deserves more than that horrible man."

"That's typical of you, Jenni," smiled Kate. "More worried about others than yourself. She will be fine. Perhaps this will be the kick up the arse she needs to get rid of that rat. He really is an obnoxious little man. She deserves better."

"I honestly can't believe this is happening to me," groaned Jenni. "We had such a lovely evening. I was having a whale of a time and then he goes and spoils it all."

"You really mustn't fret, dear." Kate patted her arm again. "Unfortunately, you have caused a bit of a stir in the village. It's been a long time since a single woman has lived here and the hot-blooded males are like stags in the rutting season."

Jenni laughed as she imagined Peter and Alaistair locking horns. "Trust me to have two of those males trying to stick their tongues down my throat. Have they no manners? At least find out if I'm interested before you try it on."

Kate sighed. Jenni had no idea what a stir she had caused. She was the open flower bud to the buzzing bees. The workers were determined to drink from her nectar and the fight was on to be first. Jenni was an innocent in all this. She was one of those people who was genuinely nice. Not in a boring, condescending way. Jenni had no agenda and did not see the badness in others. She wanted peace and tranquillity, but unfortunately, her arrival had caused speculation and more interest than she had asked for.

Jenni sipped her brandy as she thought about what had happened.

No doubt some of the party-goers had seen her run off and the gossips would draw their own conclusions. She knew what the truth was. She had nothing to be ashamed of. Despite Peter trying to wriggle out of the blame, Jenni was confident that her side of the story would be the accepted commentary, in time. The most important thing for Jenni right now was that Paula learnt the facts. She would talk to her, woman to woman. Make sure she knew what a lech her husband was.

It never entered her mind that Paula might not want to know. Surely any woman would want to find out if their husband had so little respect for them that he would be willing to risk everything to pursue his own perverted actions. Jenni was determined to enlighten poor Paula.

In terms of the wicked gossips, she may well have to weather the storm for a few days. People will have their own views on what happened. Facts would be irrelevant. But Jenni would dispel any gossip for the truth.

At least with Christmas fast approaching, people's minds might move on. Everyone will be far too busy with their festive arrangements to wonder what Peter St John had been up to.

Soon they will be last week's news.

Next week's fish and chip paper.

CHAPTER TWENTY-FIVE
THE VILLAGE HALL

The show was over.

The corridor cleared as the revellers headed back to the bar or the dance floor. Paula was left alone with her husband. The stupid wretch was hunched over on his knees with his sweaty head in his hands. Surrounding him, a pool of vomit, which Paula had no intention of dealing with.

She had frozen.

She didn't know what to do. Watching Peter snivelling at her feet, but feeling nothing at all. The anger had passed. Humiliation was waiting to make its presence felt, but right now there was nothing. Later, the hate would rush to the fore, but just now Paula was numb.

She looked down at her husband in disgust. No words had been spoken since Jenni rushed off. She didn't know what to say. Peter was clearly past holding a coherent conversation. A conversation which Paula had no desire to have. It would have to happen in time, but right now, silence was a much more powerful weapon. There was no way Paula was going to allow Peter to twist her around his little finger when he sobered up.

No, this was the end.

Paula had had enough.

She had put up with her husband's behaviour for years. She knew enough about what he got up to. She had enough knowledge of his string of affairs which had populated their marriage. Up until now, she had turned the other cheek. She ignored the gossip and rumours. She ignored the tell-tale signs; the lipstick on his collars; the smell of another woman's scent.

Unfortunately, the situation had been complicated. That had been her excuse for her turning a blind eye.

Paula didn't like what had been happening, but Peter always came home to her. She put up with his behaviour because he returned to her. Without fail. It gave her a feeling of power that he couldn't do without her. He may want a pretty bit of skirt, but he always came home to safe and reliable Paula.

But this was different.

Jenni was beautiful. Paula was not in her league. If Jenni wanted Peter, she could just click her fingers and he would be there. Paula could not face the humiliation of being discarded for a neighbour. And not such a beautiful one. Jenni was a widow, single and with means of her own. For Peter, she would be a catch.

How the hell had it got to this?

Suddenly Paula realised she was not alone. Al crept down the corridor towards the marital carnage. He stepped carefully to avoid the vomit and came to a stop at her side. His comforting arms held her as she buried her head into his shoulder. At last she could cry. Loud sobs sprung forth, convulsing her body with heaving motions. Snot dribbled from her nose. She tried to clean her face, conscious of Al's shirt. Without being asked, Al produced a huge, white handkerchief and dabbed at her nose, gently. His kindness made her cry even more.

"Come on, Paula love." Al tucked her dangling hair behind her ears. "Let me take you home."

Paula gestured towards her husband, still sat in his own vomit. "What about him?" she hiccupped, as a sob interrupted her speech.

"He can shift for himself. Stupid sod." Al pushed at Peter with his foot, trying to attract his attention. "Don't come home tonight, you idiot. You will not be welcome."

With that, he guided Paula out of the hall, into the rain. It was a short walk across the road to Laurel House. Al took charge, letting them into the house and double-locking the front door. Peter St John would not be getting in, even if he tried.

Paula had stopped crying. She led the way into the kitchen, where she grabbed a bottle of Peter's favourite whiskey. Reaching for glasses, she poured two generous measures and handed a glass to Al. She even managed a brave smile as they clinked glasses.

"What the hell happened, Paula?" asked Al.

"He was snogging Jenni Sullivan. Can you believe it? I caught them in the act."

Paula was getting angry now. The initial shock had worn off and her mind was seething, with both humiliation and disgust, at the seedy image she had witnessed.

"That doesn't sound like Jenni. Are you sure she was involved?"

Al was certain Jenni would not have welcomed Peter's drunken advances. But Paula needed careful handling. All too often she had ignored what was going on right under her nose. The last thing she would probably welcome was a huge dose of reality.

"Well, she was very much attached to my husband's lips. What a slag. Peter said she tried it on with him." Paula took another large slurp of whiskey.

"He would say that, wouldn't he?" Al shook his head slowly. He could not believe Jenni had played any part in what had happened. Peter was just trying to wriggle out of the blame. "Jenni is not interested in Peter. She told me as much when we went out for dinner recently."

"Why, what did she say? And why were you talking about Peter to her anyway?" Paula looked puzzled and angry now.

"She told me. About the night of the dinner party. Pete rubbed his leg, suggestively, up and down hers under the table. She was really pissed off about it."

Paula's mouth gaped open in shock. "He did what? Bloody hell. That was my welcome to the village dinner for Jenni. What a prat! What the hell must she think of us?"

"She really likes you, Paula. She told me that too. It's just Pete. She said he was creepy. So there is no way she was a willing participant in that drama."

The penny had finally dropped.

Paula had to face the embarrassing fact that her husband had assaulted their new neighbour. How the hell would she ever live this one down once the gossips got started? Her reputation would be in tatters. And what would it do to her business? Paula was dependent on referrals to keep the orders flowing.

"That stupid idiot. I will never take him back this time," groaned Paula. "He has gone too far. He has humiliated himself and me with his constant desire to screw anything with a pulse. Well, that's it. Over."

Paula poured another slug of whiskey, offering the bottle to Al.

"You could do so much better, Paula. He really doesn't deserve you. Perhaps it is time for you to give him the boot."

Silence greeted that last comment.

Paula sipped her whiskey as she considered Al's words. Could she manage without Peter? Would she be better without him? Al knew first-hand how difficult a marriage break up was. And despite this knowledge, he was suggesting that policy. Paula was not one for snap decisions, but a seed had lodged in her brain. She would take it out and examine it over the days ahead.

And then she would make her move.

CHAPTER TWENTY-SIX
THE RECTORY

He opened one eye, grimacing as bright light hit his retina.

Groaning, Peter gradually became aware of his surroundings. He was lying curled up on an awfully hard sofa. His body had moulded into its rigid contours. A flat pillow was double folded and wedged under his head. He was fully dressed, with a thin blanket twisted around his legs. Trying to straighten his body, he eased his legs over the arm of the sofa. He uncurled slowly. The blood started to return to his ankles as the pins and needles receded.

Unfortunately, the pain in his head was very real.

A throbbing ache started at the base of his neck and drove its way towards his temple. He winced as the pain settled behind his eyes. He felt sick. His stomach was churning, performing somersaults from the after-effects of vomiting and the subsequent empty stomach. Gradually he pushed himself up the sofa, trying to get upright. The world started to spin and he gripped hold of the arm for stability. Placed on the floor beside him was a large washing up bowl, empty thankfully. At least he hadn't disgraced himself any further last night.

The bowl served as an embarrassing reminder. The events of last night came crashing back into his brain, adding to the actual pain lodged there. Peter groaned as he remembered what had happened. Paula had gone mental at him.

She had hit him.

She'd never hit him before.

What an idiot. Why in the hell had he thought he could get away with it? He must have been so pissed. Out of his head with drink. Well that would be his excuse. He was not responsible for his actions. It was the drink.

And Jenni.

Oh God, what the hell must she think of him? Drunken Peter had thought it was such a good idea. Oh, he was very brave with a few drinks inside him. Grabbing her unawares and showing her a good time. It had backfired, big time. She would probably see him as some sleaze-bag, not a future lover. What a bloody idiot.

Look at him now. Lying on someone's sofa with a hangover the size of Europe.

Whilst he was wallowing in his own self-pity, the door opened a crack. Jeremy's face poked through, surveying any potential damage to his lounge carpet. Relieved he wasn't going to have to explain that to Kate, Jeremy entered the room and moved closer to check on the patient.

"Peter, old chap, how are you feeling this morning?" He handed Peter a glass of water with a couple of paracetamol. "Bet you have a bit of a sore head."

God, that was the understatement of the year. Thank the Lord he didn't say that out loud, Peter decided, especially as he suddenly realised he had slept over at the vicar's house. Wouldn't do to blaspheme in Jeremy's presence.

"Feel like shit, Jeremy," he groaned. "Thank you for letting me stay. I appreciate it."

"Well, there was no way you were welcome back home, old chap," replied Jeremy. He placed a comforting arm on the man's shoulder. "Paula was very angry with you. I think you may need to find some temporary lodgings until she calms down."

"She will be fine by now. She's a good girl, my wife. If you don't mind, I will just use your loo and then head home."

Peter was scrambling to stand up, using the arm of the chair as a support. The world shifted on its axis again as his brain tilted in his skull. Oh God, this was the worst hangover, ever. Never again.

"Whatever you think, old chap. You know her best. I would just recommend a big slice of humility, if I were you."

As Peter made his way to the downstairs bathroom, he clocked Kate standing on the stairs. She had the most unflattering dressing gown on and looked like she had been sucking a lemon, not literally speaking, but purely by the look on her face. He would get no sympathy there then, he thought.

He swore he heard her mutter, 'you idiot,' under her breath. Fair enough. He probably was. A reasonable assessment, he grinned to himself. Suddenly, he was starting to feel more perky. Pissing off the ever-so-perfect Kate Penrose, was giving him a spring to his step.

After a quick wash in the sink and a squeeze of toothpaste rubbed around his gums, Peter was starting to feel human again. The paracetamol must have started to kick in. Now was the time to face the music. It was a shame the village shop wasn't open on a Sunday. He could have done with a big bouquet of flowers for Paula. He would just have to settle for his innate good charms to carry the day.

Peter trudged, head down, along the high street, trying to avoid eye contact with a couple of dog walkers. He certainly didn't feel up to hearing, second hand, what a fool he had been last night. Most of the houses around the village hall still had their curtains shut. Good news. At least only a few would witness his walk of shame. The curtains were still drawn at Laurel House, which was another relief. Peter could let himself in and sneak upstairs. If he could get into bed with Paula, undetected, he could perhaps snuggle up to her and make up in the best way possible.

She would be putty in his hands.

His key wouldn't turn in the lock. He jiggled it from side to side, but no movement. The deadlock must be on. Shit, that blew his plan of smooching up to Paula. He was going to have to wake her up. Taking a deep breath, he pressed the doorbell.

Within seconds, the door swung open and Alaistair Middleton stood blocking his way. What the bloody hell was Al doing at his, this early in the morning? It was clear that he had had the same sort of night as Peter. He was wearing last night's clothes and his hair stood up on ends, in a tangled mess.

"Mate, what you are doing here?" Peter tried to step into the house, only to find his way blocked by Al. "Come on, mate. Out the way."

Al stood firm. "Sorry Peter. I'm not letting you in."

Peter pushed against his friend, angry now. "Not letting me in. Fuck off mate. It's my bloody house. You can't stop me."

Al drew himself up to full height, puffing out his chest. "Paula's orders, mate. You ain't coming in. She's packed you a bag and booked you a room in the B&B down the road. Sorry mate, but you have really screwed it up this time."

Realisation of his plight was hitting home. This situation required handling a bit more carefully. "Paula, love," he shouted. "I'm sorry, love. I know I have been a bit of a pillock. But we can sort this out. I love you, darling."

It was getting embarrassing having this conversation through the bulky form of his best friend. But needs must. He could hear movement behind Al.

"Just fuck off, Peter. I have had it with you. I want a divorce. And I mean it this time."

Paula screamed those last words so there was no mistaking her intentions. She had threatened divorce a few times before, but each time the anger had quelled and she had forgiven him. This time was different. She had never packed his bags before. She had never thrown him out before. Perhaps she wouldn't calm down this time.

What the hell was he to do?

He could tell it was serious. Al had a look of understanding and maybe even compassion on his face. He reached across to Peter and touched his shoulder.

"Think you should do as she says, Peter. I'll pop over to the B&B later and check on you. OK?"

Peter was shrinking in stature as his world imploded. He really didn't believe this was happening to him. What the hell was he going to do if Paula divorced him? He would be poor, just like his mate Al.

He didn't do poor.

This cannot be happening.

Shrugging his shoulders, he picked up his suitcase and headed for the car. He was probably well over the legal limit, but he didn't care. It was only a couple of miles down the road, and there was no way Paula was getting her hands on his F-type.

She would come round. A few days away would be good. Pub grub and a nice B&B was no big problem. Anyway, he could not handle an argument right now, with the way his head was pounding. Let it all calm down and then he would win Paula round.

He had to.

Losing everything was not an option for Peter St John.

CHAPTER TWENTY-SEVEN
THE CROFT GUEST HOUSE

The bed was hard and lumpy, which was not helping Peter's current mood.

He had tossed and turned most of the night and had finally given up. Sleep eluded him. Or was it his conscience? Making a cup of tea with the ancient teasmaid, he went back to bed, pumping the pillows, trying to get some support for his aching back. This really was the most uncomfortable bed ever. He couldn't stay here much longer, he thought. He would have to sort out the whole situation quickly, especially as he had a perfectly comfortable bed back at Laurel House.

How the hell had it come to this? Alone in a cheap B&B when he could be cuddled up in bed with his wife. Enjoying all the comforts of home.

Peter was feeling sorry for himself.

He had been such a fool on Saturday night. Drink and bravado had spurred him on to a new all-time low. Why had he even tried to snog Jenni Sullivan? It wasn't all that good anyway. He had been hugely disappointed with the kiss. It was not worth the hassle it had caused him. Just one stupid kiss and right in front of Paula. No wonder she was not in a forgiving mood. He had really blown it this time. The way Paula had been with him on Sunday really worried him. She seemed seriously pissed off with him this time.

Let's face it, he had not been a good husband. He had a history of deceit. Not something to be proud of at all. Perhaps he deserved it.

Far too often, he took Paula for granted. She had turned the other cheek on numerous occasions and he had become complacent. Was she serious when she spoke of divorce? Surely she would forgive him. She always had before. But maybe not this time.

Theirs was a good marriage, in his opinion. They rubbed along well together. They had a laugh and the sex wasn't bad either.

OK, he hadn't wanted to marry Paula. It happened by accident. The story of his life. A few drunken dates, in their post-university days, had led to Paula getting pregnant. By the time he knew anything about it, it was too late to abort. Paula's parents had insisted that they got married and Peter was dragged, kicking and screaming, down the aisle.

Well the kicking and screaming bit was only, figuratively speaking, in his head. Peter had dealt with that latest setback in the same way he had dealt with his traumatic childhood. He sucked it up and got on with it. Paula would never know that he had been reluctant to marry. She had thought they represented 'love's young dream' as she stroked her growing belly at the altar. He had smiled at her as they made their vows. The same vows he would go on to break on a regular basis.

The reason they married died in the womb at six months.

Peter had not wanted the child, but when the baby died, he was devastated. Paula appeared to cope better with the loss than her husband. Unknown to Peter, she had channelled her grief into caring for her husband. It was to be her coping mechanism over the dark days ahead. Months later, they emerged from the trauma as a tight unit. The death of a child can either make or break a marriage.

For the St John's it was the glue which held them together.

Paula never became pregnant again. They rarely spoke of the baby or their desire to have another. Peter had found a contraceptive pill box one day in her bedside drawer. She had never told him she was taking protection. He didn't raise that with Paula.

He had just got on with it, as was his way.

Peter sipped on his tea, in reflective mood. Perhaps that was part of his problem. He had never shared any of his hopes nor fears for the future with the one person who loved him. And Paula had loved him. He was sure of that. Perhaps if he had talked to Paula about his mother and his childhood, she could have helped to fix him. Because Peter needed fixing. He was gradually realising that fact.

Peter was just too scared to let anyone see his vulnerability. It gave them power over him. Even after twenty-odd years of marriage, he was too scared to let Paula see he wasn't the big man she thought he was.

And now it was too late.

Peter wiped a tear from his eye, angrily. It wouldn't do to wallow in self-pity too long. He had work to do, especially if he was going to win his wife back.

It's funny how you don't realise how special something is until you are about to lose it.

Well, Peter was not going to lose.

He didn't do losing.

CHAPTER TWENTY-EIGHT
KATE'S GENERAL STORE

Jenni had sought refuge in the village shop with Kate. The two women were ensconced in the back room with huge cups of tea and a generous helping of chocolate cake.

Sunday had been hell on earth for Jenni.

She had woken far too early with a banging headache. Those large brandies had taken their toll, especially on top of wine. She had a wicked hangover. As soon as she woke, the memories of the previous night had crashed back into her head, filling her with doubt and anxiety. She knew in her heart that she was not responsible for what had happened. She had done nothing to encourage Peter St John. Why did she feel so incredibly guilty?

She hadn't asked him to grab her like that. She didn't ask him to kiss her. And oh, what a horrible experience it was. All slobber and tongue. The man was disgusting. If Paula hadn't come along when she had, what the hell would have happened? Should she have fought back more? The shock of his assault had made her immobile. If Paula hadn't come to her rescue, how far would it have gone before her natural fight reaction kicked in? It didn't bear thinking about.

Jenni realised how it might have looked to Paula, but surely, she must know her husband's reputation. Surely she would recognise that Jenni was not a willing participant. Jenni was positive that she had been struggling to get away from his lecherous embrace when Paula had launched her attack on her husband. She must have seen Jenni trying to get away from Peter's arms.

Surely?

Jenni had not been willing, in any sense of the word. She had been too shocked to react at first. Perhaps Peter had taken that as consent? Surely not. In fact, he didn't seem interested in whether she was consenting or not. Acting like a scared rabbit in the headlights is not an open invitation to continue, not in the rationale world anyway.

And Jenni had been that scared little bunny rabbit, totally shocked by his behaviour. She had not given him any sign that she wanted him to stick his tongue down her throat or given him permission to grab her boob like he was polishing a doorknob. Stupid idiot. If it wasn't for the fact that he had been really pissed, Jenni may well have considered taking it further and reporting him for assault.

But she didn't want the fuss.

The thought of facing the rest of the community filled her with dread. She had kept the curtains drawn most of Sunday as she retreated into her own world. There was no way she would have contemplated church. She would not be alone in that. Poor Jeremy had struggled with just a few old ladies attending communion. They were fresh from an early night's sleep. Even Kate had rolled over in bed, reluctant to move. Other than the joy of seeing Peter's struggle to get up Sunday morning, Kate had retreated back to bed to wallow in her hangover.

It had taken a huge dose of courage for Jenni to venture out to the shop this morning. She knew she would always get an understanding shoulder to cry on from Kate. Her friend had the measure of that man and would not judge Jenni.

For some time they sat together in companionable silence.

Claire, Kate's assistant, was manning the till out front. The door through to the back room was ajar, as Kate kept one ear on activity in the shop. She trusted Claire implicitly, but she had only been working for her for a few months and still struggled with some of the tasks. Being available to step in was important.

The bell which hung over the shop door tinkled as Anna Fletcher strolled purposefully into the store. She grabbed a pint of milk and hot-footed it to the counter. Clearing her throat was a pointless task, especially as there was no one else in the shop and she had Claire's complete attention.

"Gosh, that was an interesting Saturday night," she started.

Anna had not even been present at the party. It really wasn't her thing. But she always had her ear to the ground and was not adverse in passing on any gossip. She had picked up the details at church on Sunday and was keen to spread the news to anyone who would spare her the time to listen.

"Sorry?" answered the shop assistant.

"That new woman. Jenni, I think her name is. Caught in flagrante with Peter St John. Can you believe it? That is certainly one way to introduce yourself to the village."

Jenni gasped as she listened to the nasty comments. Why is it always the woman who gets thrown under the bus? Even with a reputation like Peter's, this horrible woman had just assumed Jenni was the protagonist.

Kate was already on her feet and heading for the counter. Jenni could not follow. She took the coward's way out and stayed in hiding.

"Anna Fletcher. Don't you come into my shop spreading malicious gossip. I will not have it." Kate's face had turned rosy red with anger as she faced the nosy spinster.

Anna looked very disgruntled with the turn of events. She had been excited to be the first to spread the rumours. Although, she was not surprised at Kate's reaction. Everyone knew she had cosied up to the new villager, suddenly finding a new best friend.

Anna was a retired schoolteacher, who missed the thrust of working at the heart of a community. As the local teacher, she had had influence over the minds of the future generation and had loved the power she held over the parents, often frightening them with her steely stare.

She had taught Peter St John at primary school. He had been a little sod then and didn't seem to have learned any manners since he grew up. Anna was of a generation who accepted that men stray. The woman was always in the wrong. Not that Anna had much experience of men. She had never married and was much happier with her household of cats.

Anna had not warmed to Jenni Sullivan when she had first met her.

The woman was far too attractive for her age and flaunted her shapely figure with well-cut clothes and formidably high heels, which Anna would never have entertained, even in her youth. Anna judged newcomers purely on appearance rather than getting to know the individual person. It was probably one of the reasons why she was disliked by many in the community.

"I don't know why you are accusing me of being malicious, Kate. The woman was caught in the corridor kissing Peter. There is no getting away from that one, is there?"

Kate shook her head in frustration. "Ms Fletcher, I'm sorry but I need to correct you. As I understand it, you weren't there on Saturday night, but I was. So hear it from the horse's mouth. Jenni was assaulted by a very drunk Peter St John. He is incredibly lucky she didn't call the police and raise a complaint. So I would respectfully ask that you keep your opinions to yourself. Thank you."

Kate crossed her arms as she stared intently at Anna Fletcher. It was a staring competition, which only one person was ever going to win. And that person would be Kate.

Visibly crumpling under the vicious stare, Anna coughed nervously. "If you say so, Mrs Penrose." The use of formal names was further indication of the frosty atmosphere. "It is that poor woman, Paula, I feel sorry for. I hear she has thrown him out. He's at the B&B."

Kate sighed. This awful woman could not stop gossiping. She always had something to say about someone, and it was rarely favourable.

"I think it would be sensible, all round, if we leave the St John's to sort out their own issues. It's not right to speculate, in my opinion. Now, if you are all done, let me get you your change. Don't want to stop you any longer than necessary."

It was a clear dismissal, but even then, it took Anna a few moments to realise it. Snapping her purse clasp with a loud crack, she stormed from the store, milk in hand. Kate looked across at her assistant and laughed, whilst wiping her hands down the front of her apron.

Good riddance to bad rubbish, she thought.

Meanwhile, tucked in the storeroom, Jenni was in tears again.

When would this ever end? That nasty woman would not be alone in blaming Jenni for what happened. She would be the focus of gossip for days to come. Why the hell did she move here? She should have stayed in Birmingham and none of this would have happened. She was grateful to Kate for defending her, but would the neutrals be on her side or would she be ostracised by the other women in the village? Would she be seen as a threat?

Jenni Sullivan, the husband snatcher.

That expression was ridiculous enough to laugh at, but Jenni wasn't in the mood for that right now. She was feeling sorry for herself and not in the right frame of mind to rationalise what was happening. All the confidence she had built over recent months, as she had found her way to Dorset and a fresh start, was crumbling. She was not normally the type to allow gossip to hurt. Sticks and stones and all that.

But Jenni felt vulnerable and alone.

Escape back to her little, safe cottage seemed to be the best option for now. If she hunkered down until after Christmas, perhaps it would all go away. Perhaps the nasty gossips would find something else to talk about by then.

Jenni realised she needed to face Paula at some point and offer an explanation but, right now, she didn't feel strong enough. Time enough to face that when Jenni felt stronger, emotionally.

Like the coward she was feeling, Jenni let herself out of the back door. From here, she could walk around the back of the houses to her cottage. No one would see her, which meant she didn't have to face anyone else today. She just couldn't face that right now.

It was incredibly rude to leave Kate in the lurch like that, but hopefully she would understand.

CHAPTER TWENTY-NINE
ROSE COTTAGE

Jenni sneaked back into the house by the garden door. Why she behaved so surreptitiously, was anyone's guess. She was safe now. In her own home.

She had been determined not to run into anyone, so had skirted around the back of her house, across the field at the end of her garden. Feeling like a criminal, she had shimmied over the fence, catching her tights on the barbed wire. Her leg stung and, reaching down, she could feel a wetness on her thigh. Clearly the barbed wire had done more damage than just her tights.

Her day was getting worse by the minute.

Pulling her tights down, she noticed a nasty cut which was oozing blood down her leg. Hopping across the kitchen, with one leg in and one out of her tights, she resembled a three-legged race competitor, at school sports day. But performing less elegantly!

She found her first aid box and started to root around for a plaster. The whole image could have been amusing if Jenni had been in the right frame of mind, but unfortunately, she was seething with anger. She really couldn't believe this was happening to her. Moving was supposed to have been a fresh start, but it was already being totally ballsed up by some stupid guy who had the ego the size of his degenerate reputation.

Having cleaned herself up and thrown her tights in the bin, Jenni grabbed a bottle of Pinot from the wine fridge and poured a generous glass. It was far too early to start drinking, but circumstances warranted it. Okay, it was a school day and Jenni didn't drink during the week, but her head was all over the place, so something to take the edge off it was necessary.

"Alexa, play my bad day playlist."

Jenni had several playlists saved on her virtual assistant, each designed to suit her mood. Her bad day playlist was packed with angry songs and mournful tunes. It had helped her through the dark days after Reggie's death. Days like today required a tune which you could shout along to, rather than harmonise with. Eminem's Lose Yourself started to play. Jenni took a huge slug of wine and launched into song.

By the time the closing beats of the epic tune faded, Jenni was feeling a damn sight better. The fact that she had downed two large glasses already had helped to mellow her considerably. With her legs stretched out on the chair opposite, Jenni rested her head on her arm as she continued to hum a tune.

She didn't see the human shape which moved passed her kitchen window and was now hovering outside the back door. A soft knock was far too quiet to catch Jenni's attention. However, the door opening did. She spotted Henrique squeezing his body through the half-opened door, whilst trying to keep his dirty boots on the mat.

"Jenni, you OK?"

Henrique was balancing himself awkwardly on the small mat. With the stimulation of wine, Jenni couldn't help but giggle at the sight.

"Alexa, off." Jenni was surprised to find her words were a bit slurred. Wine on an empty stomach was probably not the greatest idea. "Come in, Henrique. Take those boots off and grab a glass."

Not only was it against Jenni's principles to be drinking on a Monday lunchtime, but even more seriously, she shouldn't be drinking alone. Jenni was not sure whether that was the only reason she had invited the gardener in. She wanted company and the lovely Henrique was the perfect person to cheer her mood. She was desperate for a boost and he would no doubt meet that need, if previous encounters were anything to go by. He always made her laugh with his tales of her fellow villagers, told in his broken English.

The Spaniard didn't need to be asked twice.

He had spotted Jenni arriving home in an unusually secretive fashion and had been intrigued. Why was Señorita Sullivan climbing over her back fence? He had been clipping back a rose on the side wall, unseen by Jenni. She would have been mortified to know that her gardener had had a good view of her legs as she had repaired the damage to her hosiery. He had had a good look and loved what he saw. She had some shapely pins for a woman of her age.

A glass of wine would be a welcome distraction, especially as it was freezing outside today. One of those days when a nice, warm kitchen was preferable to continuing pruning. Especially if that warm kitchen was owned by the lovely Jenni, who was clearly a little tiddly.

Jenni poured him a generous glass of Pinot and they chinked glasses in a silent toast.

"What we drinking to?" the young man asked. "Don't see you drinking during the day normally, Jenni."

Jenni groaned as the memories came rushing back into her drunken mind. "Just pissed off, Henrique. Did you not hear the rumours? I have been branded the scarlet woman."

"Scarlet woman? Me no understand," laughed Henrique. He hadn't heard any rumours yet as, fortunately, Monday was not his day for Anna Fletcher's garden. Even if it had been, he may not have understood the colour reference, which unfortunately didn't translate easily into Spanish.

Jenni's eyes filled with tears.

Unexpectedly.

It must have been the wine which had heightened her emotions.

She seemed to have spent far too much time weeping since that dreadful night. In normal circumstances, she would give herself a damn good talking to, but the events of Saturday night had really floored her. Between sobs, Jenni told her friendly gardener the whole story. Henrique remained silent as he listened to her words, carefully. Her rambling and crying didn't make it easy for him, but he got enough to understand that Peter St John had been up to his usual again and poor Señorita Sullivan was on the receiving end.

"No cry, Jenni." Henrique reached across the table to hold her hand.

It was this gentle touch of comfort which broke Jenni. The dam burst. Instead of sobs, Jenni dissolved into heart-breaking tears. All the pent up emotion since Saturday, added to a feeling of unfairness of her treatment, overtook Jenni.

"Oh no," sighed Henrique.

He hadn't seen that one coming and felt awkward watching his favourite customer so distressed. He did what came naturally to him. He took Jenni in his arms, bringing her to her feet. Embracing her, he rubbed his hands gently down her back, creating circles with his fingers as he tried to reassure the woman.

Jenni rested her head on Henrique's shoulder.

It was wonderful to be held again.

It seemed so long since she had been comforted like this by a man. Her sons obviously didn't count in the equation. She had been lonely for so long now that the feel of a man's body touching hers was amazing. She could feel his breath on her neck, which was doing wonderful things to her. She could feel her breathing co-ordinating with his as her world calmed. His fingers continued to stroke her back, sending shivers down her spine.

She turned her head slightly and found Henrique watching her intently. He smiled. She smiled. Their heads seemed to get closer and closer as their eyes remained fixed on each other. Their lips touched. A delicate kiss. Another smile.

The mood changed in an instant.

His mouth found hers. This time, the kiss was deep and powerful. She melted into his arms as she touched her tongue to his. He tasted of wine, with a hint of garlic. The kiss deepened as Henrique swept her up into his arms. Striding purposely across the kitchen, he made his way up the stairs, pushing open her bedroom door with his knee. Gently he laid her on the bed, looking deeply into her eyes for her consent. She nodded.

Any reservations she may have had flew out the window under the comforting arms of her gardener. Jenni suddenly felt the sexiest woman in the world. She did not even think about the big knickers she had on, or the white bra which had been in with one of her son's rugger socks and had turned an off-red colour. All her inhibitions had flown as she relaxed under Henrique's gaze.

Taking their time, they undressed each other. Jenni admired his physique. His young body was covered in dark hair, the hairiest chest she had ever seen. She did not feel embarrassed when he removed her bra and started to touch her breasts. The fact that she was nearly old enough to be his mother fled from her mind. Jenni was absorbed by lust.

There was no turning back now.

As they touched each other, driving their excitement to a frenzy, Henrique reached into his jeans and found a condom. Swiftly, he donned it without taking his eyes of her. She didn't have the heart to tell him she was a post-menopausal woman. That ship had sailed.

Now was not the time to remind him of her advancing years.

His eyes were hypnotic as Jenni gave in to her pent up desires. She gasped as he entered her, eyes widening with excitement. They moved together, touching, stroking and kissing.

Henrique was an expert lover.

He controlled his passion to ensure Jenni reached a peak before he allowed himself to explode into her. They fell together into a crumpled heap on the sheets, panting from their exertions.

Jenni nestled into his arms, kissing his cheek.

It had been years since Jenni had made love to a man. The last time was the night before Reggie died. A warm, comforting and familiar lovemaking with her soul mate. This was different.

This was fast and furious with a Latin lover. It was beautiful, but it didn't mean anything to either of them. They were fulfilling a need. That was all.

"That was lovely," Jenni sighed as she stroked his cheek. "Thank you."

"You are a beautiful woman, Señorita Sullivan."

"Jenni, please."

She smiled, thinking how awkward his use of a formal title sounded. It certainly did make her feel like his mother, even if, literally translated, he was implying she was a Miss. Now that they had finished, Jenni knew that she needed to set the record straight about their relationship. Or lack of a relationship. The last thing she wanted was Henrique getting any ideas.

"Henrique, I hope you realise that this was just sex." Oh God, that sounded so harsh, thought Jenni, as she watched a glance of confusion cross his face. "I really like you, but I'm not looking for a relationship."

For a moment, it looked like Henrique was relieved. Should she feel a bit miffed about that? Obviously, she wasn't looking for him to be devastated, but maybe a bit of disappointment would have been nice.

"Jenni, you are a lovely lady, but I have a girlfriend. In Barcelona. She loves me, so we have no future. Sorry."

Jenni laughed at this point.

This whole afternoon seemed surreal. A passionate sex session with no strings attached. In fact, Jenni felt pretty cool. She had never done anything so daring in her life. If it wasn't for the fact that this must remain a secret, she would love to tell Kate. They could pick the bones out of it over a few glasses of wine, and Jenni was sure her new friend would be impressed that she had slept with the village stud.

She stretched out her body across the bed, totally comfortable with her nakedness. Henrique was leaning up on one elbow as he traced his fingers across her caesarean scar. She shivered with excitement as his fingers moved lower. Perhaps more of the same was on the cards. It would be rude to refuse, especially considering that this may never happen again.

Bang, bang, bang. The front door knocker broke the sexual tension, which was building nicely.

"Oh shit," cried Jenni. She crawled across the carpet towards the window. "It's Kate. Quick Henrique, get dressed now."

CHAPTER THIRTY
ROSE COTTAGE

Kate dropped the door knocker with a satisfying bang.

She was certain Jenni was at home. There was no way she was leaving things the way they were left in the shop earlier. Lifting the letter box, she peered into the hallway. She could swear she could hear movement. Why wasn't Jenni answering the door, she wondered?

Dreadfully nosy, but Kate didn't care. She was her friend. Surely that made it acceptable to peer through the letter box. Jenni might need help.

Perhaps she had fainted or more likely, perhaps Jenni was in the bathroom. That might explain the delay in answering. The sound of feet charging down the staircase was the next thing she heard. That definitely sounds like more than one pair of feet, thought Kate.

Intriguing.

Unable to resist, Kate popped the letter box open again and gasped at what she saw. Jenni was doing up her blouse. Okay, she may have changed outfits when she got home. Reasonable assumption.

But no, what made Kate gasp was the sight of Henrique kissing Jenni as he ran past her on the stairs, heading for the kitchen door.

O-M-G. She's a dark horse.

Kate grinned as she imagined what Jenni had been up to. Lucky cow. She only just managed to compose her face before the door swung open. Jenni was smoothing her hair back into place as she acted all surprised to see her friend.

"Kate, didn't expect to see you again so soon."

Was there a hint of frustration in Jenni's voice? Had Kate interrupted something? It certainly looked like it, although Kate was not one to speculate. Of course. She would have to try and get it out of her friend over a cup of coffee.

"I was worried about you, darling. Left Claire in charge so I could come and check on you."

Kate had a way of inviting herself in before being asked. It worked perfectly as she followed Jenni into the kitchen. She could see Henrique out in the garden, happily attacking a large rose bush. Must be taking his sexual tension out on the poor plant, if that's what Kate had interrupted.

Jenni avoided her friend's inquisitive gaze by making herself busy with the coffee pot. Perhaps a full-bodied black coffee would distract Kate from questioning her further about the presence of a red-blooded male in her boudoir. As she busied herself, with her back to Kate, she quickly adjusted her clothing, tucking in her blouse.

"That's so sweet of you, Kate. I'm okay." Jenni paused. Realising that her friend did not believe a word of it, she decided to expand. The raised eyebrow was an obvious give away. "Well, I was pretty pissed off. That cow, Anna, spouting off about me was just too much. Why are some people so horrible, especially when they don't even know the facts? I just had to escape without running into anyone else. Does that make me a coward?"

Kate picked up her coffee cup and sipped the strong drink as she watched Jenni. So far, not giving away too much. Well, she would keep probing.

"Don't let people like Anna Fletcher get under your skin. She is a lonely, old woman who is very bitter. Don't think she has ever had a man warming her bed, the shrivelled old hag." Kate laughed, breaking the tension. "I put her straight and she went away with her tail between her legs. My only word of advice would be to get to Paula. Have a chat with her and put the record straight."

Jenni tucked her hair behind one ear as her fingers wandered across her face. "You are probably right. I did get a text from Alaistair earlier. He said Paula was keen to chat but was worried about making the first move."

Being an adult was not much fun sometimes. The rules of the playground still seemed to apply even when you reached your fifties. He said, she said. How tedious the whole situation was?

Kate honestly could not contain herself any longer. She had to know what was happening between Jenni and Henrique. Kate was not one for gossip, but if her eyes had seen what she thought she had seen, then it was a case of 'hats off' to Jenni.

"Anyway, what was the lovely Henrique doing in the house when I knocked? Servicing the indoor plants too now?"

Jenni blushed as Kate smirked. "Can you keep a secret?" Jenni whispered as she leant across the kitchen table.

"You know I can. Come on. Spill."

"I just had sex with the Spanish stud."

Jenni giggled like a naughty schoolgirl. Her face was a deep shade of red now but plastered with the hugest smile ever. Not that Kate could blame her for that. What an achievement.

Damn, the lucky cow.

"Bloody hell, Jen. How the hell did that happen? No, forget that. I don't need to know about the build-up. Just answer me one thing. Was it good?"

"Bloody amazing." Jenni's face was on fire now. You could have warmed crumpets on her cheeks. "Don't get any ideas though, mate. It is just a one-off. I needed a bit of a pick-me-up and Henrique obliged. You mustn't tell anyone at all, please."

Kate zipped her lips in confirmation. "Your secret is safe with me. But bloody hell, you lucky girl. Details please."

"It was lovely."

"Lovely? Are you bloody kidding me? Lovely is a bit of an insult to our Mediterranean stud, surely?"

"OK, OK. But I'm not one to kiss and tell. Let's just say that I haven't had sex since Reggie died and it was worth the wait. I was about to have seconds when you turned up."

Kate snorted with laughter. "Sorry love. What bad timing. Perhaps you can pick up where you left off when I go. Shall I go now?" She winked at the last remark.

"Bit late for that," laughed Jenni. "The moment has passed. Probably did me a favour anyway. It was a nice distraction, but that's all."

"I'm not asking you to break confidences but is his body as good as I imagine it is?" laughed Kate.

Henrique was truly the most beautiful man in the village, even if he was a boy. Most of the women still with a pulse, had lustful thoughts about him as he tended their greenery. Kate knew why her daughter, Mary, was always found with her nose struck to the window when he was in their garden. And Mary was only 13. Henrique had that effect on all the girls.

And Jenni had screwed him. Bloody hell, she is the luckiest of cows.

"Better," answered Jenni. "He's all muscle and tone and he smelt amazing. And he didn't even flinch when he saw my granny pants. Just ripped them off without a second look. Thank the Lord!" Jenni laughed, remembering her mortification when she realised she had dressed for comfort, rather than speed, that morning.

"Shit. Granny knickers? Oh Jenni, how could you." Kate dissolved into belly laughs as she imagined the scene. "My old mum always used to say 'wear your best matching knickers and bra set every day, just in case it's your last. You don't want the undertaker seeing you in an old pair'. I'm sure the same rule applies to finding yourself in bed with a young stud."

Jenni was laughing too. "He has probably never seen anything like it. But he was the complete gentleman. Perhaps if I was wearing my sexy briefs, he might have taken them off with his teeth. And he has the most amazing teeth."

"Stop it, woman. You are making me horny just thinking about it."

Kate stood up and wandered over to the kitchen stable door. There she could get a good look at young Henrique and marvel over Jenni's good luck.

Well, if you are going to get talked about by the village gossips, bedding a man half your age is surely much better than nasty talk about being caught in the clutches of Pervy Pete, Kate decided. Well done, Jenni.

The two friends relaxed in silence, absorbing the enormity of what had just happened. Kate smiled to herself as she decided that Jenni sleeping with Henrique, even if it was a one-off, was just what her friend needed right now. She looked like a new woman. Corny as it sounded, but she had a glow about her that hadn't been there before.

Perhaps this was the start of a new, exciting relationship. Kate was not totally convinced by her friend's protestations of it being just a one-night stand, or should we say, one-afternoon stand. And all power to her if it was to be a relationship. She deserved a decent chap in her bed. Lucky bloody cow.

Jenni was now gazing out the kitchen window watching Henrique.

She watched his body as he moved around the rose bush, flexing his muscles as he bent and stretched. He was beautiful. Jenni didn't feel embarrassed about the age difference or her actions today. She felt confident that Henrique would keep their secret, so there was no face-saving required.

But the real impact of their wonderful session was on Jenni's mind rather than her body, which glowed with the after-effects of good sex.

Somehow, she felt a healing of her ruptured heart. She had mourned Reggie for long enough. Today had confirmed it was time to move on. She would never stop loving him, but he was gone and she had a long time ahead of her, God willing. She could not put her life on hold for ever. Perhaps it was now time to live again.

Not with Henrique. He was just a catalyst, but he had done her a huge favour.

And her next step was to sort out the situation with Paula and face her critics. She wanted to stay in Sixpenny Bissett, and Peter St John was not going to spoil that for her.

CHAPTER THIRTY-ONE
LAUREL HOUSE

Paula was sat alone in the lounge with a mug of steaming hot tea.

The silence filling the house was wonderful. She had noticed so many improvements since Peter had left for the B&B. She could sleep soundly, without listening to his snoring and farting half the night. The bathroom was so much cleaner without all the wonder creams he used, in an attempt to reclaim his fast-departing youth. A youth which had, in fact, departed long ago. He was just far too vain to realise it.

All in all, she didn't miss him one bit.

Why she hadn't done this earlier? A decision she couldn't comprehend. She had ignored the warning signs and always seemed to have made excuses for him. A man who could happily sleep with another woman and come home to his wife, with no semblance of guilt, was not worth having. He must have had such a low opinion of Paula and she had let him perpetuate that. Well no more. She was going to get her pride back and, with it, her life.

No longer would she be in his shadow.

It would take time. First, she needed to regain her confidence in facing the world outside Laurel House. It had been a few days since the debacle on Saturday night, and Paula had not left the house since. She couldn't face the eyes of the village. Not just yet. She was also worried about running into Jenni. How embarrassing would that be? Al had tried to convince her that all would be OK, but Paula was not ready to face others yet, especially the wronged woman.

Al was a good friend. He had been a diamond.

Al had been by her side when Peter had come calling on Sunday, demanding more of his things. She had always been fond of her husband's friend. Oh yes, he could talk and it was hard to get a word in edgeways, but he had a big heart and his support over the last few days had been invaluable. He had even suggested she join him for Christmas dinner, which had been so kind. She couldn't understand how Al had put up with Peter's so-called friendship for so long. Perhaps Al had been behaving like her, clutching hold of a hint of company rather than assessing the true quality of that fellowship.

Her reflections were interrupted by the ring of the doorbell.

She wasn't expecting anyone. Al was at work and said he would pop round later this evening. Paula dragged herself off the sofa as the bell rang again. As she looked through the frosted glass, she could see it was Jenni.

Paula took a deep breath as she opened the door. She honestly didn't know Jenni well enough to anticipate what reaction she was likely to get. She was nervous but tried hard not to show it.

"Hi, Paula." Jenni had a huge, encouraging smile on her face. "Can I come in?"

Jenni was holding out a beautifully decorated chocolate cake, which looked magnificent. Clearly, she had guessed that the way into Paula's heart might be signposted by chocolate, in any form.

"Of course." Paula led the way into the lounge, offering Jenni a coffee enroute. She cut two large slices of the velvety sponge and handed a plate to Jenni. "I'm so glad you popped round, Jenni. I have been too much of a coward to come to you."

Jenni reached her hand out and touched Paula's arm. "Please, don't say that. None of this is your fault. I should have come sooner, but I was a bit scared you might slam the door in my face. Alaistair texted me the other night and gave me the kick up the arse I needed to come and break the ice."

Both women took a seat and sipped their coffee. Any perceived tension had broken. It had all been in their minds, as both women had inflated the anger of the other. They had more in common than they knew. Two women hurt by the actions of one man. Although the embarrassment Jenni was suffering could not hold a torch to the betrayal Paula was feeling.

"This cake is wonderful," sighed Paula, as she took another mouthful. "Have you ever thought of doing this professionally? You would make a fortune."

Jenni laughed at the thought. "Never. I love to bake but I don't have a head for business. I left all that to Reggie."

Paula took another bite and savoured the lightness of the sponge with the tang of the bitter chocolate. "Well, if you decide to branch out, there would be lots of people in the village who would help you get started. You have a talent, Jenni. Don't let a lack of business acumen stand in your way. And anyway, what are you going to spend your time on? You have your whole life ahead of you."

Paula could see untapped potential in Jenni.

Her situation resonated with Paula. She had struggled over the years with her own imposter syndrome when she started up the upholstery company. Peter had not helped, especially as he delighted in putting his wife down. She had succeeded despite him, not because of his support.

Coming back to the subject in hand, Paula changed the conversation. "I am so sorry about what happened to you on Saturday. My husband is a right tosser sometimes. Not sure I should even call him husband, not now I've thrown him out."

"Honestly, Paula. I haven't come round here for your apology. You are not responsible for Peter. I should have told you about him getting a bit fruity at your dinner party, but I really didn't know how to." Jenni did feel ashamed that she hadn't nipped it in the bud, right at the start. "I am just so sorry that you had to witness what you did at the weekend."

Paula kept running the scene through her mind and, as she did, it looked worse each time. No one wants to see their husband with his hands all over another woman, especially when the victim was not even welcoming the embrace.

"It wasn't the best evening of my life, but to be fair, it's probably done me a favour. I think I have gradually woken from a sleep of ignorance. I knew Peter was unfaithful to me, but it wasn't happening right under my nose before. I'm done with him." Paula sighed. "I have told him I want a divorce. I honestly don't care if I must sell up and leave here, as long as I am free of that idiot."

"Life is too short to be with someone who doesn't make you happy," sighed Jenni.

Paula nodded sagely, thinking of those few words. She had been unhappy for too long now. She just hadn't seen it. Now was the time to grasp life by the horns before it was too late. She was young enough to start over again.

Without Peter.

Jenni's situation was so very different. She had been so lucky with Reggie. He would never have been unfaithful. Jenni was certain of that. Not that he didn't have the opportunity. He had been a good-looking man and had the gift of the gab, which was particularly useful in the motor trade. One of his best qualities had been his obsession with loyalty. He valued that characteristic in those he made money with. Those values included a devotion to his wife. He was committed to his family as much as his business. Jenni had had her ups and downs with Reggie, but after every argument they always made up and they would never go to bed on a quarrel.

"Do you think you will ever marry again?" asked Paula, changing the tone of the conversation dramatically.

Probably a bit too personal a question, but Paula had made a new resolution since she had kicked out Peter. She was determined to speak frankly, never mind the consequences. She had spent too many years hiding her own thoughts behind her verbose husband. Fortunately, Jenni didn't look offended with the question.

"I honestly don't know, Paula. It's not something I have thought about really. If it happens then maybe, but it would have to be someone special to take the place of my Reggie."

"Well you certainly have caused a stir in Sixpenny Bissett," laughed Paula. "If we ignore my prat of a husband, you have attracted a fair amount of attention from the males in our community. I think Al has a bit of a crush on you. The General does nothing but talk about your qualities, and even the vicar seems to go all silly when you are around. Not that he is a threat. Kate keeps him on a close rein, even closer than his boss, a.k.a. God."

Jenni's face was a picture. She looked shocked and horrified at the same time. "Oh dear. Not much to choose from there then," laughed Jenni. "The only thing Alaistair loves is the sound of his own voice. And The General is an absolute sweetie, but he's old enough to be my dad."

Surprisingly, Paula bristled as Jenni ridiculed Al. Her reaction shocked her, but she pushed those thoughts to one side. Perhaps she would unwrap them later and examine them further.

"It's like bees round the honeypot when you are around. The men go all stupid and buzz around the queen," laughed Paula. The newcomer had definitely stirred things up. "Not that I'm jealous, of course."

Jenni smiled at the imagery. It was hard to not notice the interest her arrival in the village had created. The community was tight-knit and hadn't seen a woman, on her own, move in for such a long time.

Anyone would have caused a stir. That was her opinion, but as usual, Jenni was underestimating her personal impact.

Again.

She was a beautiful woman who didn't look her age. She had a vulnerability about her which drove men crazy. They wanted to protect her, own her, desire her. If Paula was totally honest with herself, she was jealous of Jenni. The new woman in the village was everything Paula could never be. She would never see men fall at her feet. It had never been the case in her youth and certainly wouldn't be now. She had not aged as well as Jenni. Her love of cakes had piled on the pounds, and she could not imagine carrying off the lovely dresses and high heels Jenni seemed to wear so naturally.

Paula realised that life as a singleton would be tougher for her.

But that no longer filled her with fear.

"Tell me, Paula, what's the story with Richard Samuels?"

Paula recognised the dreamy expression on Jenni's face. Oh dear, she thought. There lies nothing but disappointment.

"Richard is a lovely man, but a very broken one."

Paula was weighing up how much to share. Richard was very private and would hate to think he was the subject of gossip. Paula had known Richard since they were at secondary school together. She had been by his side during his most recent trauma and had seen the devastation of his loss. It was only fair to let Jenni down gently. Any interest in Richard would never be reciprocated.

She continued. "Richard lost his wife, Nicola, two years ago to the dreaded big C. I know it sounds a bit clichéd, but she was his one and only. There won't be another woman for Richard. Ever."

Jenni remained thoughtful. She could understand the pain of loss, especially as Reggie had been her world. But Paula seemed to be a bit dramatic. Perhaps she had her own reasons for putting Jenni off. Perhaps she had her eyes on the most eligible of bachelors in Sixpenny Bissett?

"Poor man. Life does deal some dreadful cards sometimes."

Jenni decided to leave the subject there. No point in pushing a subject which Paula seemed determined to close down quickly.

The conversation moved on to a safer place; Christmas preparations and all that entailed. Once the initial awkwardness about Peter's behaviour had been addressed, the two women had fallen into a relaxed conversation. A firm friendship was blossoming, one which both women would come to value highly over the years ahead.

CHAPTER THIRTY-TWO
ROSE COTTAGE

Jenni gazed at her son, appreciating his cleared plate, a sure sign of the success of Christmas dinner.

George had travelled down the previous afternoon, his first visit to his mother's new home. His numerous nods of the head as she showed him around, gave Jenni confidence. She was actually delighted, and somewhat relieved, that her elder son approved of her new home.

George had been strong-minded about her plans to move away from Birmingham. It had taken much persuasion, on her part, to get his agreement to sell the family home. Not that she was obliged to get his permission, but Jenni felt strongly that her boys should agree with her decision. It made life easier all round.

And Jenni would do anything to keep her boys happy.

George had, in fact, moved out of the family home some years before, taking a flat near the Gas Street Basin. His home looked out over the canal and was right in the centre of the trendy clubs and pubs, ideal for a young, single man. Not that he spent much time clubbing. He was obsessed with his job. Far too like his father, who had a strong work ethic, which he had handed down to his son.

Jimmy had been the more difficult of her sons with her decision to move. Outside of his life at university, the family house was Jimmy's only other abode. She was technically making him homeless by her decision. Fortunately, Jimmy was particularly close to his mother, both in characteristics and emotions. He gradually came to understand his mother's need to get away from Birmingham. Eventually, he dropped his objections and smoothed her path, allowing the sale of the family home to go ahead.

His desire to travel the world probably came into the equation too. Anything to keep his mother sweet with the idea of him escaping too. It became a bargaining tool for Jimmy. Jenni had to agree to cutting the apron strings and allow her baby boy to flee the nest.

Back to the present, George had decided to shut up the business on Christmas Eve lunchtime so he could be with her by late afternoon. As Jenni gave him the guided tour of the house, she could tell her son was seeing the possibilities of her new home. Jenni was succeeding in making Rose Cottage her forever home, and she could see the pride in her son's face at her efforts. His concerns about, in his eyes, her rash decision to move were disappearing as he could see how comfortable his mother looked in her new environment. All he really wanted was to see his mother happy again.

George took the wine bottle and topped up both glasses. Settling his feet out in front of him, George eased back in the chair. He raised the glass in a salute to Jenni.

"Mum, that was amazing, as usual. God, I have missed your roasts."

It had seemed a bit excessive to cook a whole turkey for just the two of them, but Jenni knew her son. It wouldn't be Christmas without the traditional turkey. George had a healthy appetite and had polished off a huge portion. Neither of them could contemplate pudding just yet. A glass of wine and The Queen's speech would probably define their day for now.

"I'm glad you enjoyed it, darling. It is so lovely to have you here, even if it's just for a couple of nights. So you approve of my new home?" Jenni reached across the gap between them to take her son's hand in hers.

"I do, Mum. It feels about right for you. And you look happy, Mum. That's all me and Jimmy want for you."

Jimmy had video-called them that morning for a chat, which had been fun, especially as it was late at night for her younger son and he had clearly had a few sherbets by the time they had talked.

"Thank you, George darling. I'm glad you understand why I wanted to move. It is so much easier for me to hide in plain sight in a new place."

There was a huge dose of irony in Jenni's words.

She hadn't wanted to share the news with George that she had been on the receiving end of Peter St John's scandalous behaviour. George certainly wouldn't have been amused and would have probably wanted to meet the man and give him a piece of his mind. She really didn't need George getting involved. She just wanted to forget. Despite the recent events, Jenni loved her new home and was excited about the friendships she was making.

Jenni had kept Henrique a secret too.

Her son would certainly not approve of her jumping into bed with the gardener. Jenni smiled to herself as she thought about that passionate lunchtime. She hadn't seen Henrique since and was determined to maintain a professional distance when they did. As much as she had enjoyed the sex, she was not interested in a relationship with someone young enough to be her son. She had caused enough of a stir in the village without adding to it. But it had been amazing whilst it lasted.

"Mum?" George interrupted her musings. "What are you going to do for the rest of your life then?"

"Whoa, where did that come from?" laughed Jenni. "That's a bit deep, isn't it?"

George grinned as he swirled his wine around the huge-bellied glass. "Sorry, that probably came out all wrong. What I meant to say was, what do you plan to do now you've moved? You spent most of your life looking after Dad and us boys. So what now?"

"Good question. I haven't really given it much thought yet. I need to do something, but having never really worked at a job before, I wouldn't know where to start." Jenni knew that her job bringing up the boys and keeping house was equally as important as any paid employment she could have been doing. Most of her old friends remained at home, even though their children had flown the nest. Jenni knew instinctively that she needed something more. "Perhaps I could do some charity work or something good for the community. I guess it's a lovely position to be in. I don't need to work as your dad has left me well provided for, but I'm only 50 so I should have a few years ahead of me. Can't see myself settling into daytime TV just yet."

"Exactly. The last thing I would want is for you to get lonely or bored, Mother dearest. Back in Brum, you had all your mates whom you could meet up with and socialise. This village seems ridiculously small compared with Birmingham. Won't you get bored?"

"I have already made a good friend in Kate, next door. She's lovely. Next time you are down, I will invite her and her husband Jeremy round." Jenni knew her son would love Kate as much as she did. "But you are right, I need to think of a fresh challenge. Someone mentioned something to me the other day, which got me thinking."

George leaned in; his attention gripped. "Oh yes, tell me more."

"Paula, one of my neighbours, was raving about one of my cakes. You remember the chocolate mirror cake you and Jimmy always wanted for your birthdays?"

"Do I remember?" laughed George. "I can taste it just thinking about it."

"Paula reckoned I should go into business, making cakes. What do you think? Is it a stupid idea?"

Jenni was renowned for talking herself out of things. It was a confidence issue for her. When Paula had first mentioned it, Jenni had been intrigued and excited, but as each day passed, she convinced herself it was a crazy idea.

"That's not a bad idea, Mum. It's the sort of thing you could do from home, so you don't need to worry about the legalities of business premises. Are there any local cafés or shops you could tap into to sell your wares?"

"Funnily enough, Kate next door runs the local village shop. Perhaps I should have a chat with her."

A kernel of an idea was starting to grow in her mind. As it took root, Jenni decided she would pick Kate's brains after the festive period. Only the other day, Kate had been moaning about how difficult it was getting to keep the village store open. Perhaps a bit of diversification was in order.

But that was for another day. Today was all about eating, drinking and spending quality time with her elder son.

"Anyway, are you ready for some Christmas pudding, son? It's homemade."

CHAPTER THIRTY-THREE
THE MANOR HOUSE

Herbert Smythe-Jones had got himself into a right pickle.

It was the night of his legendary New Year's Eve party and the caterers had let him down. He was furious and had even resorted to shouting down the phone at the boss of the company. Not his normal behaviour. He was usually calmness personified. His anger had not helped anyway. They had still told him it was impossible for them to be in two places at the same time.

Their problem, which had quickly become Herbert's.

The General was expecting thirty people for drinks and finger food at 8pm and he was not going to let them down. People couldn't rearrange their New Year's Eve plans at the last minute, could they? He had even phoned The King's Head with no success. Jacky was hugely apologetic that they couldn't help, but they had full covers booked for the evening and just couldn't spare any staff to help.

In exasperation, Herbert had made a dash for the supermarket, where the answer to his prayers had literally bumped into him. Jenni Sullivan was a vision of beauty in his eyes, as their trolleys bashed into each other. After he had explained his dilemma, Jenni had jumped to his aid. Jenni took over, helping to organise his shopping needs and agreeing to help him prepare for the party. Herbert was overcome by her generosity. There really are angels in this world, he reflected.

It was an hour until show time and, at The Manor House, Herbert was working alongside Jenni at the vast kitchen table. Jenni was an absolute star, organising him and allocating him the simpler tasks, which Herbert could not mess up even if he tried. It was a good job Jenni was on the guest list for tonight's festivities. That would have been even more embarrassing than his total failure to manage a few simple canapés. Herbert might be a good cook, but catering for a large number of guests was out of his league of expertise.

As he topped blinis with prawns in a cocktail sauce, he watched Jenni. The resemblance with his wife, Bridget, was uncanny, especially as she worked her way around the kitchen. Even some of their mannerisms were shared, and Jenni's seemingly confident command of the troublesome Aga whisked him back over the years to a happier time.

He smiled as the memories overwhelmed him.

"Right, Herbert, I think we are nearly there." Jenni interrupted his lovely musings. "I just need to put the baguettes in the Aga 10 minutes before we want to eat. The hot canapés are keeping warm in the hostess trolley and the cold are in the fridge. Just your blinis to finish and I think we are done." As she spoke, Jenni was wafting her arms around, directing his eyesight, in an orchestrated dance through the menu.

"Jenni, you are an absolute lifesaver," sighed The General. "I honestly don't know what I would have done without your help. You are so very kind, my dear."

Jenni noticed The General's eyes glazing over with moisture. Oh please don't let him cry on me, she thought. She had loved spending the last couple of hours with him. Jenni missed her own father desperately. He had died when George was a baby and that loss still felt fresh in her heart. The General reminded her of her dear father. She could quite easily fall into a big bear hug with him, although given recent events, she could not contemplate any further damage to her good character.

Even if the gossip was totally unwarranted.

She had talked to Herbert about his plan to bring her onto the Parish Council. The recent gossip had been an unnecessary set back, which had made her doubt the wisdom of such a move. Herbert had been keen for her to ignore the tittle-tattle, but understood that perhaps the timing wasn't right yet. Maybe one for the future.

The General secretly cursed Peter St John for his stupidity and the hurt caused to poor Jenni. She certainly didn't deserve that. Jenni interrupted his thoughts.

"Herbert, you are so very welcome." She smiled as she fiddled with the knot in her apron. "I have enjoyed myself this afternoon. It's been fun. Just lucky I was doing Waitrose at the same time as you, or goodness knows what would have happened. Perhaps you could have made it a 'bring your own food party'." Jenni laughed as she saw the shock on The General's face at the very thought.

"I was lost and you found me and brought me home." Herbert winked at Jenni as he realised how cringeworthy that last remark was. "Since Bridget died, I have always relied on caterers to manage my annual party. It is the only time I really entertain and I would have been so disappointed if it had been a failure this year. Especially as it was outside my control. Looks like I will have to find a new firm for next year."

"Well seriously, Herbert, I have loved helping so don't rush into making that decision. You never know, perhaps I can help again next time."

Jenni's brain was jumping ahead again.

Interestingly, she had had two conversations recently where that kernel of an idea was starting to sprout. Maybe she had found her new year's resolution. Perhaps she should consider her strengths and invest in them. She loved to bake and she was an excellent cook too, even if she said so herself. She was going to sit down with Kate next week and bash out her ideas. If her new friend didn't laugh at her plan then maybe, just maybe, she had found a new and exciting venture.

"I forgot to ask, my dear, I do hope things are all sorted with you and Paula. I have invited Paula tonight, but not Peter. Things won't be awkward, will they?"

"Don't you worry about that, Herbert. Paula is fine and understands it was all Peter's fault. I went for coffee with her before Christmas and she seems a different woman already. I think she is well rid of the guy."

The General smiled. He had heard all the gossip, courtesy of Anna Fletcher. Despite her severe telling off from Kate, Anna had still managed to spread the rumours around the village. The General had not believed a word of it. He could not imagine Jenni behaving so unacceptably and, knowing Peter St John, he was sure who was the culprit. Paula would manage very well without that man, he believed.

Unfortunately, there was far too much interest in Jenni, in The General's opinion.

A single woman was a dangerous distraction in the community. Not that it was Jenni's fault, but she had caused a stir since she moved in. Peter was obviously the extreme example of what could happen should fascination with a beautiful woman overcome a sensible mind. The General had spotted Henrique's eyes following Jenni's body as she helped to unload the car earlier. That was certainly unacceptable. He would have to have words with his gardener later. He hadn't been invited tonight. He was staff. That just wasn't the done thing in The General's world. Henrique didn't move in the same social circles as Herbert.

Jenni needs a protector, believed The General. A woman needs a chap in her life, company, and direction. The General was very set in his ways. A traditionalist. He decided he should talk to Jenni sometime about coming to an arrangement. They would work well as a couple. He could provide her with a beautiful home and security for the future. She would bring her style and caring personality to his family. He was sure that both his children would love her instantly.

The General's thoughts were way off the mark, as far as Jenni would have been concerned. She would have been horrified to know what his idea of the future could be. Jenni would never see Herbert Smythe-Jones as anything more than a father figure. A friend, but certainly not a lover.

Jenni grabbed her coat which had been hanging over a kitchen chair. "Anyway, Herbert. I must dash." She shrugged her arms into the sleeves as she picked up her handbag. "I need to grab a quick shower and a change. I will be back by 8 o'clock. Don't worry. Once I'm back, I will plate up."

The General pulled his car keys down from the shelf. "I will drive you back.

It's the least I can do and it will save you some valuable time."

"There really is no need," replied Jenni.

It would only take her ten minutes to walk back to her house. It would be a tight turnaround to make herself presentable for the evening ahead. Perhaps saving a few minutes might help.

"But if you are sure. That would be lovely. Thanks Herbert."

CHAPTER THIRTY-FOUR
THE MANOR HOUSE

Less than an hour later, Jenni accompanied by Kate and Jeremy, made her way down the winding drive to The Manor House.

It was the quickest turnaround ever. Jenni was surprised at herself.

She had hurtled back into her house, discarding her clothes as she made her way upstairs. Freddie sat by the shower door, meowing as if the world was about to end. He was most disgusted that Jenni had prioritised herself over his dinner. If it wasn't for the fact that he hated wetness of any form, he would have followed his mistress into the wet room and curled himself around her legs until she remembered her responsibilities.

Instead his cries got louder. Poor starving Freddie.

How she had managed to shower, dry and style her hair and, of course, feed Freddie before Kate came knocking, was a mystery. Jenni had chosen a red, bodycon dress, which hugged her figure in all the right places. Her hair was tied in a chignon secured with a jewelled clasp. Fake not real, unfortunately. Her trusty Christian Louboutin's had been cleaned up, after Peter had emptied the contents of his drunken stomach on them. Jenni would have been mightily pissed off if they had been ruined. That would have been far greater a sin, in her book, than plastering his sloppy lips all over her face. And that was bad enough.

During the walk, Jenni had updated Kate about her conversation with Paula. She was proud of herself for not letting that situation fester. It was all part of the new Jenni. She would not cower and hide away because of a stupid man. She was determined to face down her critics, especially those who were badly informed. Anna Fletcher was due at The General's tonight and Jenni had her strategy in place. That nasty woman was not going to spoil her fun tonight. Jenni would wipe the smug smile off Anna's face.

Jenni was not one to hold a grudge, but Anna Fletcher had been spreading her nasty barbs around the village and, even if most people didn't believe her drivel, mud sticks. Jenni was determined to take control of the gossip and dismiss it out of sight.

Herbert opened the huge front door, welcoming them with open arms. He was dressed in a tailored, black suit with pristine white shirt. The dicky bow was scarlet with white spots, a nod to The General's cheeky sense of humour.

"There she is. My angel." The General pulled Jenni into a firm embrace, splashing confusion over the Penrose's faces. Herbert spotted the look and decided to expand, saving Jenni's blushes. "My friends, this wonderful lady came to my help today when the caterers let me down."

"Oh stop it, Herbert. It was nothing. I had a lovely time." Jenni untangled herself from The General's arms. "Anyway, let me into that kitchen so I can finish off. Have many people arrived yet?"

"Anna is here but she's always first at any event. Come into the drawing room first please. Let me get your drinks before you make me feel even more guilty. Come. Come."

The General ushered the group through the hallway, taking their coats and depositing them on a chaise longue. The drawing room had been cleared of much of its normal, bulky furniture, leaving a scattering of chairs and occasional tables. The guest would have plenty of places to leave a glass whilst eating. Jenni hated those parties where you spent most of your time juggling glass, food plate and trying to attempt to eat or drink. It was not conducive to a relaxing time.

The General was obviously very practised in the art of entertaining.

Anna Fletcher was standing by the patio doors, clutching a gin and tonic. Dressed in a navy blue twinset, she looked even more like the retired teacher she was, rather than a New Year reveller. Jenni felt like a bitch for even thinking that, but oh well, the woman did not deserve anything else.

Jenni's plan was put into action immediately.

She walked confidently over to Anna with a false, beaming smile plastered on her face. Before Anna could react, Jenni laid her hands on the woman's arms and kissed her on both cheeks. The shocked look on Anna's face was a picture. It looked like she could combust right there.

"Anna, how lovely to see you. I hope you had a lovely Christmas." Jenni's voice was sickly sweet as she preened over the nasty, old lady.

Anna Fletcher was caught completely unawares.

Her plan had been to shun Jenni Sullivan. She had put as much thought into the evening's event as her enemy had. Her plan had been foiled. Thank the Lord, the only witnesses to her embarrassment were Jeremy and Kate. Luckily, The General had left the room in search of drinks for the new arrivals. Anna had a soft spot for Herbert and she would have been mortified if he had been a witness to what had just happened.

Anna had to respond, even if she didn't want to. "Jennifer, nice to see you." The smile was forced. The use of her full name, which no one but Jenni's mother ever used, was deliberate. "Christmas was quiet and peaceful, just as Our Lord would expect it."

Jenni smiled again, even though her whole being was grimacing with disgust for this hypocrite. How can she talk about the Lord when her actions were anything but Christian?

First step of Jenni's plan was completed.

It was clear that Anna was squirming inside, having been put on the spot. Jenni was doing a celebratory dance in her head, like one of those emojis she loved to add to her Twitter posts. The second part of the master plan would have to wait until Paula arrived, and then the two women would put the gossiper right back in her box.

Time to escape to the kitchen and help The General out, thought Jenni.

She left Kate and Jeremy with the unenviable task of entertaining Anna.

Jenni grinned as she caught her friend's expression. A combination of frustration and humour. Jeremy was certainly equipped with the tools of the trade to listen to the moans and groans of his congregation, but poor Kate did not have the patience. Kate had watched the play between Anna and Jenni with an increased pride for her new friend, who had stood up to the village bully with such confidence.

By the time Jenni returned to the drawing room, most of the guests had arrived. She took a moment to stand at the doorway and observe.

First to catch her eye was Richard Samuels. He looked dashing in navy chinos and a pink, tailored shirt. Not many men could pull off a pink shirt, but Richard Samuels certainly could. He wore it well. It fitted like a glove to his skin, revealing a muscular chest, straining against the fabric.

Jenni sighed as she mooned over the gorgeous man.

He really was striking, with his chiselled good looks, high cheekbones and piercing blue eyes. His dark brown hair was tousled on top and cut back around his ears, slightly longer than Jenni would prefer, but she would work on that one. A gold, hooped earring graced his left ear. Even though he was a more mature man, this trendy addition did not seem out of place.

Dragging her eyes away from the man of her dreams, she spotted Paula who was sipping a glass of red wine as she listened intently to Alaistair. Paula was initially not aware of Jenni watching her. Perhaps if she were, she would have been a bit more careful. Jenni was shocked to see the desire in Paula's gaze as she looked at Alaistair. Wow, I never saw that one coming, thought Jenni. It was clear to the casual observer that Paula was well on the way to finding a new bedfellow. And hopefully Alaistair would treat her far better than the last occupant.

Jeremy and Kate had managed to extract themselves from Anna's company and were deep in conversation with the Hadley's. Rather than interrupt, Jenni headed over towards Paula, clocking Anna who was intently watching her every movement across the room. What a nosy bitch she is, thought Jenni. Secretly she was pleased that the nasty woman was paying more interest than was necessary. I will give her something to gossip about, reflected Jenni.

As she reached Paula, Jenni placed her hand on the woman's shoulder to attract her attention. "Paula, how lovely to see you. Happy New Year." Jenni kissed her on the cheek as Paula turned and embraced her new friend.

"Happy New Year to you, Jenni."

"Hi Alaistair, good to see you," Jenni added, conscious not to leave him out.

Alaistair gave her a huge, beaming smile. Like Paula, he looked a changed person. The absence of Peter St John in both their lives seemed to have had a positive impact. They didn't seem to realise it yet themselves, but Jenni was sure that, soon enough, they would embrace the obvious attraction they felt for each other.

The three of them chatted for a while, sharing news of the Christmas period. Alaistair had cooked for Paula and they had enjoyed a quiet day together. Jenni noticed that, on occasions, they even finished each other's sentences. How adorable. They were both keen to hear about George's visit and whether he approved of her new home.

The party was in full swing.

The General circulated around his guests, enthralling them with his humorous anecdotes. He was a brilliant raconteur and could hold an audience in the palm of his hands. Many of his stories related to his time in the army. When he joined Jenni, Paula and Alaistair, he had them in stitches as he told a yarn about a private who literally lost his head in a tank accident. It really should not have been funny. It was horrific and what a way to lose your life. But The General had a way of telling the story which dismissed the dire situation, instead focused on the surrounding events, which had to be heard to be believed.

Jenni could not remember the last time she had belly laughed. Sounds pretty sick, but you had to be there!

The food was greeted with enthusiasm, as the guests lined their stomachs for the night ahead. The General felt it necessary to announce, at the top of his voice, the part which Jenni had played in digging him out of a hole. She accepted cries of congratulations and the numerous compliments on the range of canapés produced. Jenni stored that, again, in her memory to be taken out later and examined. Her plans for the future were gaining momentum, and the positive feedback was helping her confidence in deciding how she filled her time going forward.

Once Jenni had filled her plate with food, she found herself standing next to Richard. They were alone beside the heavy, red curtains which covered the drawing room patio doors. The fabric was rich, both in weave and colour. Jenni resisted the temptation to touch the weave and run it through her fingers. Fabric had such a sensuous feel to it and, standing opposite Richard Sullivan, she knew could not allow herself to feel sensual or she would be lost completely.

Richard looked decidedly uncomfortable as he slipped a prawn blini into his mouth. Jenni could not help watching the movement of his lips as he licked the cocktail sauce from its edge. His Adam's apple travelled slowly down his throat as he swallowed. Even the act of swallowing looked sexy. Jenni could feel the heat rising.

She forgot everything Kate and Paula had told her about the man. If she had remembered their words of caution, she might have realised the lust she felt would not be reciprocated. Ahead lay disappointment, but her mind could not entertain those thoughts right now. She was enjoying the chance to just be in his presence. That was enough for now.

"Great party, isn't it."

She started up a conversation, conscious of the awkwardness between them. The air was charged with electricity. In her head only. She could sense the tension, but thought it was sexually charged. How wrong could she be?

Richard had no means of escape. She had started to talk and any opportunity for him to escape was gone. He would have to humour her for now and perhaps she would leave him alone.

"Yes, very good." A long, silent gap filled the air before he continued. "The food is delicious. Herbert was not wrong."

God this was painful, thought Jenni. He may look like the man of my dreams but the conversation was stilted and uncomfortable. Was it just her or was he like it with everyone?

"Thank you, Richard. Just a few bits I pulled together this afternoon." Jenni was not one for bragging, but again, was trying the get the conversation to flow.

She noticed Richard was frantically looking around the other guests as if he was finding an escape route, away from her. Jenni was just not used to this type of behaviour from a man.

Since moving to Sixpenny Bissett, she had been overwhelmed by male attention. But the one man she craved attention from became some sort of bumbling idiot in her presence. What was so wrong with her that he was desperate to escape?

The conversation was clearly going nowhere.

One needs to know when one is flogging a dead horse.

Unfortunately for Jenni, she was slow to realise that.

CHAPTER THIRTY-FIVE
THE MANOR HOUSE

If he could have avoided the party, he would have.

Richard really wasn't in the mood to be sociable. He would be just as happy with a couple of pints down The King's Head and then a bit of Jules Holland's Hootenanny before bed. The Christmas and New Year festivities were always the worst time for Richard. Nicola had loved Christmas and had always made such a big fuss. She would plan everything out weeks in advance, buying beautiful gifts for friends and family.

They never had children. It just didn't happen.

By the time they realised one of them had a problem, their lives together were wonderfully settled. They had become used to the independence of travelling around the world. Frequently, they would load up the boat and take her off to the Greek islands for weeks on end. Days of lying in the sun and eating wonderful food at a Greek taverna brought them joy. Children would get in the way. Children didn't fit into their lives. Neither of them had ever expressed any sadness that babies didn't arrive.

Until Nicola died.

Left alone, Richard was heartbroken. Was it selfish of him to want a child, made with love, with his soulmate? A child who would carry on her genes, leaving a legacy. He had been in a quandary at the time. Part of him wished they had had a child to comfort him in his loss, but the other part of him was glad that he, alone, was grieving. Could he inflict that level of pain on a child?

But back to the subject in hand, the New Year's Eve party.

Herbert had been insistent that Richard come along, and he couldn't disappoint his dear friend. Herbert had been a good friend to Richard since Nicola's death. The two men had much in common. They shared the deep loss of their soulmates. They also both enjoyed the sea. Often Herbert would join him at the boatyard, tinkering with Richard's latest project.

Richard never objected to Herbert joining him at work. In fact, he valued his judgement and advice. In return, Richard would take The General out on his yacht. The two men were comfortable in each other's company and would happily relax with a couple of fishing rods and a beer as the day drew to a close. They didn't need to talk, just relax in each other's presence.

Richard's real problem was that he struggled to fully commit to living.

After Nicola's death, he had tried to take his own life.

Only to fail at that.

He was fated to linger in a world between life and death. Not really present in either. The only time he really felt alive was on water. There, he could appreciate the fierceness of nature and the vastness of time. He felt close to Nicola on the yacht. He was sure she would be mad at him for giving up on life. She had been so desperate to hold on when the cancer got a grip. But he just didn't want to go on alone, without her.

Less of those morbid thoughts.

Focus turned back to the party.

Richard had been caught by Jeremy and Kate as soon as he arrived at The Manor House. He did like Jeremy. The vicar was a gentle man, who understood his pain of grief. On the other hand, Richard felt intimidated by Kate. She was a ballsy character, very different to Nicola. She had a way of making Richard feel very insignificant. He was sure that Kate never intended to, but it was just the way she made Richard feel. He often thought that Jeremy must have balls of steel, with Kate as his wife.

Richard was not one to circulate around the room.

Another downside of being a widower. Everyone was in a couple except Anna Fletcher, and he could certainly do without getting caught by her. So he would act as third wheel for much of the evening. Richard felt decidedly awkward in a crowd, especially a crowd of happy couples. It made his own situation even more pronounced.

Richard had spotted Jenni as she came in, bearing trays of her delicious canapés. He was intrigued by the new woman in the village. She really was stunning. Long, straight, blond hair which she had tied up in some sort of bun. She was tall, not much shorter than him, which must make her about 6 feet. The dress she wore left absolutely nothing to the imagination. For a woman of his age, she had a cracking figure. Trim waist, long, elegant legs and a decent set of boobs.

If it wasn't that he had given up on life, especially his love life, he would have been interested.

Oh, he had heard the rumour about Peter St John having a crack at her. Poor woman. She didn't deserve that. It seemed that Jenni had the testosterone levels in the village elevating dangerously high. The other night he had overheard that Spanish gardener mooning over her in the bar. He seemed to think he stood a chance with the newcomer. What interest would a classy woman like Jenni Sullivan have in a boy?

If Richard was completely honest with himself, he was frightened of women now. Nicola had been his rock, but since she had left him, his confidence had fizzled away. He struggled to hold down a normal conversation with an attractive woman now. So even if he wanted to find a new partner, he was a lost cause.

Damn it.

Without realising how, Richard found he was alone with Jenni. She was nibbling on a finger sandwich, looking even more sexy up close. If that was even possible. What the hell should he say? He didn't have a clue. She looked so relaxed and comfortable and he just felt like running away. Fast. Why was this woman having such a strange effect on him? Her gaze was haunting and inviting at the same time.

She smelt delicious. A strong perfume wafted from her. Everything about her looked controlled and organised. Not a hair escaped from her bun and there was no sign of any grey locks to spoil her look. Her makeup was immaculate and her nails were painted a bright red colour to match her dress.

She was beautiful. She was sexy.

He fancied her.

But he couldn't do anything about it.

That was just the way it had to be. No woman could replace Nicola. It made him a lonely man, but that was the price he was prepared to pay. He would carry the torch for Nicola until his dying day.

After making a bit of small talk, which was uncomfortable in the extreme, he managed to extricate himself from her company. His relief was palpable as he attached himself to Thomas Hadley, who was discussing yields. No matter how boring the discussion would be, it was worth it to get away from Jenni.

He didn't spare a thought for how Jenni felt about his behaviour. All he was focused on was saving his own blushes. The fact that he had left the poor woman standing alone, wondering what she had done to offend him, did not enter his mind.

He was totally embarrassed at how out of his depth he felt. He was also extremely worried about how he was feeling. He thought he was immune to the charms of a sexy woman. He told himself he was off the market for ever. That strategy had never been a problem. Up until now.

Something was stirring in him. He had run away from Jenni because she had made him feel something. Something he didn't think he possessed any more.

Desire.

CHAPTER THIRTY-SIX
ROSE COTTAGE

It was mid-morning before Jenni awoke.

She had been exhausted, finally crawling into her bed around 2am. She had drunk far more than she had intended. Luckily, she had been sober enough to stick to her practised hangover cure: drinking a pint of water with a couple of painkillers before bed usually headed off the worst of the dehydration which, all too often, makes the alcohol hurt so much.

As she rolled onto her side to look at the bedside clock, she noticed Freddie. He had the whole of the left hand side of the bed and was stretched out lengthwise, as if to stake his claim. Freddie was deeply asleep and, as she watched her beautiful puss, his nose twitched and ears flicked as he dreamed. Feeling a tad wicked, she gently stroked his head, tickling behind his ears, which he adored. Freddie went from sleep to wide awake in seconds, as only a cat can. He stretched his hind legs upwards as he rolled onto his side. Making his way up the bed, he buffeted Jenni's face with his.

A gesture of affection along with a reminder that, now he was awake, he was hungry. When was he not hungry?

Jenni plumped her pillows and sat up, pulling Freddie into her arms. The poor feline soon realised that he would have to perform before his mistress decided to shake a leg and get out of bed. His routine started with a great deal of head rubbing, wiping his dribble all over Jenni's fingers, followed with the offering of his belly for a rub. If that didn't make her feel guilty and feed him, then nothing would.

As Jenni pandered to Freddie's needs, she was thinking about the previous night.

It had been a good evening with friends. The food had gone down well and she was proud of her part in that. Herbert had been vociferous in his praise, which had been lovely, if a little embarrassing. Other than Anna Fletcher, everyone else at the party had been such good company. They had chatted, drank, and even danced as the night wore on. At midnight, everyone had come together in a circle, holding hands as a raucous rendition of Auld Lang Syne rang out. Neighbours kissed neighbours as they greeted a new year.

The evening had restored her faith in the decision to move to Sixpenny Bissett. She had started to doubt whether the plan had been wise, or whether her self-confidence could cope, after the recent debacle of Peter's behaviour. Mixing with the community last night was a positive step towards her acceptance into the parish.

Interestingly, Jenni noticed that there was one person missing at midnight. Well, if truth be told, there were two people missing. Anna Fletcher had left about 11pm, complaining that she never stayed out past 10pm, as that was far too late. Perhaps she changed into a pumpkin at midnight. There was a communal sigh of relief as she departed.

The other person, missing at midnight, was Richard Samuels.

Jenni had watched him disappear out of the drawing room with five minutes to spare. An impeccably timed toilet break, perhaps. What a strange man. She couldn't make him out. But Jenni was intrigued. His rudeness was confusing. They only spoke for a fleeting time and it was clear he could not wait to get away from her.

And that was the confusing part.

His eyes watched her with a hidden passion. He was smouldering with pent up emotion, but somehow, he was stopping himself. Even after he left her side, she kept catching him looking at her. His eyes followed her around the room. He might have been talking to another villager, but his eyes sought her out. The reality was that both of them had been dancing around each other with their eyes all evening.

So why was he incredibly rude when he had the chance to talk to her. Had he heard the rumours about Peter St John? Did he think she was somehow complicit? God knows what he might think if Anna Fletcher had been bending his ear.

Despite everything, Jenni had decided Richard Samuels could be the man to mend her broken heart. He was the most beautiful guy she had met since

Reggie's death. Not that Jenni was purely driven by looks. Looks were important to her. Reggie had been a handsome man and attraction played a big part in their lives together. Reggie had the looks and the personality to go with it.

Unfortunately, Richard Samuels had the looks, but not the personality.

That was Jenni's judgement from the little conversation they had shared last night. Perhaps he was just painfully shy. Kate and Paula had both spoken to her about Richard being damaged goods. Jenni could not dismiss the pain of the loss of his wife. She had been through the same grief, so she was well placed to understand the hurt of being left behind. But eventually, that loss got easier to manage.

At their age, they were far too young to stay alone for ever.

Jenni believed that Reggie would expect her to move on at some point. Not that they had spoken about it when he was alive. They had been so present that they had lived each day with a passion, and the thought of one of them leaving the other behind was incomprehensible. But having loved someone that deeply, you get to know their thoughts and dreams. Reggie was very much the alpha male in their relationship. It never really bothered Jenni. She enjoyed being looked after. That had been one of the most difficult things for her to deal with after his sudden death.

Reggie would expect Jenni to seek out a new mate to care for her.

Since Reggie's death, Jenni had changed. She had had to learn how to manage her life without a man to sort out any problems. She enjoyed the new freedoms and, whilst there were times when she wanted to crawl into a ball and let someone else take over, she forced herself to be strong. That forced behaviour was soon becoming habit. In the last two years she had become a stronger woman.

But that strength did not mean she wanted to remain alone forever.

She had needs. She wanted a companion who could fulfil those needs. Having steamy sex with Henrique was nice, but that wasn't her future. Henrique was simply a trial run. He had shown her that she could still be sexy. She could still be desired.

Henrique had awoken a passion in her which had been sleeping for too long. She needed to do something about that.

Richard Samuels was going to be the man to complete her new life. He was her future. Together they would heal each other.

Richard just didn't know it.

Yet.

CHAPTER THIRTY-SEVEN
KATE'S GENERAL STORE

The shop had been quiet that morning, which had allowed Kate to take the opportunity to do an impromptu stocktake.

Unfortunately, this was not helping the owner feel any better about the current state of the shop's finances.

Counting the tins, which had gathered dust on the shelves, was a reminder that footfall was reducing. Kate was not sure how much longer she could keep the shop open if the lack of customers continued. Employing Claire to serve on the till, whilst Kate took some time away, was proving to have been a dangerous decision. It had seemed the right thing at the time, but now she was not so sure. Claire only worked 15 hours a week, but the cost of her wages was putting even more strain on the paltry profit Kate was making.

It was clear that, all too soon, Kate would have to make a decision about Claire's future.

It was a decision which was causing her sleepless nights. She liked Claire and giving her the boot would hurt. Claire was a single mum and the money she earned from the shop helped to supplement her Universal Credit. Finding a job, which was flexible enough to avoid the need for childcare, was always going to be difficult. But Kate did not have deep pockets. If things didn't change soon, she would have to make one of the toughest decisions ever, in order to save the village shop.

Deep in thought, Kate didn't hear the bell tinkle as the door opened.

"Penny for them." Jenni popped her head around the aisle, finally catching her friend's attention.

"Sorry mate but I can't afford a penny," laughed Kate.

Despite the laughter, it was impossible not to see the anxiety which was dragging Kate down. Her brave face was not convincing at all.

"Shall I put the kettle on and you can tell me all about it?" Jenni suggested.

The friendly smile, which lit up Jenni's face, had a soothing quality. With some reluctance, Kate decided that she should probably talk to her friend about her troubles. A problem shared is a problem halved. Perhaps Jenni may have some words of wisdom to help. Kate was not keen on sharing her private financial troubles, but Jenni was discrete, and had a sensible head on her shoulders. Sometimes it's easier for an impartial observer to see the root cause of a problem in a business and maybe offer valuable solutions.

Kate needed a solution. And quickly, if she was going to save her business.

"Perfect," smiled Kate.

She cleaned her dusty hands on her apron as she followed Jenni into the back room. Jenni took command, making the tea, while Kate sat down wearily at the table. Her sigh and the droop to her shoulders spoke volumes about the worry which was troubling her. It was only a few days into the new year and Kate had had her fill of it already. This year was probably going to be the one where she had to admit defeat and shut up shop.

Literally.

Once the tea was poured, Jenni opened the conversation. She could tell her new friend was wrangling with a problem and was desperate to help. Jenni was determined to try and coax it out of her.

"Come on, Kate. Why the long face? January blues or what?"

Kate shrugged her shoulders. If only it was just 'a winter blues' feeling. She could cope with that.

"It's all a bit of a pickle," she started. "I'm so worried about the shop, Jenni. It's just not bringing in enough money. With all the bills and paying Claire's salary, I haven't made any money for months now. And at this rate, it will be making a loss soon. That's just not sustainable."

The telling had been rushed and garbled as if she knew that, if she didn't just say it, the words wouldn't come out.

Jenni looked shocked. Of course she was. It certainly wasn't common knowledge.

Kate had been fairly good at keeping the state of affairs quiet. Only Jeremy had an inkling of how bad things were, and he had been avoiding asking his wife questions. Jeremy had been the one who had persuaded Kate that it was their duty to take on the village shop, a lifeline to the local community. He was reluctant to admit their involvement in the shop was just prolonging its life, rather than saving it.

"Oh, Kate, I am so sorry to hear that. You have been shouldering one hell of a burden. Surely the Parish Council could help in drumming up business." Jenni took a sip of tea as the wheels of her mind started to whirl with ideas. "We need people to know how important their custom is to keep such a valuable resource going."

"You may well be right, Jenni. But I don't think I can carry on alone." Kate sighed wearily.

Now that she was talking, it became even more clear to Kate that the weight of the problem had been sitting so heavily on her shoulders.

"Other than The General and Anna Fletcher, who do all their shopping with me, so many villagers just use me for emergencies. If the shop folds, the slack will be picked up by one of the other community shops or home deliveries, but it just doesn't feel right. It's like another nail in the coffin for Sixpenny Bissett." Kate was picking at a thread on her apron as she spoke, a clear sign of worry. She sighed again, deeply. "It is just so desperately sad, especially after all the work I have put into this venture."

Jenni realised the time was right to speak to her friend about her idea. If she didn't share her thoughts now, it could be too late.

"Kate, I had been meaning to talk to you for weeks now. I have an idea. It may not be something you want to do, but just hear me out."

"Go on." Kate's interest was piqued.

"Look, I have been thinking about what to do with my time. I'm too young to retire, but I don't want to try and get a proper job." Jenni motioned bunny fingers as she used the expression. "I wouldn't know where to start. I was thinking about what I am good at. What I could use my skills for. Baking cakes. Cooking in general. That's my thing."

Jenni was struggling to shape her thoughts into a coherent sentence. It sounded so disjointed as she skirted around the issue. She wanted to impress Kate with her idea. It needed to sound considered and sensible rather than garbled. Just because they were friends didn't give her any advantage when it came to someone trusting you to be part of their business. Especially a business in such a precarious position. Jenni paused as she gathered her thoughts and tried to get them into some sort of order.

"OK, where are you going with this?" Kate actually looked interested now. It was all the encouragement Jenni needed.

"Why don't I rent some of your space? To sell cakes. You have the extra room you aren't using and I could make use of it. The rent may help your profitability and, of course, there would be cross-sale opportunities." Jenni was watching Kate's expression to determine how far to push it. So far, so good. Kate seemed interested. "I haven't really planned anything out yet, but I'm quite excited about the idea."

"I like the idea. What sort of scale are you thinking? Could you make and stock enough cake to make it viable for you?" Kate's brain was ticking over at speed as she rattled the questions off.

"I seriously haven't shaped the idea out yet, but I was hoping that, between us, we could come up with something. I would probably use my kitchen to do the cooking and the shop to do the selling. What's your gut feel?"

Jenni could feel her own excitement increasing now that she had started the discussion. The fact that Kate had not laughed at her idea was a start. She seemed interested and perhaps now was a good time to try a new venture.

Kate could see a chink of light. A small kernel of an idea was burrowing deep into her brain, weaving the tendrils of possibility across her mind. Maybe, just maybe, Jenni was on to something.

"Why not go a step further?" cried Kate. "A café."

"A café?" Jenni mused.

"Yes, why not? I don't use that whole space at the front left of the shop and it would be plenty big enough to set up some chairs and tables. We would need a counter and coffee making equipment, but oh my God, I think it would be brilliant."

Kate's mind was bounding ahead now. She could see possibilities for the future, even extending the café out into the front yard, which would help to draw more customers in. Suddenly, her mind hit upon the fly in the proverbial ointment.

Money.

"Oh shit, what am I thinking?" she gasped. "I haven't got two beans to rub together as it is, so how the hell am I going to pay for improvement work to adjust the space to be suitable for a café? Stupid cow."

Kate dropped her head into her hands in frustration.

"Don't worry about the money, Kate. If we are going to do this then I will invest in the work. I can pay for the adjustments and, of course, the equipment we will need to set it up."

The idea of investing in the business was exciting Jenni now. She was already forming ideas about a theme, colours and types of crockery. Her enthusiasm was bouncing about like Tigger. This plan was so much more than she expected and could be something which would keep her occupied in the months ahead.

"Are you sure, Jenni? Look, I've just told you my business is on the brink. Isn't it dangerous for you to put money in when the shop is hardly a going concern?"

Kate winced as she started to wave goodbye, figuratively, to the opportunity. She could not let her friend waste money on a venture which may not succeed and may prove to be very costly. As much as the idea could throw her a lifeline and keep the shop open for a bit longer, could she really let her friend throw good money after bad?

"Don't start backing out just when I have started to get excited!" cried Jenni. "I think it's a brilliant idea. It just needs some thought. Why don't I start by doing some investigation into how much it would cost to adapt part of the shop into a café? I'm sure Alaistair would be willing to give me a quote. Then you and me can sit down and look at the figures. Make some decisions."

Kate could see the enthusiasm written all over Jenni's face. She had been totally honest with her friend about the dangerous position the shop was in and, even that fact, didn't seem to be putting her off. Perhaps the plan did have merit. Perhaps this was her saviour, or should she say, the village's saviour.

"Okay, if you are sure. I honestly don't want you to go into this blind. I would rather you know how tough things have been to make money out of the shop before you make a decision."

"Look, Kate. Not being funny, but my Reggie left me in a reasonably comfortable position, so money isn't the problem. I can afford to pay for the work. We just need to decide if we can make a shop and café combination work."

"What about your boys? Should you speak to them first before you do anything? I really wouldn't want them to think I have coerced you into anything."

Jenni flicked her hair behind her ears as if she meant business.

"Firstly, the money is mine. George has the family business and Jimmy is well provided for, so this would be my own personal money. Which I have." As she spoke, Jenni reached across the table to take Kate's hand. "And if truth be told, I spoke to George about my idea when he was at home for Christmas. He was fully supportive of me trying a business venture. He had said about buying a small café or something like that, but, initially, I was a bit scared of going that one step further than just a bit of baking and selling."

"So how come you aren't scared of my idea for the café?" asked Kate.

Her line of questioning was designed to pick any possible holes in Jenni's plan. Emotionally, she was not prepared to throw herself into planning a future if Jenni was likely to get cold feet once she looked more fully at the costs.

"Because it's you," laughed Jenni. "I think we would make a great team. Work would be fun. Please let's try this out."

The two women embraced.

Kate rubbed her hand up and down Jenni's back, reassuring both of them for the challenges which lay ahead. Their friendship had blossomed in the few months they had known each other. They had already created a strong bond and now, with the idea of setting up a business together, those ties would become stronger still.

Kate felt a huge weight shifting off her shoulders. If they could make this work, she may not have to make that dreadful decision to let Claire go. If anything, they may need more staff to help run the expanded business. One step at a time, she cautioned herself.

This could be the start of something special.

Both women were excited. "I think we should crack a bottle to celebrate," smiled Jenni.

"Already drinking the profits," laughed Kate, as she pulled a Pinot out of the fridge. "I think this could be the start of something special, Jenni love. So, yes, let's celebrate."

CHAPTER THIRTY-EIGHT
ROSE COTTAGE

Jenni picked up her handbag, doing her usual check for phone and purse before she dashed out of the house.

She was off to the supermarket to do her weekly shop. That, in itself, was the most blatant case of double standards. She should be ashamed of herself. Only the other day, Jenni had been frustrated about the lack of support from the community for the village shop, and yet here she was, off to the local supermarket. Jenni felt a twinge of guilt as she berated herself silently.

Since her talk with Kate, Jenni had literally been floating on air. She was incredibly excited about the idea and spent every waking moment working on her plans. She was determined to prove to both her and Kate that they could make this work. If her determination alone was all they needed, then the café would be an instant success.

Jenni had spoken to Alaistair as soon as she left the General Store. He had agreed to pop into the shop the next day and do a preliminary survey. From that initial look, he would be able to estimate the work required and the all-important costs. He could see Jenni's excitement about the plan and was keen to move things forward as quickly as he could for her. Interestingly, he believed it would also provide him with some much need brownie points with Paula. She did seem very fond of Jenni and was constantly extolling her new friend's good points to him, when they were together.

And they were together a lot, now.

Something that was bringing Alaistair a much needed boost, both to his confidence and his view on womankind in general. Paula had brought joy to his life when he had thought any chance for happiness had waned. For now, he was playing it cautiously in case Paula just saw him as the friend to lean on.

Taking Kate's counsel, Jenni had spoken to George too.

As much as she had been full of bravado when speaking with her prospective business partner, Jenni would never consider putting money into the shop without seeking the advice of her elder son. He had his father's head for business, and rightly challenged her on a number of points, his way of ensuring she was doing this for the right reasons and not just to please a friend. Once he had finished questioning her motives, George gave her his blessing.

Secretly, he believed this was one of the best decisions Jenni had made recently. He had had his doubts about her moving to Dorset. The distance between them being the main factor. But this latest venture sounded just what his mother needed to embed her in a new community and give her a new focus after her loss.

Things were moving at pace now.

Jenni had spent hours online looking at crockery. She had found a site which sold beautiful, bone china cups and saucers. The sets were all mixed in design and colours, which would add an eclectic feel to the café. She had also found some beautiful mugs but had resisted her compulsion to just go ahead and make the orders. Everything had been saved on her laptop, so she could share with Kate in due course. Jenni had also found a reasonably priced coffee machine, which also had the option for them to lease rather than buy. Thinking the lease option might be a sensible approach, Jenni had then fallen down a rabbit hole as she investigated lease agreements.

To say that Jenni was excited was an understatement.

Saying farewell to Freddie, who was not taking any notice as he had found a suntrap on the dining room windowsill, Jenni shut the front door. It was at this point that she noticed the tyre. Her back left tyre was as flat as a pancake.

"Oh damn," she cried as she kicked the rubber. "Why now?"

Muttering under her breath, Jenni circled the car looking for anything else. The mechanics of a car were simply beyond Jenni. That had been Reggie's department. She had never changed a tyre in her life and she certainly wasn't going to start now. She knew she had a spare in the boot, but that was as far as it went.

Wracking her brains, Jenni tried to remember what George had told her when she had picked up the car from him. It had various warranties and guarantees, but how would that help when she was miles away from Birmingham? She had breakdown cover, but did this situation really warrant a call out?

"Bloody hell," she vented, as the tyre got another kick.

"Everything OK, Jenni?" Richard Samuels walked up her drive. A knight in shining armour, riding to her rescue.

"No not really." Jenni pointed at the offending tyre. "Stupid tyre. I was just about to call my breakdown company."

"Don't worry about that," interrupted Richard. "Have you got a spare? I will have that sorted for you in no time."

Jenni smiled at the man as he took control. Just what she was secretly hoping he would do.

"Are you sure, Richard? I really don't want to put you to any trouble."

"No trouble at all. I will have this changed in a jiffy."

Jenni realised that she had managed more of a conversation with the elusive Richard Samuels in the last few minutes than she had managed since moving in. Amazing what a little car trouble can do.

Richard smiled at her and she went weak at the knees. Bloody hell, she thought. He is the sexiest man ever. A vision in dark jeans, which hugged his bottom and showed off his slim legs. He was wearing a navy, North Face jacket, which he was shrugging out of as he surveyed the job. Handing his jacket to Jenni, he rolled up the sleeves of his jumper. He had remarkably hairy arms. I wonder how hairy the rest of him is, thought Jenni? Her line of thought was certainly not helping her state of heightened desire.

Calm down! Calm down!

Within minutes, Richard had located the jack and had the car elevated. It took some time to remove the nuts, which looked like they had been almost welded on. Whoever had fixed them on had no intention of them being removed quickly in an emergency. Unfortunately, this was no F1 tyre change. Richard cursed as he struggled to get them to move. Jenni felt incredibly embarrassed that he was getting all mucky, while she just stood and watched. His immaculately manicured hands were already covered in oil.

Richard didn't seem bothered. He whistled a tune as he knelt in her gravel, dirtying his jeans. He really was all man. Just how she liked them.

Poor Jenni was literally transfixed as she watched him. She didn't say a word. If truth be told, she couldn't form a sentence. How could this man make her feel so unnecessary and have no inkling of the impact he was having?

The new tyre was in place and tightened. Richard stood up, rubbing his mucky hands together with a wide grin on his face.

"All done. Now, could I trouble you for some soap and water?"

Jenni was galvanised into action. Unlocking the front door, she led him into the kitchen, handing over soap and a fluffy towel. Richard was looking around the room as he washed.

"You have made some excellent improvements to this place, Jenni. I remember it as being pretty outdated and sad before."

"Thank you, Richard. I love this place. It didn't take me long to get settled and stamp my personality on it."

A safe conversation so far. Jenni blushed as her eyes continued to admire the man stood at her kitchen sink. Every movement he made was sexy, even washing his hands. O-M-G. What was she becoming?

A sex-starved old fool, who should know better.

"Well, I better get going." Richard interrupted her musings. "Need to get back to work."

"What sort of work do you do, Richard?" Jenni had heard various bits from Kate, but work chat was a safe avenue, she decided.

"I own a boatyard down on Poole Harbour, but I don't necessarily need to be down there every day. Got a good team of lads who do the builds. I was in the middle of doing a design this morning. Don't know about you, but my attention span is getting worse as I get older. I find a little walk mid-morning helps to get the old juices flowing."

Jenni blushed a deep shade of red as she imagined his juices flowing. Coughing to hide her discomfort, she found her voice. "Oh that sounds really interesting. I would love to see some of your designs sometime."

"Maybe next time I take The General out for a trip on the boat, you can come too," smiled Richard.

Jenni was not a great sailor but she nodded enthusiastically, like some deranged, nodding dog. She would just have to overcome her motion sickness if she wanted to spend time on the water with this heartthrob. Pleasure or pain, always in perfect synergy.

"I cannot thank you enough for your help today, Richard. I would have been totally lost without you. In return, perhaps you would let me cook your supper one evening."

Richard looked slightly uncomfortable at the suggestion, but obviously covered that uncertainty quickly so as not to offend. "That's very kind, but you don't have to."

Jenni was not being put off. This might be her one opportunity. "I insist. How about Friday night? Shall we say 7pm?"

Richard could not refuse without being rude. She had backed him into a corner and he had to oblige. "Perfect. I will see you then. Red or white?"

"Either would be lovely," replied Jenni.

"Well. I must get going. See you Friday."

Richard was edging towards the front door and Jenni followed. The trip to the supermarket was even more important now. She needed to plan out something special for them.

CHAPTER THIRTY-NINE
THE RECTORY

Jenni and Kate joined Alaistair at the kitchen table to view his proposed plans.

Over the last few days, Kate had started to let herself get excited about the idea of the café. Whilst it had been her idea, she was surprised how Jenni had jumped on it without hesitation. The conversation had moved from selling a few cakes to an expansion of the business, in what had seemed like seconds.

When Kate had spoken to Jeremy about the idea, he was extremely positive too. He saw this as a means for the shop to remain a viable business proposition, but more importantly, in his role as leader of the village's pastoral care, he saw the café as a huge opportunity. It could be a place for local groups to meet. A place where those who were lonely could find a friendly face. Everyone Kate spoke to about the plan seemed to see huge possibilities for the village.

Anticipation and excitement were building.

Now they had to make it happen. And from Kate's perspective, she was desperate for the plan to work so that the shop could survive. Since the two women had talked, a huge weight had lifted from Kate's shoulders. She had slept properly last night, the first time in weeks. Life always seemed so much easier to tackle after a decent night's kip.

Fortunately for Kate, Jenni had been keen to do most of the research to follow up on their idea. It wasn't that Kate didn't want to be involved, but she knew her limitations. She had so much on with the shop and the children at the moment and letting Jenni run with the plans had worked for her. Now was the time for her to become more involved. Plans needed deciding on and Kate was intrigued to see what Al and Jenni had come up with.

Alaistair had pulled together a floor plan of the shop, with expanded detail of the area which was to be designated as the café. It was huge sheet of paper and covered most of the table. As he spoke, he used his pen as a pointer.

"Ladies, I think we only need to make limited alterations to this area. The flooring is sound and in good condition. I am assuming you want to keep the open-plan feel of the store, so the main alterations involve building a counter area. I think you could do with some additional power connections for your equipment."

Both Kate and Jenni nodded.

"For the counter, I suggest you keep it fairly basic. Putting it in this corner allows you to maximise the floor space for your customers. The side entrance would have a flip-up top to allow you behind and keep your customers out, especially any children. Thinking health and safety." Al grinned.

Jenni had been doing the required research on all health and safety requirements. It was a minefield, but one she would have to grasp before they could open up that part of the business. Rather than putting her off, it had galvanised Jenni. She now had a separate notepad where she jotted down all the legal requirements she needed to cover off, in order to make the business compliant. Jenni was in her element with her notepad and 'to do' list. She had never felt so organised.

Alaistair continued. "I suggest a glass panel across the top half of the main counter, so you can display cakes and tempt those just buying a coffee to indulge in your goodies." He paused, almost with dramatic effect. "So, all in all, it's about a couple of day's work and the cost would be this."

Alaistair pushed an itemised bill towards Jenni. She quickly picked it before Kate could see it. In terms of the building work, Jenni was determined to cover those costs and she was keen to keep any worry, about finance, from Kate's door. The last thing she wanted was for Kate to get cold feet, especially if she saw the price of the work. As Jenni looked at the bill though, she was pleasantly surprised. Alaistair was obviously being kind to them on the labour charges. Overall, the amount she would need to spend was well within what she had expected.

"That looks very reasonable, Alaistair. I'm happy to go with your suggestions. Kate?"

Kate reached out for the draft bill but Jenni shook her head. Kate sighed with a sense of resignation. Jenni was obviously keeping true to her word that she wanted to cover the building costs. If she was honest with herself, Kate was hugely relieved and was certainly not going to argue with her new partner.

"Without seeing the bill, the plan you have drawn up looks excellent, Al. I think putting the counter where you suggest is the best place. It will keep a natural flow to the shop and, hopefully, mean that people will move between the two businesses, benefiting us both."

Jenni was determined to reach a decision that day and was relieved that Kate was supportive of Alaistair's ideas.

She was not impulsive by nature, but the suggestion of opening a café had engaged her and she was incredibly excited to get going. Of course, she realised it would be a few months before they could officially open the café, but between now and then, she would have plenty to do.

"It looks like we are in agreement then, Alaistair." Jenni still didn't feel close enough to abbreviate Alaistair's name as her friend had done. She was also a bit 'old-school' when it came to business and didn't want her friendship with the builder to get in the way of the work. "When do you think you would be able to start?"

Alaistair had an old-fashioned diary. No electronic scheduling for him. He flicked through the pages with a look of concentration fixed on his face. A couple of times he stopped and hovered over a page, then moved on. The weeks were virtually flicking past as he moved through his diary.

"I am going to be totally honest with you ladies, my diary is pretty jammed at the moment. I would prefer to do the work in two days solid rather than the odd bit of time here and there. Hopefully, that will minimise the impact on the shop."

Kate interrupted at that point. "Sorry Al, when it comes to doing the work, will you need me to shut the shop up?"

"Good point, Kate. No, we should be able to work round you, but I will try to start early and finish late if that's OK. I will hang a plastic sheeting over the divide between the shop and café to avoid any dust and muck impacting on you. Does that work for you?"

"Sure, sounds good to me," smiled Kate. She could see Jenni itching to find out when the work would be done. "So timescales, Al?"

"Right. I think I can do 24th and 25th March. I know that's a month or two off, but that really is the earliest I can do. Obviously, if you are getting anyone else to quote on the work and they can do it sooner, I do understand."

Kate had not even considered asking anyone else to quote for the work and looked across at Jenni to see what she was thinking. Al was a friend but also the best builder around. She could not imagine going to anyone else, but it was Jenni's money. She must decide.

Jenni had a very serious expression on her face. "Alaistair, we trust you and want you to do the work. If that's the timescale, then we are happy with that. I'm not underestimating the amount of work we will need to do before we can start the café operating, so this buys me some time to work on my plans."

Kate heaved a sigh of relief. It looked like things were going to progress. It wasn't just the future of the shop Kate was keen to get sorted out, she was also incredibly excited to be working with her new best friend.

The thought of spending time with Jenni every day was bringing joy to her heart.

CHAPTER FORTY
ROSE COTTAGE

Friday afternoons were Henrique's favourite time of the week.

Why?

Because it was his time to do Señorita Sullivan's garden. He loved going to Jenni's house. From a work viewpoint, her garden was well-stocked and easy to maintain. It was not a difficult job for Henrique. It usually involved a bit of grass cutting and tidying the bushes. A nice, slow end to the week. During the winter months, he had been working on the numerous trailing roses which covered the walls of the thatch. They were getting a good pruning, allowing the roses to come back strongly in the spring.

It wasn't just a work preference; the true reason was Señorita Sullivan. He had a crush on Jenni. A big crush. She was gorgeous and sexy. He couldn't get her out of his mind. At night, he lay in his caravan, thinking of them together. He relived the one and only time, over and over.

It was a stupid crush. He understood there was no future for them. She was a proper grown-up, whilst he was still young and wanting to sow his oats. But she had gotten under his skin. He couldn't help what he was thinking or feeling. It wasn't rational, but he could dream.

He found that he was ignoring his girlfriend's calls from Barcelona. He really didn't want to lie to her, not while they were trying to make long-distance romance work. The last few times they had spoken, he had found it hard to talk about what he was up to, without talking about Jenni. He had been conscious that his girlfriend had seemed far too interested in his new client and he had had to close down the chat quickly, which had probably made her even more suspicious.

As Henrique made his way through the side gate into Jenni's garden, he spotted her at the kitchen sink. She caught his eye and waved, gesturing her signal for tea. He nodded. Any excuse to spend some time in Jenni's company, even if it meant a later finish tonight.

Their routine on a Friday had become quite practised.

Jenni would make the tea and he would join her in the kitchen for a chat. Jenni had a vast range of books, which she was allowing him to borrow to improve his English. Often, their conversations would revolve around the latest novel he was absorbed in and any observations he had.

Jenni's love of books was a passion they shared. A common interest, as well as the amazing sex. Even if the sex was only a one-off. For now.

Their lovemaking had been amazing and was the reason Henrique was fixated on this woman. If she wasn't sexy enough, Jenni's passion for stories was another turn-on for the Spaniard. Jenni had an eclectic range of books and he was gradually working his way through. She was his own, private librarian. At night, when his fantasies took over, the image of Jenni naked with a book in hand was obsessing him to the point of distraction.

He was in too deep. Way too deep, especially as he realised Jenni didn't see their relationship as a relationship. It had just been sex. For her.

Back to reality, Henrique entered the utility room, kicking off his boots.

"Hola, Jenni," he cried, as he wandered into the main kitchen. The heat from the Aga hit his cold face, providing instant warmth. "How are you today?"

"Hola, Henrique. I'm super, thank you. Tea? And I have a slice of Vikki sponge cake if you fancy?"

Henrique nodded enthusiastically at the thought of Jenni's cakes. They really were the best. As soon as the plate was placed in front of him, he was stuffing his face with the crumbling sponge. If it wasn't for the fact that Jenni was such a polite lady with standards, he would have been inclined to lick the plate. He resorted to mopping up with his finger, then sucking it rather suggestively.

It wasn't working, he decided. Jenni didn't throw herself at him, turned on by his sensuous sucking. What a shame.

"How are you getting on with Wuthering Heights then?" Jenni enquired. "It's a tough read that one, but one of my favourites."

Jenni was a fan of Emily Brontë and had read her most famous offering several times. She found that a second or third reading of any book gave fresh perspective, but the Brontës could be read over and over again without boredom kicking in.

"It is going good."

"Going well or it is good," corrected Jenni.

She had become accustomed to picking up on some of Henrique's vocabulary. He never seemed to be upset with her suggestions, thankfully. Jenni's intention was never to be condescending. She cared for the lad and just wanted to help.

"I am reading with my laptop on. I can look up words into Spanish when I don't understand. It makes me slow but it is good."

Henrique smiled as he looked at Jenni.

She really was the most beautiful woman he had seen since he arrived in England. Even without make-up, her face shone with a light of happiness. He took a slurp of his tea, enjoying its fragrant taste. Tea was a drink he had developed a taste for at university. It seemed to be the staple brew in his student accommodation and, once he had overcome the various nuances of milk intake, he had found a good builder's tea was his preference.

"What are your plans for the weekend, Jenni?" He continued to sip his drink.

"Richard Samuels is coming for dinner tonight, so I do need to get on soon and do the prep." Jenni didn't notice the look of devastation which appeared on Henrique's face. "He was my knight in shining armour the other day, when I got a flat tyre."

Henrique grimaced.

Richard Samuels was much nearer Jenni's age and was a very handsome chap. Even though he knew the brief interlude with Jenni was a one-off, the last thing he wanted to contemplate was some other fellow enjoying her delights. The one saving grace was that he had never seen Richard with a woman.

Hopefully, he is gay and won't be interested in Jenni. Let's face it, a man as good-looking as Richard Samuels without a woman, must be gay, thought Henrique. It was all very simple in his mind.

"That will be lovely." Henrique's words were forced. Hopefully, it would be a disaster. Not the nicest thing to be thinking. He was not proud of his thoughts. They smacked of juvenile jealously. When he was around Jenni, he was irrational. "If you get bored this weekend, I'm not working so feel free to give me a shout out." Henrique picked up his vocabulary from numerous sources and radio was one of them.

Jenni smiled, somewhat resignedly.

She tried her hardest not to encourage Henrique. It had been a mistake to fall into bed with him and she really didn't want to give him any 'come-on' signs. It wouldn't be fair. He was a lovely lad and she really didn't want to hurt his feelings. It was extremely flattering to find that someone that young could want to sleep with her, a middle-aged woman. But that was all it was. Flattering and fun. It would not be repeated. It could not.

Jenni was still embarrassed about her behaviour that day. It was so out of character. She had never had a one-night stand in her life. Well, she had been married to Reggie from a young age. Sex between her and Reggie had been loving and mutual. When she had lost her husband, she could not imagine being naked with another man.

It would be far too embarrassing.

She had stretch marks!

Reggie had loved those marks as symbols of the two wonderful babies she had given him. He had never minded if she put a bit of weight on, which was rare. They had celebrated their mutual love handles. They were familiar with each other's bodies. God knows, Reggie even used to fart in bed to make her giggle, so there were no bodily secrets kept from each other. After nearly thirty years of marriage, they had become used to what they liked and could meet each other's needs.

Sleeping with Henrique had been something else.

Her inhibitions had flown out the window as the young man worshipped her body. She was so caught up in the moment that she didn't even think about the difference in the tone of their bodies. His was so young and fresh compared to her 'lived-in' frame. Henrique did not seem to notice or, if he did, he was far too wrapped up in the passion to notice the difference.

After the event, Jenni had felt embarrassed just thinking about their differing circumstances. But Henrique had made things so easy for her. He had never mentioned it since. He acted completely cool with the whole situation, saving her blushes.

But he did seem quite obsessed with her company now. No words were spoken, but she caught his furtive looks when he didn't think she was watching. There was something going on in Henrique's head which she couldn't make out. There was no way she was starting that conversation up.

Let sleeping dogs lie. That was the safest and kindest policy.

CHAPTER FORTY-ONE
ROSE COTTAGE

The doorbell rang, right on time

Jenni loved a man who was punctual. It was a prerequisite for her in a relationship. Not that this was a relationship.

Not yet.

Jenni was one of the most organised people she knew and became hugely frustrated when people didn't apply the same courtesy to her. Timekeeping was a basic. If you promise to be somewhere at a certain time, then be there.

"Richard, come in."

Jenni greeted him with a welcoming smile and a proffered cheek to kiss. Awkwardly, Richard took her hand and shook it.

Not a great start.

Richard passed her a bottle of Beaujolais. No flowers. Again, another signal which Jenni really should have picked up on. It could have saved her huge embarrassment later.

Richard looked and smelt amazing. He was wearing chinos, dark blue, with a white polo shirt under a leather jacket. Whatever aftershave he was wearing was a heady mix, which hit her nostrils as she took his jacket. He started to take his shoes off but Jenni stopped him. She was never too fussy about people being barefoot in her house. Only Henrique, who always sported filthy boots. Although to be honest, his socks were never too clean either.

Richard followed Jenni into the kitchen.

She had decided to serve dinner in that room, rather than the dining room, so they could enjoy the warmth from the Aga and to make the setting more informal. She was determined to make Richard relax in her company, so she could get to know him better. Perhaps if he got to know her properly, then his rudeness at The General's party might be a thing of the past.

And if he relaxed a bit, perhaps he could see her as a future girlfriend rather than some sort of enemy. The mixed messages she had received at the party had confused her. But her woman's intuition told her he fancied her, so what was stopping him? If he made a move, she certainly wouldn't stop him.

They made small talk, while Jenni put the finishing touches to dinner. Richard disguised his nervousness by opening the wine and pouring generous glasses. Jenni had decided on lamb shanks, slow cooked in a mint gravy, with roast potatoes and green beans. It was one of those dishes which needed little watching so that she could devote her full attention to Richard.

"Tell me Jenni, what made you decide on Dorset?" Richard appeared to be relaxing as he sipped the wine.

Jenni had her back to him as she plated up. "We had been here on holiday before, when the boys were little, and I remembered the small, chocolate-box type villages. When Reggie died, I wanted to get as far away from Birmingham as possible. Too many memories."

Richard nodded, understanding her pain. "When did you lose your husband?" His voice was soft and it took her a moment to realise he had spoken.

"Nearly two years ago now. We had a car accident. Reggie didn't make it. I spent about two months in hospital having treatment for my injuries. It was dreadful." Other than her friend, Kate, Jenni hadn't spoken to anyone else in the village about the accident. It's not the sort of thing that comes up in general conversation, and Jenni was not one to seek out sympathy. "Reggie died beside me when we were trapped in the car. One minute he was there with me and the next, he was gone."

"I'm so sorry," whispered Richard. "I can only imagine how hard that was. You say you have boys. That must have been a comfort to you."

He was thinking about his own desolation when Nicola had died and he was left all alone.

Jenni paused, thinking back to George's discomfort with any type of caring activity. "It is probably so wrong of me to say this but, at that time, I really wished I had daughters. George and Jimmy are my entire world, but they were not ideal when I needed a hand in the bathroom. We spent the first week of me being home from hospital suitably embarrassed until I got a care worker in to help. The relief on my boys' faces when they no longer had to try and help me put my underwear on was so funny."

Richard laughed at the telling. Jenni could speak about her tragedy with humour, something he had really struggled with, and still did.

He was starting to relax in her company.

"What do your boys do? I guess they are all grown up as they don't live with you."

"Big, strapping boys, yes. George is 26. He took over the family business after his father died. Reggie was a car dealer." Jenni spotted Richard's grin, a sure sign that the stereotypical view of car dealers was forefront of his mind. "An honest one. And a highly successful one. Reggie left me in an extremely comfortable position, which gave me choices. One of which was to move home. Escape those memories. I wanted to be somewhere I hadn't shared with Reggie. A chance to almost reinvent myself for the second part of my life."

Richard nodded at that. His own home was still a shrine to Nicola. He had given her clothes and personal effects to charity, but every piece of furniture and the ornaments, which adorned their home, were picked by Nicola. Each item held memories for him, which ate away at his soul.

"What about your other son? Is he in the family business too?"

"Now that's a whole different story," sighed Jenni. "My younger son, James, or Jimmy is 22. Just finished university and is travelling the world, living on his dad's inheritance. I have absolutely no idea what he will do when he grows up. I honestly don't see him as a car salesman. He's far too idealistic and opinionated. He and George would end up falling out if they worked together."

Richard liked the sound of Jimmy already. He had been the black sheep of his family, not conforming to what his parents wanted. He had taken to the sea for his gap year. It was this trip of a lifetime which had given him his love of the open waves. He had been determined to make it his career after university. "Where in the world is he then? Don't you worry about him?"

"The last time we spoke, he was in Australia. Surfing the waves and enjoying the weather. I haven't spoken to him since Christmas though. Just messages since he went to Australia. He must be really enjoying himself. He is usually more reliable when it comes to keeping his old mum up to date with his movements. I try not to worry. He may well be 22 but he's still my little baby."

The love shone from Jenni's face as she spoke of Jimmy. Parents don't have favourites but her Jimmy had a special place in his mother's heart.

As they had been chatting, Jenni had served up dinner, which Richard was tucking into with gusto.

"Um, this is wonderful. The lamb simply melts in your mouth. Thank you, Jenni."

Jenni always appreciated praise for her cooking. Having lived with three men, she knew the importance of feeding their bellies. The way to a man's heart and all that.

Whilst Jenni had happily shared some of her background with Reggie, she was not picking up any signs that Richard would voluntarily speak of his wife. She decided it was best to avoid that subject unless he brought it up. The fact that he was conversing naturally with her was a bonus. He was clearly a shy man, who struggled in social situations, so her plan was to keep him relaxed and see how things developed.

"Tell me a bit more about your boatyard. Do you actually make boats or just repair them?"

Another safe option in the conversation stakes. Work. You can't go too far wrong with that.

"Most of the work we do is repairs, but I design too. That's the work which makes the money, to be fair." Richard's face was animated as he shared his passion for his boats. He looked even more attractive, if that were possible. "I tend to be working on a new design every six months. Most of the people I work for have deep pockets and are very demanding. It takes several iterations before the client is satisfied."

"I can imagine," replied Jenni.

She remembered going to the Boat Show at the NEC some years before. The money sloshing around that venue was overwhelming. It was clear that Richard loved his work. Suddenly, he had become relaxed, engaged, a totally different person.

"Once we have nailed down the design, my team will do the actual build. I subcontract out the interior work, as that's where it gets really silly. Gold plated handles and granite surfaces, you know what I mean. The cost of the inside of some of these boats is quite scary. I really don't need the hassle. Give me the hull and overall structure and I'm happy. That's where the beauty of a craft lies."

As he spoke, his hands were creating a boat shape, helping him describe the process. Jenni watched his hands, imagining them shaping her body. He had man's hands, bearing the signs of his trade. At the same time, they were well kept, with nicely manicured fingernails and smooth skin. She noticed he wore a gold band on his ring finger.

Not a good sign.

Jenni had reluctantly put her wedding band aside as she started her new life in Sixpenny Bissett. She still wore her engagement ring, but the band hung on a chain around her neck. Taking off her wedding ring wasn't a signal that Jenni had forgotten Reggie. No, it was her way of letting him go, gradually.

"So how long does it take to build a boat?" asked Jenni.

She wasn't overly interested, but her ploy was to keep him talking and thus keep him relaxed. It sounded very premeditated, her approach to the evening. It wasn't. Jenni wanted to get to know the man in front of her and, hopefully, help him see past his grief and into the future.

"That really does depend on the spec, but it averages around six months. I have three permanent guys, who are master boat builders, and I can bring in extra temps when we have a rush on. Ray, who is the most senior of the team, runs the yard day-to-day. It's great because it means I don't have to go in every day. I work from home at least three days a week."

Jenni started to serve up dessert as they spoke. She had made a fruit roulade, hoping Richard would notice that it was homemade.

"I bet you get to visit some pretty exotic locations then when you are looking for new clients."

"Unfortunately not," he grinned. "The majority of my clients are UK based. Shame, as those Arabs will spend a fortune on their yachts, but that's out of my league. Umm, this meringue is to die for. Did you make it yourself?"

Jenni was delighted. "I did. I'm so glad you like it. You are a bit of a guinea pig. I hope you don't mind."

"How so? Not that I mind, of course." Richard laughed.

He stretched back in his seat, another indication her plan was working.

"Well, hot off the press. I'm going into business with Kate Penrose. I'm going to set up a café in part of the village shop. The plan is to make and sell cakes, but I'm also thinking of expanding it to cover dinner parties and small catering events." Jenni was fairly animated herself, now that she was talking about her passion. "I decided I needed to do something for me. I spent most of my married life caring for Reggie and the boys. Now is my time."

"What a great idea," agreed Richard. "If your cakes are as good as this, then I have no doubt you will be a resounding success. I fear for my waistline though, as I think I will be a regular visitor."

His smile beamed and Jenni was lost in its glistening shine. She could feel a tingle in her tummy and her heart rate seemed to be racing. The attraction was obvious.

Surely, he could see it too.

"Why don't I put the coffee on and we can take them through to the lounge. Get a bit more comfortable."

Jenni didn't give him the chance to reply as she tried to hide her pent-up excitement.

CHAPTER FORTY-TWO
ROSE COTTAGE

Jenni's lounge was warm and welcoming.

A log fire burnt slowly within a light-coloured stone fireplace, the main feature of the room. Large, cream sofas sat against two walls, with a huge mat covering the empty floor space. Richard settled on one of the sofas as he waited for Jenni to return with coffee.

So far, the evening had been excellent. Relaxed and fun. Not what he had expected, if he was honest with himself.

Richard had been worried about accepting the invitation. His feelings for Jenni were confusing. He had been in a whirl as he tried to understand what his head, and heart, were telling him. If he couldn't understand what he was feeling, what hope did anyone else have?

Jenni was a beautiful woman and seemed really kind and generous. In his state of confusion over his own feelings, he was determined not to lead her on. He couldn't open his heart to another woman and the last thing he wanted was to play with her emotions. But as fast as his head was telling him that he could not let his guard down and risk his heart in another's hands, his emotional side was fascinated by this woman.

She was beautiful and incredibly sexy. He was attracted to her. Big time.

His body yearned for her touch. Not only was she stunning to look at, but she had character. The way she had stood up to the gossip around Peter St John showed her inner strength. He liked that in her. She had balls. Her personality lit up a room. At Herbert's party, she was the life and soul of the room. Unfortunately, he had not covered himself in glory that night. He had behaved like a bumbling idiot in her presence, and he really couldn't believe she had invited him round after such a poor performance.

Richard longed to get to know her better. But at the same time, he didn't want to. If he knew the person, Jenni, it would make it so much harder to reject her. Was it not better to keep that distance now and build the ice wall of defence to prevent him feeling anything?

Oh God, he was one fucked-up human being.

Jenni seemed interested in him. He wasn't that stupid that he couldn't see the desire in her eyes. It turned him on, big time. Whatever he did now, he would probably be hurting her feelings.

What a bastard. Why couldn't he just sort his bloody head out.

"Do you take it black or white?" Jenni's voice interrupted his confused thoughts.

"Black please," Richard smiled, trying to banish the concerns haunting his mind.

Jenni had pulled over a coffee table and taken a seat next to him on the sofa. Her close proximity unnerved him. He could smell her perfume as she leant forward to pour the coffee. He could make out the dip in her cleavage as she passed him a cup, brimming with rich coffee. The sight was enticing, with a glimpse of lace teasing his eyes. Jenni crossed her legs as she sank back onto the sofa. Her legs were shapely and long, covered in sheer, black tights.

Or were they stockings?

O.M.G., he groaned silently, tormenting himself with desire. A desire he could do nothing about.

The situation was getting dangerous. Richard decided to refocus back to their conversation about Jenni's aspirations for the café. Perhaps if he kept their chat on things which she was interested in, he could get through the rest of the evening with little or no damage.

"Tell me a bit more about your plans for the café. Are you going to run it independently to the shop?"

Jenni was oblivious to Richard's scheme to keep the conversation on safe ground. She quite happily picked up and ran with his opening line. "Good question, Richard. And not one that I know the answer to yet. I have a whole list of things to look at in the coming weeks. I need to work out the financial side of things, business accounts and everything to do with the banking side of running a business. Maybe I can pick your brains sometime?"

Damn. He wasn't expecting to open up another avenue for them to be thrust together. "Of course," he smiled. "Happy to help."

Oh if only she knew!

Jenni touched his arm as she leant forward to replace her coffee cup on the table. "You are too kind," she purred. Her voice dripped with sexual enticement as she continued. "I do miss having a man around to help with the decision making. I'm certainly no weak damsel in distress, but it is so lovely to bounce ideas off another person. Especially a man with experience."

How can the word experience carry so much sensual connotation?

Her hand rested on his leg as she gazed into his eyes. Richard felt like a rabbit in the headlights. He was trapped in her stare.

Hypnotised.

Paralysed.

Slowly she edged closer to him. Her lips were slightly parted and he could feel her breath on his face. She was panting with excitement. Slowly she kissed him, butterfly kisses which flitted across his lips. The movement was sensual. He desired her. The charge between them was electric.

Exquisite.

He could have been lost. He could have kissed her back. He could have enjoyed the moment.

But he didn't.

He shrugged her off, moving away from her on the sofa. Reacting as if she were a leper. Tainted. Dirty.

"No. Stop." Richard gasped as his head dropped into his hands. "I'm sorry, Jenni. I can't."

Jenni stopped and pulled back. She searched his face, looking for understanding. How could he reject her so obviously? Jenni was mortified. What the hell was happening?

Richard stood up, looking at Jenni who was trying her hardest not to cry. He felt like a complete bastard. What was wrong with him? A beautiful woman throws herself at him and he acts like she is a monster.

He had hurt her, it was obvious. He should never have allowed it to go so far.

It was all his fault.

But would she ever understand that?

How could she? He barely understood himself.

Jenni whispered with a quiver in her voice. "Why? What's wrong with me?"

Richard sat back down. There was no way she was going to repeat the kissing attempt, not after his reaction. She deserved an explanation. It was the least he could do.

"I'm so sorry, Jenni. It's not you. It's me." That old cliché sounded so insignificant to describe his reaction and the hurt caused. "I really like you. You're so very beautiful and if things were different, I could fall for you big time." He paused, collecting his thoughts. "I'm just not ready for a relationship."

"Who said I wanted a relationship?" said Jenni.

He could hear the hurt in her voice and he felt even more of a bastard.

"You are too special a woman for a stupid one-night stand. I cannot give you what you want or deserve. I'm sorry."

God that sounded dreadful. He knew he was making things ten times worse. He really should retreat now before he embarrassed himself further.

Jenni was picking at a loose thread on the throw which covered the sofa. Her head was down and she hadn't looked him in the eye since he had spurned her kisses. Her cheeks had gone a dark shade of red and a tear squeezed out of the side of her eye. She looked totally lost and vulnerable.

And it was all his stupid fault.

He had relaxed in her company. Perhaps he had flirted with her. Perhaps he had led her on without realising it. Whatever, he felt dreadful.

"Look, I'd better go. Thank you for such a lovely meal, Jenni. I am so very sorry."

Jenni didn't move as he walked towards the lounge door. He looked back and saw sadness, humiliation, and a touch of anger. There was no going back now. His bridges were well and truly burned.

Silently, Richard walked away.

CHAPTER FORTY-THREE
THE CARAVAN IN THE WOODS

"Shit," cried Jenni, as she heard the front door closing.

Screaming at the top of her voice might make her feel slightly better, but the rational part of her brain did not want Richard hearing her anguish. Grabbing a cushion, she folded herself inwards, cocooning her body to make it as small as possible. It was then that she allowed the tears of sadness to fall.

She sobbed. Letting the pain flow.

At first, she cried at the rejection. How could Richard spurn her like that? He reacted as if she was repulsive, whereas minutes before he appeared to be attracted to her. How could she have got it so very wrong?

Then she cried for the humiliation of the Peter St John episode. The disgust for the lecherous fool who had nearly wrecked her arrival into the community.

And finally she cried for Reggie. Why did he have to go and leave her to deal with all this shit? Life had been so easy before his death. She hadn't appreciated how lucky she had been before.

Sobs racked her body. Healing cries washed away the pain. Freddie had heard her weeping and jumped up onto the sofa. His furry head knocked against her, reassuring her of his loving presence. Automatically she stroked his feline shape, drawing comfort. As her crying slowed, she sniffed, wiping her dripping nose across her hand. Her mascara came away in black streaks, making her look like some desolate panda.

Once the worst of her sadness had washed away, anger hit her with full force.

How dare he treat her like that. Richard bloody Samuels. OK, she fancied him, but his rejection was nasty. He was so full of himself. As if she gave a damn about him. He wasn't all that, anyway! She didn't fancy him that much.

He might be good-looking but he had nothing else going for him. Rude bastard.

Jenni was not sure she was convincing herself. It was a good try, but it wasn't making her feel any better. She considered getting drunk but ruled that one out pretty quickly. The hangover tomorrow was not worth the moment of oblivion tonight. The last thing she wanted right now was to sit and wallow in self-pity. It was only 8.30pm.

The night might be ruined, but it wasn't over yet.

A walk in the crisp, night air. That's what she would do. She had taken to this odd night-time routine recently, something she would never have contemplated in Birmingham. She had invested in a powerful torch and, once you were clear of the high street, the surrounding woods and fields were full of night-time activity. She would find a fallen tree and sit and stare up at the stars.

Imagining the hugeness of the universe would bring her troubles into perspective. She would seek consolation in the constellations.

Jenni grabbed her bright-red ski jacket and welly boots and let herself out of the front door. Once she was away from the houses, she flicked on her torch and headed for the woods. It didn't take her long to find a suitable place to sit, a fallen tree stump.

She stretched back to gaze upwards. The night sky was clear of clouds, allowing her to see the vast expanse of the constellations. She located the Plough and Orion's Belt easily. Those were the ones most people could find. Jenni traced her way across the sky, picking out Ursa Major and Minor, along with Andromeda. Her childhood knowledge rushed to the forefront of her mind as she tried to forget about Richard bloody Samuels.

Stargazing always reminded her of her father.

As a child, she would often join him on the hill above their home to watch the twinkling delights. Her father was a bit of a closet gazer and had loads of facts and figures which blew her teenage mind. At that age, the idea of something millions of miles away, back in time, was incomprehensible. To be fair, Jenni was unsure she understood that concept now. She just enjoyed the idea of watching the movement of the constellations during the year. Tonight it was providing her with happy memories, chasing away the disappointments of earlier that evening.

Breathing slowly and consciously, Jenni could feel her body relaxing. It was a tried and tested habit, letting the stress leave her body with each outward breath. The embarrassment and humiliation of earlier was dissolving into the crisp, winter evening.

One day she would laugh at her attempt to seduce the man who would not be seduced.

But not today. It was still too raw.

She was losing her touch. If she had ever had the touch in the first place. Jenni had literally fallen at the first hurdle. A pathetic attempt at seduction and one that should never be repeated.

Suddenly she heard the snap of a breaking twig.

Someone was moving towards her in the shadows. She could see the trace of a light as it moved, side to side, across the ground. A tuneful whistle broke the silence as the light drew closer. Jenni was not afraid. She felt safe living here in the countryside, where everyone knew each other and, unfortunately, knew each other's business. Sometimes far too much. But she was conscious of not frightening the walker if they stumbled across her in the dark. She turned her torch on and wafted it in the direction of the sound.

Out of the darkness, the shadow grew larger. It didn't take her long to recognise the youthful shape of her gardener, Henrique. He was strolling purposefully towards her, one hand in the pocket of his tight jeans. He spotted Jenni and a smile beamed through the gloom.

"Jenni, what are you doing out here in the dark?" His voice carried an edge of concern. "I thought you had Richard round for dinner."

Jenni groaned. "Long story and one I would rather not think about, just now."

Henrique held his hand out to her. "Come on then. I have a beautiful bottle of Rioja which is perfect for sharing. Let me distract you from your troubles, lovely lady." His voice was soft and sultry.

Jenni was fully aware that she really shouldn't.

But she did.

Grabbing hold of his hand, she pulled herself up, excitement bubbling in her belly. They walked deeper into the woods. Jenni assumed they were heading for the caravan, a place she had seen before on her walks, but never ventured further towards. His home was located at the edge of the coppice, far away from the village and all its amenities. Obviously, Henrique was not scared of the dark, she thought. He liked his own company and the solitude of remoteness. It added to his air of mystery which made him even more desirable to the women of Sixpenny Bissett.

"Were you coming back from the pub?" Jenni asked.

"I was," answered the Spaniard. "Geoff, he asked me to help out for a couple of hours tonight. Cash in the hand, he said. It was lucky I walked back the long way around or I may have missed you."

Jenni could swear he winked, although the darkness around them made it hard to tell for sure.

It didn't take them long to reach the caravan. Henrique flicked a switch and lights, dotted around the interior, sprung into life. The left-hand side of the mobile home was clearly the living space with a large, curved seating area and fold-down table. A small kitchenette, with cooker and sink, was situated opposite the door. To the right was obviously the bedroom area, with two closed doors.

"Can I use your bathroom, Henrique?" asked Jenni.

She was keen to check out her panda eyes in case there was still evidence of her earlier breakdown. Jenni was not vain but bad eye makeup is never a good look. She didn't want Henrique to think she had been devastated tonight. Her pride would not let that happen.

Henrique gestured to the first of the closed doors, as he manhandled the cork from the bottle of wine. Luckily, the mascara which had ringed her eyes had rubbed away and there was little evidence of the sorrow she had felt from her earlier rejection. Tousling her fingers through her hair, she checked herself out in the mirror, pleased with the results. There is life in the old dog yet, she decided. The bathroom was small and compact, so she wriggled around to use the loo before returning to join Henrique.

He was sat on the sofa area with two large glasses in front of him. He patted the seat next to him. Jenni thought how vastly different his approach was to Richard's. Henrique was obviously pleased to see her and to be in her company.

She could tell how pleased he was from the bulge in his jeans. Wow, that really helped heal her dented pride. She can't be that bad if she could excite a young lad without even touching him. Bloody Richard Samuels, he doesn't know what he has just turned down.

As she sat down, his arm gently came to rest on her shoulder as his other hand passed her the wine. Jenni took a taste, savouring the flavour as it slipped down her throat.

"Oh that is lovely," she sighed. "Nectar of the gods."

Henrique looked confused. "Nectar? No, I don't understand."

"It's one of those English expressions which is hard to explain," Jenni said. "Means something wonderful to taste. Seductive on the lips."

She was flirting with him. And enjoying it immensely.

"Tell me, what happened tonight, Jenni."

Henrique's arm tightened slightly around her shoulders. She moved in closer, resting her head on his shoulder. It felt good to be held, comforted. Jenni missed the reassuring hold of a man and lapped up the attention she was getting right now.

"Oh, it was a disaster," groaned Jenni. "It started off okay. We had a nice meal and a chat. I definitely misread the signs though. I tried to kiss him. Don't laugh, but he rejected me. Pulled away."

Henrique's face was a picture. A mix of surprise and glee all at the same time.

"Serious? That man must like men. He cannot be a real man if he could reject you, sexy lady."

Jenni was tingling with excitement.

If there was one thing that this man was good at, it was the seductive voice. It turned her on without even the need for his touch. She knew what would happen next and despite her resolutions not to mislead Henrique, she knew she would put them to the back of her mind for the next few hours.

Jenni looked deeply into his eyes as she took another sip of wine. Henrique's finger traced her pout, touching the wine which moistened her lips. He sucked his finger then returned to tracing her lips. Jenni opened her mouth slightly with a sigh as the touching became more alluring. He put his finger in her mouth and she closed her lips around it, sucking gently.

Henrique groaned.

Placing her wine back on the table, he took her head in his hands. They gazed deeply into each other's eyes as the tension built. Slowly his lips touched hers. Gentle kisses which increased in velocity until he encircled her mouth with his, thrusting his tongue between her moist lips.

She sucked on his tongue, enjoying the taste of wine on his breath.

His hands moved down her body as they continued to kiss. She shivered as his fingers circled her nipples through her jumper. He gently pulled it over her head, revealing that infamous lacy, black bra. Breaking away from her lips, his mouth kissed her throat and worked down towards her breasts. Jenni ran her fingers through his thick, black hair, pressing his head into her cleavage.

"Come," he gasped, as he rose from the sofa, taking her hand.

She didn't need any persuasion.

They made their way into his bedroom. Jenni couldn't see anything but the bed. Remarkably large for such a small space and covered in cushions. With one hand, Henrique swept everything off the bed then turned to her again. Jenni pulled his tee-shirt over his head, running her fingers across his hairy chest. Their eyes were locked on each other's faces as their hands explored. He unzipped her skirt, dropping it to the floor She stepped out of it and kicked it to the corner of the room. Unzipping his jeans, he wiggled them down his legs and performed the same kick.

They laughed, breaking the sexual tension momentarily.

"You are one sexy woman, Jenni," whispered Henrique. His eyes roamed from her lace-covered breasts to the lacy panties and stockings. "Richard does not know what he is missing. He is probably at home now, playing with himself." He laughed at his rival's defeat in the stakes of love.

"Richard who?" laughed Jenni.

She pulled him against her as she kissed him again. His hands fiddled with her bra, releasing her breasts to his hands. Pushing him backwards onto the bed, they fell together, landing in a tangled heap. Giggling, they threw their underwear off.

Jenni was relieved that she had chosen her best lacy lingerie for the evening, hoping that Richard may have appreciated it. His loss was the Spaniard's gain. At least she was not wearing her comfy granny knickers, which she had been sporting the last time she took the young man to her bed.

Not that Henrique paid much attention to the expensive lace. He was more intent on what was hidden within.

Breaking the intensity of the moment, Henrique rolled across the covers in search of a condom. She grabbed hold of his balls as he donned the latex sheath. He groaned as desire built. Rolling Jenni beneath him, he raised himself onto his forearms and entered her.

Jenni was totally consumed with desire. She knew it was wrong. But she didn't care. What harm were they doing anyone? Neither of them was committed to the other.

It was just sex.

Hot, steamy sex.

But just sex.

There were no declarations of love. Just two adults enjoying each other's bodies.

And God, was she enjoying his body.

She didn't want him to stop. Grabbing his hair, she held on tight as he pumped away. They came together.

Henrique was a shouter. He gasped with release as he grabbed her arse and squeezed tight.

Jenni panted as she came down from a high. Her body was covered with a light film of sweat. God, that was one hell of a workout.

They collapsed together.

Curling around her back, Henrique held her against his chest. "Wow Jenni, you are one hell of a woman. I can't get enough of you."

Jenni felt like the cat who got the cream. She couldn't help smiling, as every part of her body seemed to glow with the after-effects of their lovemaking.

He was a beautiful man, with a beautiful body, which he had used to worship at her temple. What is there not to like about that? How many women of her age would die to have a younger man lust after their body?

They were both exhausted and content to cuddle together in post-coital harmony.

Gradually, they both slipped into a comforting doze.

CHAPTER FORTY-FOUR
ROSE COTTAGE

It wasn't fully light when she woke.

The faint traces of darkness were receding, as dawn approached. Yawning, she stretched out her limbs. She ached all over, but in a nice way. Turning onto her side, Jenni watched her bedfellow as he slept.

Henrique was lying on his back, with one arm draped over his head. He had pushed the duvet from his body in sleep, allowing her to get one final view of his beautiful physique. Henrique could have been the model for Michelangelo's David. Perfection. Powerful, muscular arms and the proverbial six pack. Everything about him screamed sexual desire.

Of course Jenni could not resist him.

She was only human.

And she had not resisted him three times last night.

After their first entanglement, they had dozed for an hour, only to wake and enjoy each other again. And again. Jenni had never had sex more than once in a night before. Up until now, her wants had been conservative in the extreme. She wasn't entirely sure where she had got the energy from last night. Touching her body, she could feel a pleasant soreness from their activity.

But in the cold light of day, she felt her age.

She could never keep up with the youth of her lover. Jenni knew she would pay for her exertions of last night and would probably hit her bed for a nap by the afternoon. It was just a plain fact of life that she had over twenty years on Henrique. She kept herself trim and tried to exercise regularly, but nothing could disguise the ravages of time on her bones.

Her body craved a bath, not something Henrique's home could offer her.

She was also conscious about not wanting to face the walk of shame in the bright glare of daylight. Checking her watch, she could see it was 5am. Despite it being a Saturday morning, she was certain that Anna Fletcher would catch her out if Jenni was stupid enough to leave it any later. Also, and more importantly, she was hardly dressed for an early morning walk in a tight, black pencil skirt.

She didn't want to wake Henrique.

He looked so peaceful. She dropped the faintest of kisses on his brow as she slid from the bed. In her mind she was saying farewell. Her sensible head must win the emotional struggle over her heart. It wasn't right to keep leading Henrique on.

Finding her clothes within the tangle of garments on the floor, she slipped out of the bedroom to dress. She quietly let herself out of the caravan, into the cold chill of a pre-dawn, winter morning.

The air slapped her in the face with a ferocity, waking her up to reality. Pulling her ski jacket tightly around her, she put her head down and set off into the wind, making her way to the shelter of the coppice. The clearing, where Henrique's van was located, formed a natural vortex for the wind to swirl around. She was wide awake now as she battled the elements.

As she trudged home, she thought about the previous evening.

Sex with Henrique was fun. Huge fun. He was a lovely man, but she didn't want a relationship with him. Oh God, the gossips would have a field day with her, if she did. He fulfilled a need and fulfilled it with aplomb. She had told herself that the first time was a one-off, but she was starting to form a bit of a habit. Every time she faced a setback, emotionally, she ended up seeking out the young stud.

He didn't seem to mind being the crutch she leant on, but was she being fair?

Jenni was not worried that Henrique might consider her behaviour as mercenary, out for what she could get. He had a partner back in Barcelona, so he was the one doing the dirty, if truth be told. OK, he had developed some sort of crush on Jenni, but they were adults. They both knew what they were doing and it was completely consensual.

It was just sex.

What Jenni wanted was a real relationship with a man who was in love with her.

She had thought that man was Richard Samuels.

Well that's where thinking gets you! Jenni doubted she would ever be able to look him in the eye again. In the cold light of day, her embarrassment descended on her like a shackle around her neck. What a bloody fool she had been. Kate and Paula had tried to warn her that he wasn't ready for a relationship, but she had ignored their words of caution.

She had ploughed on regardless and had paid the price for her selfish actions.

If she were a man and had behaved like she had last night, she would rightly be accused of sexual exploitation. What made her behaviour different? Surely a woman can also be a manipulator of another's emotions? And she was ashamed to admit it to herself, but she was the epitome of that behaviour.

She had invited Richard to dinner, not just to thank him for his help, but with the specific aim of winning his affection. What he wanted hadn't come into her thinking. She had thrown herself at him when he had made no attempt to entice her onwards.

She had totally misread the whole situation.

She tried to rationalise that it was her own lack of experience in relationships. She had become comfortable with Reggie. He knew what she liked, and she knew how to please him. Jenni didn't know how to play the game and had cocked up big time. She had decided to be an assertive and confident woman and take what she wanted.

But that wasn't her.

It just wasn't her style. She was not an arrogant woman. She didn't over-rate herself. She was just a middle-aged woman who fancied a chap and thought she would take the lead for a change. Not wait for the man. Try and seduce him with her charms.

But her plan had fallen flat on its face.

Total humiliation.

Jenni should have invested the time in getting to know Richard. Spent time together as friends. Find things that they had in common and do those things together. They had had such a lovely evening together and she felt they were finding common ground. But then she went and blew it. Jumping in before he was ready and probably destroying any chance she had of becoming his friend, let alone his lover.

Which was such a big shame.

Of course, her attraction to Richard had initially been physical, rather than understanding the man, respecting his values and being familiar with his wants and desires. She had expected those things to follow.

And now she had blown her chances.

The really sad part of all of this pitiful story was that she had enjoyed Richard's company last night. Once their shyness of each other had been overcome, they had had a lovely time together. She had felt relaxed in his company.

Once you got to know him, Richard was an interesting man. He shared her experience of grief so could understand how difficult it was to dip your toe in the water again. Their shared experience could have been the foundation of their friendship and who knows where that could have led to. But Jenni's impatience to have the man probably meant that her friendship with him was over too.

She really regretted that outcome.

It sucked.

As she wallowed in self-pity, she hadn't noticed her surroundings. A hard frost covered the ground, the leaves cracking as she walked. The sun was starting its journey above the horizon, glimmering as its rays bounced off the steep hills on either side of their valley. All was quiet. The village was still asleep, thankfully. Not even the early dog-walkers had ventured out yet into the chilly morning.

It didn't take Jenni long to reach Rose Cottage.

As she turned up her garden path, she spotted what looked like a tramp wedged against her front door. A body wrapped in a sleeping bag, sitting up in her porch but clearly asleep. The head of the person was covered by a thick bobble hat, which had been pulled down to cover their face. Beside the sleeping bag was an enormous backpack which looked familiar.

"Jimmy?" Jenni lent over placing her arm on the stranger's shoulder. "Is that you Jimmy?"

It moved.

A groan escaped its mouth as the body came to life. James Sullivan woke from his fitful sleep. He looked at his mother in puzzlement, at first, as his mind woke.

"Mum." Jimmy pushed his hat off and shook his hair out.

Jenni noticed how long and unruly her younger son's locks had got. No wonder she had mistaken him for a tramp. He looked a right mess. And he didn't smell too good either. Reaching across him to unlock the front door, she climbed over his pile of luggage.

"Come inside, Jimmy. Let's get you in from the cold."

Jimmy didn't even attempt to get out of the sleeping bag. Like a giant caterpillar, he slid into the kitchen, dragging his backpack with him. The warmth from the Aga was like a magnet, drawing him in. He settled himself on the floor, lapping up the warmth from its cast-iron doors. Freddie came to investigate, sniffing Jimmy. The sniff must have ignited a memory as, all too soon, the cat had wormed his way onto Jimmy's lap and was reminding him how much he had been missed.

"Bloody hell, Mum, where were you last night? It was bloody freezing sleeping on the doorstep. I could have frozen to death."

Jimmy was gradually working his way out of the sleeping bag and his parka jacket. A dirty pair of jeans and layers of tee-shirts and jumpers covered the rest of his body, hence the smell. Jenni decided he had probably been wearing those garments for a few days now.

"Firstly, I had no idea that you were coming home and secondly, mind your own business," she grinned.

"Oh, Mum, you dirty cow. I have only been gone less than six months and what do I find? My own Mother arriving home in the early hours, all dishevelled. I hope he was worth it. Leaving your poor son to freeze his balls off."

"Language, James." Jenni only really used his proper name when he was in trouble, although her face told a different story. "Why didn't you tell me you were coming home? I didn't expect you for months. If I had known, I would have picked you up from the airport."

Jenni risked life and limb and pulled her son into her arms. He had lost weight. He felt all skin and bones. Once she had got over the smell of his clothes, the scent of her baby boy got the maternal juices flowing. She stroked his hair in an attempt to tame it and gave him a huge kiss on the cheek.

"God, I have missed you, Jimmy. I didn't realise how much until just now. There has been a big Jimmy-sized hole in my heart while you have been off on your travels."

"Calm down, woman," Jimmy laughed. He would never admit it, but he had missed his Mum and George more than he could have imagined. He looked around, taking in his Mum's new home. "This place looks cool, Mum. It's in the middle of nowhere though. Thankfully, the taxi driver took a credit card as it cost me a fortune to get here."

"So what time did you land? Why didn't you ring me?" Jenni was feeling guilty that her poor boy had spent the night on the doorstep. She just hoped that none of the neighbours had seen him.

"It's a long story, but I did a few stops enroute so I arrived into Heathrow from Düsseldorf at about ten last night. I did ring your mobile and text you, but obviously you were too busy." He winked knowingly.

Jenni noticed her mobile, connected to the charger, sat on the island. Five missed calls and texts confirmed Jimmy's actions. There was also a text from Richard Samuels. Surreptitiously, she clicked on it. *'Sorry I rushed off last night. Let's talk x.'*

Shit, that's not what she expected. Well, he would have to wait for now. There was only one man on her mind right now and that was her boy.

"I'm sorry darling. I honestly had no idea you would be home anytime soon. If I had, then I would have got your room ready. Now, do you want to jump in a shower and I'll get you some breakfast?"

"Thanks Mum, I do stink. Been travelling for days without changing. Soz. Can I have a cuppa first, if you can cope with the smell?" His cheeky grin always got him out of trouble.

"Of course, darling."

Jenni fussed around him as she made tea and found his favourite chocolate biscuits. She always had an emergency pack stored in the cupboard for her favoured son. Jimmy had pulled off a couple of jumpers, now that the warmth of the kitchen had penetrated his body. Once the tea was poured, he reached across to take her hand.

"Mum, I need to talk to you. Before I shower." His expression had become serious. "Don't be angry."

Jenni was worried now. "What do you mean, Jimmy? What's happened?"

"I'm in a bit of trouble."

"Oh, Jimmy." Jenni sighed.

Why is life never easy? Her mind was forming various scenarios and none of them would end up being the right one.

"Look, this girl I've been travelling with recently. She's only gone and got herself up the duff and says it's mine."

Jenni's heart sank.

The casual way her son had just thrown that remark at her was not what she and Reggie would have expected of their offspring. Her sons had been brought up to respect others, especially the women in their lives, and accept responsibility for their actions.

Jimmy's flippant remark was obviously intended to soften the blow but, if anything, it had made her furious. She had to think carefully. How to react? Her whole being was screaming with anger, but that wouldn't help either of them. He had come home for help and somehow, she needed to deal with it.

Calmly and stoically she responded, "And is it yours?"

Jimmy's face spoke volumes.

"Oh, James," she sighed again. "So why are you home? Where is she? And does she even have a name?"

"Charlie. That's her name. She's gone home to Essex to speak to her parents. Then she's coming here, if that's OK?"

Jimmy was looking contrite as he watched the emotions play across his mother's face.

He and Charlie had not made any plans yet. It hadn't been serious between them, but the consequence of a few drunken nights was now growing in her belly. Charlie had told him that her dad would go apeshit when she told him, so Jimmy had played the coward's card and come home to Mum rather than face an angry father.

"You stupid boy." Jenni's voice was controlled, but he could hear the tremble of emotion. "Well, I guess it will have to be alright, her coming here. I don't suppose I have a choice in the matter. Oh, bloody hell, Jimmy. What a mess."

Jimmy held both her hands and looked deeply into her eyes.

"I'm so sorry, Mum. I honestly don't know how it happened. Well, I do know how it happened." He grinned, although the humorous interlude was not helping. "I will sort it out. Trust me."

Jenni let go of his outstretched hand and stood up. "Go and have a shower and we will talk later." She nodded towards the stairs. "Second door on the right and there is a towel in the cupboard on the landing. I'll do us some breakfast and we can talk some more."

Once he had left the room, Jenni sat down again, wearily. What had she done to deserve this? She and Reggie had brought the kids up well, taught them values, guided them in the right direction.

And now this.

Jenni was just getting her own life together. A fresh start in a new home. New friends. A new business idea. Okay, her own love life was a disaster but she could live with that. She loved living in Sixpenny Bissett.

This was to be her forever home. She was putting down roots.

Her plan for the future had not included her younger son living with her. And it certainly hadn't included his girlfriend and baby in tow. She had no desire to be a grandmother, not just yet.

Let's face it, last night she was screwing a guy young enough to be her son, and now Jimmy's actions reminded her of the ridiculousness of her relationship with Henrique. How could she carry on a liaison with the Spaniard with her son back home?

How could she carry on any relationship with Jimmy back home?

Perhaps this act of stupidity had solved her problem with relationships, once and for all. The priority would have to be to support her son and his new family. All thoughts of herself would have to wait.

Her life in Sixpenny Bissett had taken an unexpected turn.

Who knew what the future might hold?

One thing she was certain about. Jimmy and his new family would not stop her plans for the café. She would need her new career to help her cope with the sudden promotion from mother to grandmother. She would support Jimmy, but she would not give up her future for her son's mistakes.

Jimmy would have to find a way to fit into the community of Sixpenny Bissett. His presence would no doubt shake up the community. Jenni and her family making waves again. Wouldn't Anna Fletcher love that!

Jimmy wouldn't find it easy settling in, especially as he had been used to the delights of travelling the world. Sixpenny Bissett was a quiet backwater. It probably wouldn't be his first choice of hometowns. The mistakes he and Charlie had made meant that they were probably stuck with it.

And of course Jenni was stuck with her son. And his mistakes.

CHAPTER FORTY-FIVE
EPILOGUE

The arrival of the newcomer, Jenni Sullivan, had stirred up the community of Sixpenny Bissett.

The quiet backwater had been turned on its head over recent events. The normal pace of change in the village was usually akin to a snail's pace. Slow, ponderous and on a 'need to' basis. Gossip and scandal had been unknown, but in the space of a few months, the village had witnessed an inappropriate assault and at least one relationship breakdown.

The village had awakened from its slumber and was being shaken into the 21st century. Jenni had no idea of the seismic shock waves her arrival had started. She had wanted to hide away in her beautiful cottage and had accidently found herself the centre of attention.

Sixpenny Bissett was no longer a quiet backwater. Things were changing and Jenni was at the heart of those developments.

Peter St John had finally fallen on his sword. For years, he had gained a reputation for his illicit affairs. Most of the community had turned a blind eye, feeling sorry for his poor wife. There was very little concern for Peter's well-being. He had messed with the newcomer and come out with two black eyes. Now that Paula had kicked him out, the speculation that he would leave the area completely was gathering pace. How could Peter show his face at the golf course when most of his golf buddies had taken his wife's side?

Paula St John was a new woman. She had a lightness in her step and a smile on her face, which had been missing for years. She had been dragged down by her lecherous husband. Her friendship with Alaistair Middleton had been noted. Could the two people, who had both been on the receiving end of deception, find comfort in each other?

THE NEWCOMER

The General had found a new thirst for life since Jenni had come into his life. He had mourned Bridget for so many years. He could see many of his wife's characteristics in the newcomer. He could provide her with friendship and security from the village gossips. Jenni just needed to see him differently from the father figure fixed in her head. Would their friendship blossom into something more?

Kate Penrose loved her new friend, Jenni. From the moment they had met, the two women had found that they shared a bond. They laughed and cried together. Two women, from quite different backgrounds, who had become inseparable. Would the café get off the ground and save the village shop? With the determination of these two strong women, it would be a brave person who would bet against them.

Henrique Gonzales had a crush on the newcomer. Jenni was giving him mixed signals. Telling him that their sexual encounter was a one-off, only to jump back into bed with him. He was loving the experience of the older woman and would love them to go official. Would Jenni let that happen?

Richard Samuels had spurned the newcomer. He was facing his own demons, struggling to accept that there may be life after his beloved Nicola. Could he see Jenni as anything more than a friend? Would she even be his friend after he had spurned her so cruelly?

The newcomer was confused with all the fuss about her. She had been on an emotional rollercoaster and was enjoying the ride. She was making friends, enemies, and lovers. She didn't regret her decision to move to Sixpenny Bissett.

Not everything was perfect, but life isn't, is it?

Jenni was looking forward to setting up the new café and making a positive impact on the village. She was not afraid to make mistakes along the way, as long as she had her friend, Kate, by her side. She would have to face the shock of becoming a grandmother, but that would not hold her back.

Sixpenny Bissett was her future.

Just what that future held, Jenni would have to wait and see.

The End

For Now

AFTERWORD
A MESSAGE FROM CAROLINE

Thank you for reading The Newcomer. I really hope you enjoyed it as much as I loved writing it.

The book is the first in a three part series based on the fictional village of Sixpenny Bissett. I was inspired by our recent house move into a small village in Wiltshire and the lovely way that a village community can envelops you in its arms. Life in rural countryside is very different and can take some getting used to. We love it. To my friends and neighbours, none of the characters are based on real people. I pick characteristics from everyone I meet and they find their way into my writing

I also wanted to write about relationships for those of us probably classed as middle-aged – even if we don't feel it. Jenni encapsulates all those women who find they are widowed at an age where dating is a challenge and living alone for ever more is not the best prospect. Jenni is not based on me. She is far too glamourous.

If you enjoyed The Newcomer, the second book in the series should be out in spring/summer 2023. The Café at Kate's follows Jenni as she opens the new café in the village store, working alongside her new best friend Kate. Jenni becomes a grandmother. The challenges of running a new business and supporting her son, as he becomes a father, will focus Jenni's attention, helping to put her passion for Richard Samuels to one side. But has she given up on love? Or is it a temporary pause?

As an independent published author, reviews are important to help grow my audience. I would be delighted if you could leave me a review on either Amazon or Goodreads. Your reviews will help me to develop my craft and shape my stories as I continue on my writing journey. Thank you.

L would love to hear from you on social media where you will find out more about my books.

Twitter: @Carolinerebisz

Facebook: www.facebook.com/crebisz

Website: www.crebiszauthor.co.uk

ABOUT THE AUTHOR
CAROLINE REBISZ

Caroline lives in Wiltshire with her husband and their cat Elsie. She has two grown up daughters who inspire and support her work. Family is important to Caroline and features strongly in all her books.

Throughout her career, Caroline worked in high street banking in a variety of roles. Her passion centred around leading teams of staff and using her communication skills to motivate and inspire. Since taking early retirement she has directed that passion towards writing novels.

Caroline doesn't like to restrict herself into a specific genre. Stories come to her and have to be written. All her stories feature strong-minded women and their families. Hopefully that variety of genres keeps the reader interested, alongside the author. Other books in her portfolio include A Mother's Loss and A Mother's Deceit which are both based in their old home in Norfolk, a renovated ex-pub. A Costly Affair is a psychological drama.

Caroline is currently working on The Sixpenny Bissett series.

Printed in Great Britain
by Amazon